ROGER ZELAZNY

The recipient of over 20 Hugo and Nebula nominations and awards...the celebrated author of such science fiction masterpieces as the *Amber* series, *Lord of Light*, and *This Immortal*...now Avon Books presents his newest, most stunning collection—

UNICORN VARIATIONS

"Science fiction has produced few great masters. I genuinely envy those who encounter Roger Zelazny."

Theodore Sturgeon

"He breaks rules most writers only suspect exist. His concepts are fresh, his attacks bold..."

Harlan Ellison

ROGER ZELAZNY

UNICORN VARIATIONS

◆ AVON
PUBLISHERS OF BARD, CAMELOT, DISCUS AND FLARE BOOKS

This assemblage is for Phil and Marsha Higdon

AVON BOOKS
A division of
The Hearst Corporation
1790 Broadway
New York, New York 10019

First Avon Printing: April 1987

AVON TRADEMARK REG. U.S. PAT. OFF. AND IN OTHER COUNTRIES, MARCA REGISTRADA, HECHO EN U.S.A.

Printed in the U.S.A.

K-R 10 9 8 7 6 5 4 3 2 1

Contents

Introduction

Here is another collection of things written by me, drawn from various points over the past two decades. Some I recall fondly; others I had all but forgotten.

In reviewing the stories included here, I was surprised by the number of tales written to order, i.e., to go behind a magazine's cover painting (of which more anon) or to qualify for inclusion in a theme anthology.

I pause to reflect upon the phenomenon of the theme anthology: In the Old Days (circa forties and fifties) collections of science fiction stories were just collections of science fiction stories, none of them necessarily resembling any of the others in major particulars. In recent years, however, collections of stories possessed of a common theme have become the rule in the science fiction anthology. I cannot look upon writing such stories as a bad thing. Some very good work has appeared in theme anthologies. But such volumes might fairly be viewed as something of a constraint upon writers.

And thinking back, I began writing for magazines in the days when they were considered family publications—meaning that one did not use profanity beyond occasional hells and damns, describe sexual acts, have one's characters discuss politics in any but the broadest terms or indulge in religious speculation.

Earlier this year I visited the Soviet Union in the company of some other people connected with science fiction. We met with a number of Russian and Ukrainian writers and editors. When we were told that they preferred to publish stories with happy endings, stories containing a minimum of violence, our first reaction was a knowing nod. Really.

There are always restrictions. I do not feel any imposed upon me now in the sense of editorial censorship. But there are restrictions in the form of my own limitations as a writer, and there are self-imposed restrictions having to do with story structure and matters of my temperament and taste. I am free to work within these limits. When I write the first sentence to any story, though, I surrender a lot more freedom. I have set a course. I have restricted myself even further. Freedom of expression must also bow to the necessity for clear communication, as many of science fiction's failed experiments of the sixties demonstrate.

Gore Vidal has suggested that a writer has a limited cast of characters—his own repertory company, so to speak—and that, with different makeup, they enact all of his tales. I feel he has a point there, and that this constitutes yet another limitation (though I like to feel that over the years one can pension off a few, and I do try to seek out new talent).

All of these things considered, it is not surprising that one can detect echoes, correspondences and even an eternal return or two within the work of a single author. The passage of time does bring changes, yea and alas; but still, I would recognize myself anywhere. In this sense, any writer's total output might be looked upon as a series of variations. . . .

All of that to justify a title.

I want to thank all of those people who've offered me employment in hardware stores, but I'd really prefer to keep on writing.

Unicorn Variation

*This story came into being in a somewhat atypical fashion. The
first movement in its direction occurred when Gardner Dozois
phoned me one evening and asked whether I'd ever done a short
story involving a unicorn. I said that I had not. He explained
then that he and Jack Dann were putting together a reprint
anthology of unicorn stories, and he suggested that I write one
and sell it somewhere and then sell them reprint rights to it. Two
sales. Nice. I told him that I'd think about it. Later, I was asked
by another anthologist whether I'd ever done a story set in a
barroom—and if so, he'd like it for a reprint collection he was
doing. I allowed that I hadn't. A week or so after that, I attended
a wine tasting with the redoubtable George R. R. Martin, and
during the course of the evening I decided to mention the
prospective collections in case he had ever done a unicorn story
or a barroom story. He hadn't either, but he reminded me that
Fred Saberhagen was putting together a reprint collection of
stories involving chess games (Pawn to Infinity). "Why don't
you," he said, "write a story involving a unicorn and a chess
game, set it in a barroom and sell it to everybody?" We chuckled
and sipped. A few months later, I went up to Vancouver, B.C., to
be the guest of V-Con, a very pleasant regional science fiction
convention. I had decided to take my family on the Inland
Passage Alaskan cruise after that. Now right before I left New
Mexico I had read Italo Calvino's Invisible Cities, and when I
read the section titled "Hidden Cities. 4." something seemed to
stir. It told of the city where the inhabitants exterminated all of
the vermin, completely sanitizing the place, only to be haunted
then by visions of creatures that did not exist. Later, during the
convention, things began to flow together; and on my way down
to the waterfront to board the Prinsendam, I stopped at a number*

of bookstores, speed reading all of the chess sections until I found what I wanted, two hours before sailing time. I bought the book. I sailed. I wrote "Unicorn Variation" in odd moments during what proved a fine cruise. My protagonist is named Martin—any similarity to George (who is a chess expert) is not exactly unintentional. (I'll include a note on the game itself as an afterpiece to the tale.) Later that year the Prinsendam *burned and sank. The story didn't. I sold it a sufficient number of times to pay for the cruise. Thanks, George.*

A bizarrerie of fires, cunabulum of light, it moved with a deft, almost dainty deliberation, phasing into and out of existence like a storm-shot piece of evening; or perhaps the darkness between the flares was more akin to its truest nature—swirl of black ashes assembled in prancing cadence to the lowing note of desert wind down the arroyo behind buildings as empty yet filled as the pages of unread books or stillnesses between the notes of a song.

Gone again. Back again. Again.

Power, you said? Yes. It takes considerable force of identity to manifest before or after one's time. Or both.

As it faded and gained it also advanced, moving through the warm afternoon, its tracks erased by the wind. That is, on those occasions when there were tracks.

A reason. There should always be a reason. Or reasons.

It knew why it was there—but not why it was *there*, in that particular locale.

It anticipated learning this shortly, as it approached the desolation-bound line of the old street. However, it knew that the reason may also come before, or after. Yet again, the pull was there and the force of its being was such that it had to be close to something.

The buildings were worn and decayed and some of them fallen and all of them drafty and dusty and empty. Weeds grew among floorboards. Birds nested upon rafters. The droppings of wild things were everywhere, and it knew them all as they would have known it, were they to meet face to face.

It froze, for there had come the tiniest unanticipated sound from somewhere ahead and to the left. At that moment, it was again phasing into existence and it released its outline which faded as quickly as a rainbow in hell, that but the naked presence remained beyond subtraction.

Invisible, yet existing, strong, it moved again. The clue. The cue. Ahead. A gauche. Beyond the faded word SALOON on weathered board above. Through the swinging doors. (One of them pinned alop.)

Pause and assess.

Bar to the right, dusty. Cracked mirror behind it. Empty bottles. Broken bottles. Brass rail, black, encrusted. Tables to the left and rear. In various states of repair.

Man seated at the best of the lot. His back to the door. Levi's. Hiking boots. Faded blue shirt. Green backpack leaning against the wall to his left.

Before him, on the tabletop, is the faint, painted outline of a chessboard, stained, scratched, almost obliterated.

The drawer in which he had found the chessmen is still partly open.

He could no more have passed up a chess set without working out a problem or replaying one of his better games than he could have gone without breathing, circulating his blood or maintaining a relatively stable body temperature.

It moved nearer, and perhaps there were fresh prints in the dust behind it, but none noted them.

It, too, played chess.

It watched as the man replayed what had perhaps been his finest game, from the world preliminaries of seven years past. He had blown up after that—surprised to have gotten even as far as he had—for he never could perform well under pressure. But he had always been proud of that one game, and he relived it as all sensitive beings do certain turning points in their lives. For perhaps twenty minutes, no one could have touched him. He had been shining and pure and hard and clear. He had felt like the best.

It took up a position across the board from him and stared. The man completed the game, smiling. Then he set up the board again, rose and fetched a can of beer from his pack. He popped the top.

When he returned, he discovered that White's King's Pawn had been advanced to K4. His brow furrowed. He turned his head, searching the bar, meeting his own puzzled gaze in the grimy mirror. He looked under the table. He took a drink of beer and seated himself.

He reached out and moved his Pawn to K4. A moment later, he saw White's King's Knight rise slowly into the air and drift forward to settle upon KB3. He stared for a long while into the emptiness across the table before he advanced his own Knight to his KB3.

White's Knight moved to take his Pawn. He dismissed the novelty of the situation and moved his Pawn to Q3. He all but forgot the absence of a tangible opponent as the White Knight dropped back to its KB3. He paused to take a sip of beer, but no sooner had he placed the can upon the tabletop than it rose again, passed across the board and was upended. A gurgling noise followed. Then the can fell to the floor, bouncing, ringing with an empty sound.

"I'm sorry," he said, rising and returning to his pack. "I'd have offered you one if I'd thought you were something that might like it."

He opened two more cans, returned with them, placed one near the far edge of the table, one at his own right hand.

"Thank you," came a soft, precise voice from a point beyond it.

The can was raised, tilted slightly, returned to the tabletop.

"My name is Martin," the man said.

"Call me Tlingel," said the other. "I had thought that perhaps your kind was extinct. I am pleased that you at least have survived to afford me this game."

"Huh?" Martin said. "We were all still around the last time that I looked—a couple of days ago."

"No matter. I can take care of that later," Tlingel replied. "I was misled by the appearance of this place."

"Oh. It's a ghost town. I backpack a lot."

"Not important. I am near the proper point in your career as a species. I can feel that much."

"I am afraid that I do not follow you."

"I am not at all certain that you would wish to. I assume that you intend to capture that Pawn?"

"Perhaps. Yes, I do wish to. What are you talking about?"

The beer can rose. The invisible entity took another drink.

"Well," said Tlingel, "to put it simply, your—successors—grow anxious. Your place in the scheme of things being such an important one, I had sufficient power to come and check things out."

"'Successors'? I do not understand."

"Have you seen any griffins recently?"

Martin chuckled.

"I've heard the stories," he said, "seen the photos of the one supposedly shot in the Rockies. A hoax, of course."

"Of course it must seem so. That is the way with mythical beasts."

"You're trying to say that it was real?"

"Certainly. Your world is in bad shape. When the last grizzly bear died recently, the way was opened for the griffins—just as the death of the last aepyornis brought in the yeti, the dodo the Loch Ness creature, the passenger pigeon the sasquatch, the blue whale the kraken, the American eagle the cockatrice—"

"You can't prove it by me."

"Have another drink."

Martin began to reach for the can, halted his hand and stared.

A creature approximately two inches in length, with a human face, a lionlike body and feathered wings was crouched next to the beer can.

"A minisphinx," the voice continued. "They came when you killed off the last smallpox virus."

"Are you trying to say that whenever a natural species dies out a mythical one takes its place?" he asked.

"In a word—yes. Now. It was not always so, but you have destroyed the mechanisms of evolution. The balance is now redressed by those others of us, from the morning land—we, who have never truly been endangered. We return, in our time."

"And you—whatever you are, Tlingel—you say that humanity is now endangered?"

"Very much so. But there is nothing that you can do about it, is there? Let us get on with the game."

The sphinx flew off. Martin took a sip of beer and captured the Pawn.

"Who," he asked then, "are to be our successors?"

"Modesty almost forbids," Tlingel replied. "In the case of a species as prominent as your own, it naturally has to be the loveliest, most intelligent, most important of us all."

"And what are you? Is there any way that I can have a look?"

"Well—yes. If I exert myself a trifle."

The beer can rose, was drained, fell to the floor. There followed a series of rapid rattling sounds retreating from the table. The air began to flicker over a large area opposite Martin, darkening within the glowing flamework. The outline continued to brighten, its interior growing jet black. The form moved, prancing about the saloon, multitudes of tiny, cloven hoofprints scoring and cracking the floorboards. With a final, near-blinding flash it came into full view and Martin gasped to behold it.

A black unicorn with mocking, yellow eyes sported before him, rising for a moment onto its hind legs to strike a heraldic pose. The fires flared about it a second longer, then vanished.

Martin had drawn back, raising one hand defensively.

"Regard me!" Tlingel announced. "Ancient symbol of wisdom, valor and beauty, I stand before you!"

"I thought your typical unicorn was white," Martin finally said.

"I am archetypical," Tlingel responded, dropping to all fours, "and possessed of virtues beyond the ordinary."

"Such as?"

"Let us continue our game."

"What about the fate of the human race? You said—"

". . . And save the small talk for later."

"I hardly consider the destruction of humanity to be small talk."

"And if you've any more beer . . ."

"All right," Martin said, retreating to his pack as the creature advanced, its eyes like a pair of pale suns. "There's some lager."

Something had gone out of the game. As Martin sat before the ebon horn on Tlingel's bowed head, like an insect about to be pinned, he realized that his playing was off. He had felt the pressure the moment he had seen the beast—and there was all that talk about an imminent doomsday. Any run-of-the-mill pessimist could say it without troubling him, but coming from a source as peculiar as this . . .

His earlier elation had fled. He was no longer in top form. And Tlingel was good. Very good. Martin found himself wondering whether he could manage a stalemate.

After a time, he saw that he could not and resigned.

The unicorn looked at him and smiled.

"You don't really play badly—for a human," it said.

"I've done a lot better."

"It is no shame to lose to me, mortal. Even among mythical creatures there are very few who can give a unicorn a good game."

"I am pleased that you were not wholly bored," Martin said. "Now will you tell me what you were talking about concerning the destruction of my species?"

"Oh, that," Tlingel replied. "In the morning land where those such as I dwell, I felt the possibility of your passing come like a gentle wind to my nostrils, with the promise of clearing the way for us—"

"How is it supposed to happen?"

Tlingel shrugged, horn writing on the air with a toss of the head.

"I really couldn't say. Premonitions are seldom specific. In fact, that is what I came to discover. I should have been about it already, but you diverted me with beer and good sport."

"Could you be wrong about this?"

"I doubt it. That is the other reason I am here."

"Please explain."

"Are there any beers left?"

"Two, I think."

"Please."

Martin rose and fetched them.

"Damn! The tab broke off this one," he said.

"Place it upon the table and hold it firmly."

"All right."

Tlingel's horn dipped forward quickly, piercing the can's top.

". . . Useful for all sorts of things," Tlingel observed, withdrawing it.

"The other reason you're here. . . ." Martin prompted.

"It is just that I am special. I can do things that the others cannot."

"Such as?"

"Find your weak spot and influence events to exploit it, to—hasten matters. To turn the possibility into a probability, and then—"

"*You* are going to destroy us? Personally?"

"That is the wrong way to look at it. It is more like a game of chess. It is as much a matter of exploiting your opponent's weaknesses as of exercising your own strengths. If you had not already laid the groundwork I would be powerless. I can only influence that which already exists."

"So what will it be? World War III? An ecological disaster? A mutated disease?"

"I do not really know yet, so I wish you wouldn't ask me in that fashion. I repeat that at the moment I am only observing. I am only an agent—"

"It doesn't sound that way to me."

Tlingel was silent. Martin began gathering up the chessmen.

"Aren't you going to set up the board again?"

"To amuse my destroyer a little more? No thanks."

"That's hardly the way to look at it—"

"Besides, those are the last beers."

"Oh." Tlingel stared wistfully at the vanishing pieces, then remarked, "I would be willing to play you again without additional refreshment. . . ."

"No thanks."

"You are angry."

"Wouldn't you be, if our situations were reversed?"

"You are anthropomorphizing."

"Well?"

"Oh, I suppose I would."

"You could give us a break, you know—at least let us make our own mistakes."

"You've hardly done that yourself, though, with all the creatures my fellows have succeeded."

Martin reddened.

"Okay. You just scored one. But I don't have to like it."

"You are a good player. I know that. . . ."

"Tlingel, if I were capable of playing at my best again, I think I could beat you."

The unicorn snorted two tiny wisps of smoke.

"Not *that* good," Tlingel said.

"I guess you'll never know."

"Do I detect a proposal?"

"Possibly. What's another game worth to you?"

Tlingel made a chuckling noise.

"Let me guess: You are going to say that if you beat me you want my promise not to lay my will upon the weakest link in mankind's existence and shatter it."

"Of course."

"And what do I get for winning?"

"The pleasure of the game. That's what you want, isn't it?"

"The terms sound a little lopsided."

"Not if you are going to win anyway. You keep insisting that you will."

"All right. Set up the board."

"There is something else that you have to know about me first."

"Yes?"

"I don't play well under pressure, and this game is going to be a terrific strain. You want my best game, don't you?"

"Yes, but I'm afraid I've no way of adjusting your own reactions to the play."

"I believe I could do that myself if I had more than the usual amount of time between moves."

"Agreed."

"I mean a lot of time."

"Just what do you have in mind?"

"I'll need time to get my mind off it, to relax, to come back to the positions as if they were only problems. . . ."

"You mean to go away from here between moves?"

"Yes."

"All right. How long?"

"I don't know. A few weeks, maybe."

"Take a month. Consult your experts, put your computers onto it. It may make for a slightly more interesting game."

"I really didn't have that in mind."

"Then it's time that you're trying to buy."

"I can't deny that. On the other hand, I will need it."

"In that case, I have some terms. I'd like this place cleaned up, fixed up, more lively. It's a mess. I also want beer on tap."

"Okay. I'll see to that."

"Then I agree. Let's see who goes first."

Martin switched a black and a white Pawn from hand to hand beneath the table. He raised his fists then and extended them. Tlingel leaned forward and tapped. The black horn's tip touched Martin's left hand.

"Well, it matches my sleek and glossy hide," the unicorn announced.

Martin smiled, setting up the white for himself, the black

pieces for his opponent. As soon as he had finished, he pushed his Pawn to K4.

Tlingel's delicate, ebon hoof moved to advance the Black King's Pawn to K4.

"I take it that you want a month now, to consider your next move?"

Martin did not reply but moved his Knight to KB3. Tlingel immediately moved a Knight to QB3.

Martin took a swallow of beer and then moved his Bishop to N5. The unicorn moved the other Knight to B3. Martin immediately castled and Tlingel moved the Knight to take his Pawn.

"I think we'll make it," Martin said suddenly, "if you'll just let us alone. We do learn from our mistakes, in time."

"Mythical beings do not exactly exist in time. Your world is a special case."

"Don't you people ever make mistakes?"

"Whenever we do they're sort of poetic."

Martin snarled and advanced his Pawn to Q4. Tlingel immediately countered by moving the Knight to Q3.

"I've got to stop," Martin said, standing. "I'm getting mad, and it will affect my game."

"You will be going, then?"

"Yes."

He moved to fetch his pack.

"I will see you here in one month's time?"

"Yes."

"Very well."

The unicorn rose and stamped upon the floor and lights began to play across its dark coat. Suddenly, they blazed and shot outward in all directions like a silent explosion. A wave of blackness followed.

Martin found himself leaning against the wall, shaking. When he lowered his hand from his eyes, he saw that he was alone, save for the knights, the bishops, the kings, the queens, their castles and both the kings' men.

He went away.

Three days later Martin returned in a small truck, with a generator, lumber, windows, power tools, paint, stain, cleaning compounds, wax. He dusted and vacuumed and replaced rotten wood. He installed the windows. He polished the old brass until it shone. He stained and rubbed. He waxed the floors and buffed them. He plugged holes and washed glasses. He hauled all the trash away.

It took him the better part of a week to turn the old place from a wreck back into a saloon in appearance. Then he drove off, returned all of the equipment he had rented and bought a ticket for the Northwest.

The big, damp forest was another of his favorite places for hiking, for thinking. And he was seeking a complete change of scene, a total revision of outlook. Not that his next move did not seem obvious, standard even. Yet, something nagged. . . .

He knew that it was more than just the game. Before that he had been ready to get away again, to walk drowsing among shadows, breathing clean air.

Resting, his back against the bulging root of a giant tree, he withdrew a small chess set from his pack, set it up on a rock he'd moved into position nearby. A fine, mistlike rain was settling, but the tree sheltered him, so far. He reconstructed the opening through Tlingel's withdrawal of the Knight to Q3. The simplest thing would be to take the Knight with the Bishop. But he did not move to do it.

He watched the board for a time, felt his eyelids drooping, closed them and drowsed. It may only have been for a few minutes. He was never certain afterward.

Something aroused him. He did not know what. He blinked several times and closed his eyes again. Then he reopened them hurriedly.

In his nodded position, eyes directed downward, his gaze was fixed upon an enormous pair of hairy, unshod feet—the largest pair of feet that he had ever beheld. They stood unmoving before him, pointed toward his right.

Slowly—very slowly—he raised his eyes. Not very far, as it turned out. The creature was only about four and a half feet in height. As it was looking at the chessboard rather than at him, he took the opportunity to study it.

It was unclothed but very hairy, with a dark brown pelt, obviously masculine, possessed of low brow ridges, deep-set eyes that matched its hair, heavy shoulders, five-fingered hands that sported opposing thumbs.

It turned suddenly and regarded him, flashing a large number of shining teeth.

"White's Pawn should take the Pawn," it said in a soft, nasal voice.

"Huh? Come on," Martin said. "Bishop takes Knight."

"You want to give me Black and play it that way? I'll walk all over you."

Martin glanced again at its feet.

". . . Or give me White and let me take that Pawn. I'll still do it."

"Take White," Martin said, straightening. "Let's see if you know what you're talking about." He reached for his pack. "Have a beer?"

"What's a beer?"

"A recreational aid. Wait a minute."

Before they had finished the six-pack, the sasquatch—whose name, he had learned, was Grend—had finished Martin. Grend had quickly entered a ferocious midgame, backed him into a position of dwindling security and pushed him to the point where he had seen the end and resigned.

"That was one hell of a game," Martin declared, leaning back and considering the apelike countenance before him.

"Yes, we bigfeet are pretty good, if I do say it. It's our one big recreation, and we're so damned primitive we don't have much in the way of boards and chessmen. Most of the time, we just play it in our heads. There're not many can come close to us."

"How about unicorns?" Martin asked.

Grend nodded slowly.

"They're about the only ones can really give us a good game. A little dainty, but they're subtle. Awfully sure of themselves, though, I must say. Even when they're wrong. Haven't seen any since we left the morning land, of course. Too bad. Got any more of that beer left?"

"I'm afraid not. But listen, I'll be back this way in a month. I'll bring some more if you'll meet me here and play again."

"Martin, you've got a deal. Sorry. Didn't mean to step on your toes."

He cleaned the saloon again and brought in a keg of beer which he installed under the bar and packed with ice. He moved in some bar stools, chairs and tables which he had obtained at a Goodwill store. He hung red curtains. By then it was evening.

He set up the board, ate a light meal, unrolled his sleeping bag behind the bar and camped there that night.

The following day passed quickly. Since Tlingel might show up at any time, he did not leave the vicinity but took his meals there and sat about working chess problems. When it began to grow dark, he lit a number of oil lamps and candles.

He looked at his watch with increasing frequency. He began to pace. He couldn't have made a mistake. This was the proper day. He—

He heard a chuckle.

Turning about, he saw a black unicorn head floating in the air above the chessboard. As he watched, the rest of Tlingel's body materialized.

"Good evening, Martin." Tlingel turned away from the board. "The place looks a little better. Could use some music. . . ."

Martin stepped behind the bar and switched on the transistor radio he had brought along. The sounds of a string quartet filled the air. Tlingel winced.

"Hardly in keeping with the atmosphere of the place."

He changed stations, located a country and western show.

"I think not," Tlingel said. "It loses something in transmission."

He turned it off.

"Have we a good supply of beverage?"

Martin drew a gallon stein of beer—the largest mug that he could locate, from a novelty store—and set it upon the bar. He filled a much smaller one for himself. He was determined to get the beast drunk if it were at all possible.

"Ah! Much better than those little cans," said Tlingel, whose muzzle dipped for but a moment. "Very good."

The mug was empty. Martin refilled it.

"Will you move it to the table for me?"

"Certainly."

"Have an interesting month?"

"I suppose I did."

"You've decided upon your next move?"

"Yes."

"Then let's get on with it."

Martin seated himself and captured the Pawn.

"Hm. Interesting."

Tlingel stared at the board for a long while, then raised a cloven hoof which parted in reaching for the piece.

"I'll just take that Bishop with this little Knight. Now I suppose you'll be wanting another month to make up your mind what to do next."

Tlingel leaned to the side and drained the mug.

"Let me consider it," Martin said, "while I get you a refill."

Martin sat and stared at the board through three more refills. Actually, he was not planning. He was waiting. His response to Grend had been Knight takes Bishop, and he had Grend's next move ready.

"Well?" Tlingel finally said. "What do you think?"

Martin took a small sip of beer.

"Almost ready," he said. "You hold your beer awfully well."

Tlingel laughed.

"A unicorn's horn is a detoxicant. It's possession is a universal remedy. I wait until I reach the warm glow stage, then I use my horn to burn off any excess and keep me right there."

"Oh," said Martin. "Neat trick, that."

". . . If you've had too much, just touch my horn for a moment and I'll put you back in business."

"No, thanks. That's all right. I'll just push this little Pawn in front of the Queen's Rook two steps ahead."

"Really. . ." said Tlingel. "That's interesting. You know, what this place really needs is a piano—rinkytink, funky. . . . Think you could manage it?"

"I don't play."

"Too bad."

"I suppose I could hire a piano player."

"No. I do not care to be seen by other humans."

"If he's really good, I suppose he could play blindfolded."

"Never mind."

"I'm sorry."

"You are also ingenious. I am certain that you will figure something out by next time."

Martin nodded.

"Also, didn't these old places used to have sawdust all over the floors?"

"I believe so."

"That would be nice."

"Check."

Tlingel searched the board frantically for a moment.

"Yes. I meant 'yes.' I said 'check.' It means 'yes' sometimes, too."

"Oh. Rather. Well, while we're here . . ."

Tlingel advanced the Pawn to Q3.

Martin stared. That was not what Grend had done. For a moment, he considered continuing on his own from here. He had tried to think of Grend as a coach up until this point. He had forced away the notion of crudely and crassly pitting one of them against the other. Until P-Q3. Then he recalled the game he had lost to the sasquatch.

"I'll draw the line here," he said, "and take my month."

"All right. Let's have another drink before we say good night. Okay?"

"Sure. Why not?"

They sat for a time and Tlingel told him of the morning land, of primeval forests and rolling plains, of high craggy mountains and purple seas, of magic and mythic beasts.

Martin shook his head.

"I can't quite see why you're so anxious to come here," he said, "with a place like that to call home."

Tlingel sighed.

"I suppose you'd call it keeping up with the griffins. It's the thing to do these days. Well. Till next month . . ."

Tlingel rose and turned away.

"I've got complete control now. Watch!"

The unicorn form faded, jerked out of shape, grew white, faded again, was gone, like an afterimage.

Martin moved to the bar and drew himself another mug. It was a shame to waste what was left. In the morning, he wished the unicorn were there again. Or at least the horn.

It was a gray day in the forest and he held an umbrella over the chessboard upon the rock. The droplets fell from the leaves and made dull, plopping noises as they struck the fabric. The board was set up again through Tlingel's P-Q3. Martin wondered whether Grend had remembered, had kept proper track of the days. . . .

"Hello," came the nasal voice from somewhere behind him and to the left.

He turned to see Grend moving about the tree, stepping over the massive roots with massive feet.

"You remembered," Grend said. "How good! I trust you also remembered the beer?"

"I've lugged up a whole case. We can set up the bar right here."

"What's a bar?"

"Well, it's a place where people go to drink—in out of the rain—a bit dark, for atmosphere—and they sit up on stools before a big counter, or else at little tables—and they talk to each other—and sometimes there's music—and they drink."

"We're going to have all that here?"

"No. Just the dark and the drinks. Unless you count the rain as music. I was speaking figuratively."

"Oh. It does sound like a very good place to visit, though."

"Yes. If you will hold this umbrella over the board, I'll set up the best equivalent we can have here."

"All right. Say, this looks like a version of that game we played last time."

"It is. I got to wondering what would happen if it had gone this way rather than the way that it went."

"Hmm. Let me see. . . ."

Martin removed four six-packs from his pack and opened the first.

"Here you go."

"Thanks."

Grend accepted the beer, squatted, passed the umbrella back to Martin.

"I'm still White?"

"Yeah."

"Pawn to King six."

"Really?"

"Yep."

"About the best thing for me to do would be to take this Pawn with this one."

"I'd say. Then I'll just knock off your Knight with this one."

"I guess I'll just pull this Knight back to K2."

". . . And I'll take this one over to B3. May I have another beer?"

An hour and a quarter later, Martin resigned. The rain had let up and he had folded the umbrella.

"Another game?" Grend asked.

"Yes."

The afternoon wore on. The pressure was off. This one was just for fun. Martin tried wild combinations, seeing ahead with great clarity, as he had that one day. . . .

"Stalemate," Grend announced much later. "That was a good one, though. You picked up considerably."

"I was more relaxed. Want another?"

"Maybe in a little while. Tell me more about bars now."

So he did. Finally, "How is all that beer affecting you?" he asked.

"I'm a bit dizzy. But that's all right. I'll still cream you the third game."

And he did.

"Not bad for a human, though. Not bad at all. You coming back next month?"

"Yes."

"Good. You'll bring more beer?"

"So long as my money holds out."

"Oh. Bring some plaster of Paris then. I'll make you some nice footprints and you can take casts of them. I understand they're going for quite a bit."

"I'll remember that."

Martin lurched to his feet and collected the chess set.

"Till then."

"Ciao."

Martin dusted and polished again, moved in the player piano and scattered sawdust upon the floor. He installed a fresh keg. He hung some reproductions of period posters and some atrocious old paintings he had located in a junk shop. He placed cuspidors in strategic locations. When he was finished, he seated himself at the bar and opened a bottle of mineral water. He listened to the New Mexico wind moaning as it passed, to grains of sand striking against the windowpanes. He wondered whether the whole world would have that dry, mournful sound to it if Tlingel found a means for doing away with humanity, or—disturbing thought—whether the successors to his own kind might turn things into something resembling the mythical morning land.

This troubled him for a time. Then he went and set up the

board through Black's P-Q3. When he turned back to clear the bar he saw a line of cloven hoofprints advancing across the sawdust.

"Good evening, Tlingel," he said. "What is your pleasure?"

Suddenly, the unicorn was there, without preliminary pyrotechnics. It moved to the bar and placed one hoof upon the brass rail.

"The usual."

As Martin drew the beer, Tlingel looked about.

"The place has improved, a bit."

"Glad you think so. Would you care for some music?"

"Yes."

Martin fumbled at the back of the piano, locating the switch for the small, battery-operated computer which controlled the pumping mechanism and substituted its own memory for rolls. The keyboard immediately came to life.

"Very good," Tlingel stated. "Have you found your move?"

"I have."

"Then let us be about it."

He refilled the unicorn's mug and moved it to the table, along with his own.

"Pawn to King six," he said, executing it.

"What?"

"Just that."

"Give me a minute. I want to study this."

"Take your time."

"I'll take the Pawn," Tlingel said, after a long pause and another mug.

"Then I'll take this Knight."

Later, "Knight to K2," Tlingel said.

"Knight to B3."

An extremely long pause ensued before Tlingel moved the Knight to N3.

The hell with asking Grend, Martin suddenly decided. He'd been through this part any number of times already. He moved his Knight to N5.

"Change the tune on that thing!" Tlingel snapped.

Martin rose and obliged.

"I don't like that one either. Find a better one or shut it off!"

After three more tries, Martin shut it off.

"And get me another beer!"

He refilled their mugs.

"All right."

Tlingel moved the Bishop to K2.

Keeping the unicorn from castling had to be the most important thing at the moment. So Martin moved his Queen to R5. Tlingel made a tiny, strangling noise, and when Martin looked up smoke was curling from the unicorn's nostrils.

"More beer?"

"If you please."

As he returned with it, he saw Tlingel move the Bishop to capture the Knight. There seemed no choice for him at that moment, but he studied the position for a long while anyhow.

Finally, "Bishop takes Bishop," he said.

"Of course."

"How's the warm glow?"

Tlingel chuckled.

"You'll see."

The wind rose again, began to howl. The building creaked.

"Okay," Tlingel finally said, and moved the Queen to Q2.

Martin stared. What was he doing? So far, it had gone all right, but . . . He listened again to the wind and thought of the risk he was taking.

"That's all, folks," he said, leaning back in his chair. "Continued next month."

Tlingel sighed.

"Don't run off. Fetch me another. Let me tell you of my wanderings in your world this past month."

"Looking for weak links?"

"You're lousy with them. How do you stand it?"

"They're harder to strengthen than you might think. Any advice?"

"Get the beer."

They talked until the sky paled in the east, and Martin found himself taking surreptitious notes. His admiration for the unicorn's analytical abilities increased as the evening advanced.

When they finally rose, Tlingel staggered.

"You all right?"

"Forgot to detox, that's all. Just a second. Then I'll be fading."

"Wait!"

"Whazzat?"

"I could use one, too."

"Oh. Grab hold, then."

Tlingel's head descended and Martin took the tip of the horn between his fingertips. Immediately, a delicious, warm sensation flowed through him. He closed his eyes to enjoy it. His head cleared. An ache which had been growing within his frontal sinus vanished. The tiredness went out of his muscles. He opened his eyes again.

"Thank—"

Tlingel had vanished. He held but a handful of air.

"—you."

"Rael here is my friend," Grend stated. "He's a griffin."

"I'd noticed."

Martin nodded at the beaked, golden-winged creature.

"Pleased to meet you, Rael."

"The same," cried the other in a high-pitched voice. "Have you got the beer?"

"Why—uh—yes."

"I've been telling him about beer," Grend explained, half-apologetically. "He can have some of mine. He won't kibitz or anything like that."

"Sure. All right. Any friend of yours . . ."

"The beer!" Rael cried. "Bars!"

"He's not real bright," Grend whispered. "But he's good company. I'd appreciate your humoring him."

Martin opened the first six-pack and passed the griffin and the sasquatch a beer apiece. Rael immediately punctured the can with his beak, chugged it, belched and held out his claw.

"Beer!" he shrieked. "More beer!"

Martin handed him another.

"Say, you're still into that first game, aren't you?" Grend observed, studying the board. "Now, *that* is an interesting position."

Grend drank and studied the board.

"Good thing it's not raining," Martin commented.

"Oh, it will. Just wait a while."

"More beer!" Rael screamed.

Martin passed him another without looking.

"I'll move my Pawn to N6," Grend said.

"You're kidding."

"Nope. Then you'll take that Pawn with your Bishop's Pawn. Right?"

"Yes . . ."

Martin reached out and did it.

"Okay. Now I'll just swing this Knight to Q5."

Martin took it with the Pawn.

Grend moved his Rook to K1.

"Check," he announced.

"Yes. That *is* the way to go," Martin observed.

Grend chuckled.

"I'm going to win this game another time," he said.

"I wouldn't put it past you."

"More beer?" Rael said softly.

"Sure."

As Martin passed him another, he noticed that the griffin was now leaning against the tree trunk.

After several minutes, Martin pushed his King to B1.

"Yeah, that's what I thought you'd do," Grend said. "You know something?"

"What?"

"You play a lot like a unicorn."

"Hm."

Grend moved his Rook to R3.

Later, as the rain descended gently about them and Grend beat him again, Martin realized that a prolonged period of silence had prevailed. He glanced over at the griffin. Rael had tucked his head beneath his left wing, balanced upon one leg, leaned heavily against the tree and gone to sleep.

"I told you he wouldn't be much trouble," Grend remarked.

Two games later, the beer was gone, the shadows were lengthening and Rael was stirring.

"See you next month?"

"Yeah."

"You bring any plaster of Paris?"

"Yes, I did."

"Come on, then. I know a good place pretty far from here. We don't want people beating about *these* bushes. Let's go make you some money."

"To buy beer?" Rael said, looking out from under his wing.

"Next month," Grend said.

"You ride?"

"I don't think you could carry both of us," said Grend, "and I'm not sure I'd want to right now if you could."

"Bye-bye then," Rael shrieked, and he leaped into the air, crashing into branches and tree trunks, finally breaking through the overhead cover and vanishing.

"There goes a really decent guy," said Grend. "He sees everything and he never forgets. Knows how everything works —in the woods, in the air—even in the water. Generous, too, whenever he has anything."

"Hm," Martin observed.

"Let's make tracks," Grend said.

"Pawn to N6? Really?" Tlingel said. "All right. The Bishop's Pawn will just knock off the Pawn."

Tlingel's eyes narrowed as Martin moved the Knight to Q5.

"At least this is an interesting game," the unicorn remarked. "Pawn takes Knight."

Martin moved the Rook.

"Check."

"Yes, it is. This next one is going to be a three-flagon move. Kindly bring me the first."

Martin thought back as he watched Tlingel drink and ponder. He almost felt guilty for hitting it with a powerhouse like the sasquatch behind its back. He was convinced now that the unicorn was going to lose. In every variation of this game that he'd played with Black against Grend, he'd been beaten. Tlingel was very good, but the sasquatch was a wizard with not much else to do but mental chess. It was unfair. But it was not a matter of personal honor, he kept telling himself. He was playing to protect his species against a supernatural force which might well be able to precipitate World War III by some arcane mind manipulation or magically induced computer foul-up. He didn't dare give the creature a break.

"Flagon number two, please."

He brought it another. He studied it as it studied the board. It was beautiful, he realized for the first time. It was the loveliest living thing he had ever seen. Now that the pressure was on the verge of evaporating and he could regard it without the overlay of fear which had always been there in the past, he could pause to admire it. If something *had* to succeed the human race, he could think of worse choices. . . .

"Number three now."

"Coming up."

Tlingel drained it and moved the King to B1.

Martin leaned forward immediately and pushed the Rook to R3.

Tlingel looked up, stared at him.

"Not bad."

Martin wanted to squirm. He was struck by the nobility of the creature. He wanted so badly to play and beat the unicorn on his own, fairly. Not this way.

Tlingel looked back at the board, then almost carelessly moved the Knight to K4.

"Go ahead. Or will it take you another month?"

Martin growled softly, advanced the Rook and captured the Knight.

"Of course."

Tlingel captured the Rook with the Pawn. This was not the way that the last variation with Grend had run. Still . . .

He moved his Rook to KB3. As he did, the wind seemed to commence a peculiar shrieking above, amid, the ruined buildings.

"Check," he announced.

The hell with it! he decided. I'm good enough to manage my own end game. Let's play this out.

He watched and waited and finally saw Tlingel move the King to N1.

He moved his Bishop to R6. Tlingel moved the Queen to K2. The shrieking came again, sounding nearer now. Martin took the Pawn with the Bishop.

The unicorn's head came up and it seemed to listen for a moment. Then Tlingel lowered it and captured the Bishop with the King.

Martin moved his Rook to KN3.

"Check."

Tlingel returned the King to B1.

Martin moved the Rook to KB3.

"Check."

Tlingel pushed the King to N2.

Martin moved the Rook back to KN3.

"Check."

Tlingel returned the King to B1, looked up and stared at him, showing teeth.

"Looks as if we've got a drawn game," the unicorn stated. "Care for another one?"

"Yes, but not for the fate of humanity."

"Forget it. I'd given up on that a long time ago. I decided that I wouldn't care to live here after all. I'm a little more discriminating than that."

"Except for this bar." Tlingel turned away as another shriek sounded just beyond the door, followed by strange voices. "What is that?"

"I don't know," Martin answered, rising.

The doors opened and a golden griffin entered.

"Martin!" it cried. "Beer! Beer!"

"Uh—Tlingel, this is Rael, and, and—"

Three more griffins followed it in. Then came Grend, and three others of his own kind.

"—and that one's Grend," Martin said lamely. "I don't know the others."

They all halted when they beheld the unicorn.

"Tlingel," one of the sasquatches said, "I thought you were still in the morning land."

"I still am, in a way. Martin, how is it that you are acquainted with my former countrymen?"

"Well—uh—Grend here is my chess coach."

"Aha! I begin to understand."

"I am not sure that you really do. But let me get everyone a drink first."

Martin turned on the piano and set everyone up.

"How did you find this place?" he asked Grend as he was doing it. "And how did you get here?"

"Well . . ." Grend looked embarrassed. "Rael followed you back."

"Followed a jet?"

"Griffins are supernaturally fast."

"Oh."

"Anyway, he told his relatives and some of my folks about it. When we saw that the griffins were determined to visit you, we decided that we had better come along to keep them out of trouble. They brought us."

"I—see. Interesting. . . ."

"No wonder you played like a unicorn, that one game with all the variations."

"Uh—yes."

Martin turned away, moved to the end of the bar.

"Welcome, all of you," he said. "I have a small announcement. Tlingel, a while back you had a number of observations concerning possible ecological and urban disasters and lesser dangers. Also, some ideas as to possible safeguards against some of them."

"I recall," said the unicorn.

"I passed them along to a friend of mine in Washington who used to be a member of my old chess club. I told him that the work was not entirely my own."

"I should hope so."

"He has since suggested that I turn whatever group was involved into a think tank. He will then see about paying something for its efforts."

"I didn't come here to save the world," Tlingel said.

"No, but you've been very helpful. And Grend tells me that the griffins, even if their vocabulary is a bit limited, know almost all that there is to know about ecology."

"That is probably true."

"Since they have inherited a part of the Earth, it would be to their benefit as well to help preserve the place. Inasmuch as this many of us are already here, I can save myself some travel and suggest right now that we find a meeting place—say here, once a month—and that you let me have your unique viewpoints. You must know more about how species become extinct than anyone else in the business."

"Of course," said Grend, waving his mug, "but we really should ask the yeti, also. I'll do it, if you'd like. Is that stuff coming out of the big box music?"

"Yes."

"I like it. If we do this think-tank thing, you'll make enough to keep this place going?"

"I'll buy the whole town."

Grend conversed in quick gutturals with the griffins, who shrieked back at him.

"You've got a think tank," he said, "and they want more beer."

Martin turned toward Tlingel.

"They were your observations. What do you think?"

"It may be amusing," said the unicorn, "to stop by occasionally." Then, "So much for saving the world. Did you say you wanted another game?"

"I've nothing to lose."

Grend took over the tending of the bar while Tlingel and Martin returned to the table.

He beat the unicorn in thirty-one moves and touched the extended horn.

The piano keys went up and down. Tiny sphinxes buzzed about the bar, drinking the spillage.

The game itself. Okay. It was Halprin v. Pillsbury in Munich, in 1900. Pillsbury was the stronger player. He'd beaten a number of very good players and only had Halprin, a weaker player, left to face. But two other players, running very close to Pillsbury for first prize, decided to teach him a lesson. The night before this game they got together with Halprin and coached him, teaching him everything they had learned concerning Pillsbury's style. The following day, Pillsbury faced a much better—prepared Halprin than he had anticipated playing. He realized this almost too late. The others chuckled and felt smug. But Pillsbury surprised them. Even caught off guard initially, he managed a draw. After all, he was very good. Martin is playing Halprin's game here, and Tlingel Pillsbury's. Except that Martin isn't really weak. He was just nervous the first time around. Who wouldn't be?

The Last of the Wild Ones

I did a story a long time ago that Fred Pohl published in Galaxy as "Devil Car." (My original title had been "Morning of the Scarlet Swinger." C'est la guerre.) Fifteen years passed, and I read Ross Santee's book Apache Land. In it, there was a chapter on the passing of the herds of wild mustangs. As I read it, I kept thinking of "Devil Car/Swinger." Then I realized why, and it all fell into place; I knew that my earlier story required a sequel—set, of course, fifteen years later. I called it "The Last of the Wild Ones", and so did Omni.

Spinning through the dream of time and dust they came, beneath a lake-cold, lake-blue, lake-deep sky, the sun a crashed and burning wreck above the western mountains, the wind a whipper of turning sand devils, chill turquoise wind out of the west, taking wind. They ran on bald tires, they listed on broken springs, their bodies creased, paint faded, windows cracked, exhaust tails black and gray and white, streaming behind them into the northern quarter whence they had been driven this day. And now the pursuing line of vehicles, fingers of fire curving, hooking, above, before them. And they came, stragglers and breakdowns being blasted from bloom to wilt, flash to smolder, ignored by their fleeing fellows. . . .

Murdock lay upon his belly atop the ridge, regarding the advancing herd through powerful field glasses. In the arroyo to his rear, the Angel of Death—all cream and chrome and bulletproof glass, sporting a laser cannon and two bands of armor-piercing rockets—stood like an exiled mirage glistening in the sun, vibrating, tugging against reality.

It was a country of hills, long ridges, deep canyons toward which they were being driven. Soon they would be faced with a choice. They could pass into the canyon below or enter the one farther to the east. They could also split and take both passages. The results would be the same. Other armed observers were mounted atop other ridges, waiting.

As he watched to see what the choice would be, Murdock's mind roamed back over the previous fifteen years, since the destruction of the Devil Car at the graveyard of the autos. He had, for twenty-five years, devoted his life to the pursuit of the wild ones. In that time he had become the world's foremost authority on the car herds—their habitats, their psychology, their means of maintenance and fueling—learning virtually everything concerning their ways, save for the precise nature of the initial flaw that one fatal year, which had led to the aberrant radio-communicable program that spread like a virus among the computerized vehicles. Some, but not all, were susceptible to it, tightening the disease analogy by another twist of the wrench. And some recovered, to be found returned to the garage or parked before the house one morning, battered but back in service, reluctant to recite their doings of days past. For the wild ones killed and raided, turning service stations into fortresses, dealerships into armed camps. The black Caddy had even borne within it the remains of the driver it had monoed long ago.

Murdock could feel the vibrations beneath him. He lowered the glasses, no longer needing them, and stared through the blue wind. After a few moments more he could hear the sound, as well as feel it—over a thousand engines roaring, gears grinding, sounds of scraping and crashing—as the last wild herd rushed to its doom. For a quarter of a century he had sought this day, ever since his brother's death had set him upon the trail. How many cars had he used up? He could no longer remember. And now...

He recalled his days of tracking, stalking, observing and recording. The patience, the self-control it had required, exercising restraint when what he most desired was the immediate destruction of his quarry. But there had been a benefit in the postponement—this day was the reward, in that it would see the passing of the last of them. Yet the things he remembered had left strange tracks upon the path he had traveled.

As he watched their advance, he recalled the fights for supremacy he had witnessed within the herds he had followed. Often the defeated car would withdraw after it was clear that it was beaten: grill smashed, trunk sprung, lights shattered, body crumpled and leaking. The new leader would then run in wide circles, horn blaring, signal of its victory, its mastery. The defeated one, denied repair from the herd supply, would sometimes trail after the pack, an outcast. Occasionally it would be taken back in if it located something worth raiding. More often, however, it wandered across the Plains, never to be seen mobile again. He had tracked one once, wondering whether it had made its way to some new graveyard of the autos. He was startled to see it suddenly appear atop a mesa, turn toward the face that rose above a deep gorge, grind its gears, rev its engine, and rush forward, to plunge over the edge, crashing, rolling, and burning below.

But he recalled one occasion when the winner would not settle for less than a total victory. The blue sedan had approached the beige one where it sat on a low hillock with four or five parked sports cars. Spinning its wheels, it blared its challenge at several hundred meters' distance, then turned, cutting through a half circle, and began its approach. The beige began a series of similar maneuvers, wheeling and honking, circling as it answered the challenge. The sports cars hastily withdrew to the sidelines.

They circled each other as they drew nearer, the circle quickly growing smaller. Finally the beige struck, smashing into the blue vehicle's left front fender, both of them spinning and sliding, their engines racing. Then they were apart again, feinting—advancing a brief distance, braking, turning, backing, advancing.

The second engagement clipped off the blue vehicle's left rear taillight and tore loose its rear bumper. Yet it recovered rapidly, turned, and struck the beige broadside, partly caving it in. Immediately it backed off and struck again before the other had completely recovered. The beige tore loose and spun away in reverse. It knew all the tricks, but the other kept rushing in, coming faster now, striking and withdrawing. Loud rattling noises were coming from the beige, but it continued its circling, its feinting, the sunlight through the risen dust giving it a burnished look, as of very old gold. Its next rush creased the right side of the blue vehicle. It sounded its horn as it pursued it and commenced an outward turn.

The blue car was already moving in that direction, however, gravel spewing from beneath its rear wheels, horn blasting steadily. It leaped forward and again struck the beige upon the same side. As it backed off, the beige turned to flee, its horn suddenly silent.

The blue car hesitated only a moment, then sped after it, crashing into its rear end. The beige pulled away, leaking oil, doors rattling. But the blue car pursued it and struck again. It moved on, but the blue swerved, ran through a small arc, and hit it yet again upon the same side it had earlier. This time the beige was halted by the blow, steam emerging from beneath its hood. This time, as the blue car drew back, it was unable to flee. Rushing forward, the blue struck it once more upon the badly damaged left side. The impact lifted it from the ground, turning it over onto the slope falling away sharply to its right. It rolled sideways, tumbling and bouncing, to be brought up with a crash upon its side. Moments later its fuel tank exploded.

The blue car had halted, facing downhill. It ran up an antenna from which half a dozen spinning sensors unfurled, a fairy totem pole shimmering in the fume-filled air. After a time it retracted the sensors and withdrew the aerial. It gave one loud blare of the horn then and moved away to round up the sports cars.

Murdock remembered. He put his glasses in their case as the herd neared the turning point. He could distinguish individual members now, unassisted. They were a sorry-looking lot. Seeing them, he recalled the points of the best that he had come across over the years. When their supplies of parts had been larger, they had used their external manipulators to modify themselves into some magnificent and lethal forms. Kilo for kilo, the wild ones had become superior to anything turned out in the normal course of production.

All of the car scouts, of course, went armed, and in the early days a number of them had experimented. Coming upon a small herd, they would cut out a number of the better ones, blasting the rest. Disconnecting the think boxes, they would have their partners drive them back. But attempts at rehabilitation had been something less than successful. Even a complete

wipe, followed by reprogramming, did not render the susceptible individuals immune to relapse. Murdock even recalled
one that had behaved normally for almost a year, until one day
in the midst of a traffic jam it had monooed its driver and taken
off for the hills. The only alternative was to discard the entire
computational unit and replace it with a new one—which was
hardly worthwhile, since its value was far greater than that of
the rest of the vehicle.

No, there had been no answer in that direction. Or any
other but the course that he had followed: track and attack, the
systematic destruction of the herds. Over the years his respect
for the cunning and daring of the herd leaders had grown. As
the wild ones had dwindled in number, their ferocity and guile
had reached the level of legend. There had been nights, as he
lay sleeping, that he dreamed of himself as a wild car, armed,
racing across the Plains, leader of a herd. Then there was only
one other car, a red one.

The herd began its turn. Murdock saw, with a sudden pang
of regret, that it was heading into the far eastern canyon. He
tugged at his white-streaked beard and cursed as he reached
for his stick and began to rise. True, there would still be
plenty of time to get over to the next canyon for the kill but—

No! Some of them were splitting off, heading this way!

Smiling, he drew himself upright and limped rapidly down
the hill to where the Angel of Death waited for him. He heard
the exploding mines as he climbed into the vehicle. Its motor
began to hum.

"There are a few in the next canyon," came the soft, well-
modulated, masculine voice of his machine. "I have been
monitoring all bands."

"I know," he answered, stowing his stick. "Let's head over
that way. Some will make it through."

Safety restraints snapped into place around him as they
began to move.

"Wait!"

The white vehicle halted.

"What is it that you wish?"

"You are heading north."

"We must, to exit here and enter the next canyon with the
others."

"There are some connecting side canyons to the south. Go that way. I want to beat the others in."

"There will be some risk involved."

Murdock laughed.

"I've lived with risk for a quarter of a century, waiting for this day. I want to be there first for the end. Go south!"

The car swung through a turn and headed southward.

As they cruised along the arroyo bottom's sand, Murdock asked, "Hear anything?"

"Yes," came the reply. "The sounds of those who were blasted by the mines, the cries of those who made it through."

"I knew some would make it! How many? What are they doing now?"

"They continue their flight southward. Perhaps several dozen. Perhaps many more. It is difficult to estimate from the transmissions."

Murdock chuckled.

"They've no way out. They'll have to turn sooner or later, and we'll be waiting."

"I am not certain that I could deal with a mass attack by that many—even if most lack special armaments."

"I know what I'm doing," Murdock said. "I've chosen the battleground."

He listened to the muffled thuds of the distant explosions.

"Prime the weapons systems," he announced. "Some of them could have located the sideway we'll be taking."

A twin band of yellow lights winked out on the dashboard and were replaced by a double row of green ones. Almost immediately these faded and were succeeded by two lines of steady, red points.

"Ready on rockets," came the voice of the Angel.

Murdock reached out and threw a switch.

A larger light had also come on—orange and pulsing faintly.

"Cannon ready."

Murdock threw a larger switch beside a pistol grip set in the dash below it.

"I'll keep this one on manual for now."

"Is that wise?"

Murdock did not answer. For a moment he watched the

bands of red and yellow strata to his left, a veil of shadow being drawn slowly upward over them.

"Slow now. The sideway will be coming up shortly. It should be up there on the left."

His car began to slow.

"I believe that I detect it ahead."

"Not the next one. It's blind. There's one right after it, though. It goes through."

They continued to slow as they passed the mouth of the first opening to the left. It was dark and angled off sharply.

"I've become aware of the next one."

"Very slowly now. Blast anything that moves."

Murdock reached forward and took hold of the pistol grip.

Angel braked and made the turn, advancing into a narrow pass.

"Dim the ready lights. No transmissions of any sort. Keep it dark and quiet."

They moved through an alley of shadow, the distant explosions having become a pulsing more felt than heard now. Stony walls towered on either hand. Their way wound to the right and then to the left.

Another right-hand twisting, and there was a bit of brightness and a long line of sight.

"Stop about three meters before it opens out," Murdock said, not realizing until moments later that he had whispered.

They crept ahead and came to a halt.

"Keep the engine running."

"Yes."

Murdock leaned forward, peering into the larger canyon running at right angles to their own. Dust hung in the air— dark, murky below, sparkling higher above, where the sun's rays could still reach.

"They've already passed," he reflected, "and soon they should realize they're in a box—a big one, but still a box. Then they'll turn and come back and we'll open up on them." Murdock looked to the left. "Good place right over there for some more of our people to lay up and wait for them. I'd better get in touch and let them know. Use a fresh scrambler this time."

"How do you know they'll be coming back? Perhaps they'll lay up in there and make you come in after them."

"No," Murdock said. "I know them too well. They'll run for it."

"Are you sure there aren't any other sideways?"

"None going west. There may be a few heading east, but if they take them, they'll wind up in the other trap. Either way, they lose."

"What if some of those others cut down this way?"

"The more the merrier. Get me that line. And see what you can pick up on the herd while I'm talking."

Shortly after that, he was in touch with the commander of the southern wing of the pursuers, requesting a squad of armed and armored vehicles to be laid up at the point he designated. He learned that they were already on their way to the western canyon in search of those vehicles observed entering there. The commander relayed Murdock's message to them and told him that they would be along in a matter of minutes. Murdock could still feel the shock waves from the many explosions in the eastern canyon.

"Good," he said, and he ended the transmission.

"They've reached the end," the Angel announced a little later, "and are circling. I hear their broadcasts. They are beginning to suspect that there is no way out."

Murdock smiled. He was looking to his left, where the first of the pursuing vehicles had just come into sight. He raised the microphone and began giving directions.

As he waited, he realized that at no time had he relaxed his hold on the pistol grip. He withdrew his hand, wiped his palm on his trousers, and returned it.

"They are coming now," the Angel said. "They have turned and are headed back this way."

Murdock turned his head to the right and waited. The destruction had been going on for nearly a month, and today's should be the last of it. He suddenly realized just how tired he was. A feeling of depression began to come over him. He stared at the small red lights and the larger, pulsing orange one.

"You will be able to see them in a moment."

"Can you tell how many there are?"

"Thirty-two. No, hold it . . . thirty-one. They are picking up speed. Their conversations indicate that they anticipate an interception."

"Did any come through from the eastern canyon?"

"Yes. There were several."

The sound of their engines came to him. Hidden there in the neck of the ravine, he saw the first of them—a dark sedan, dented and swaying, half of its roof and the nearest fender torn away—come around the canyon's bend. He held his fire as it approached, and soon the others followed—rattling, steaming, leaking, covered with dents and rust spots, windows broken, hoods missing, doors loose. A strange feeling came into his breast as he thought about the more magnificent specimens of the great herds he had followed over the years.

Still, he held his fire, even as the first in line drew abreast of him, and his thoughts went back to the black and shining Devil Car and to Jenny, the Scarlet Lady, with whom he had hunted it.

The first of the pack reached the place where the ambushers waited.

"Now?" the Angel asked, just as the first rocket flared off to the left.

"Yes."

They opened up and the destruction began, cars braking and swerving into one another, the canyon suddenly illuminated by half a dozen blazing wrecks, a dozen, two.

One after another, they were halted, burned. Three of the ambushers were destroyed by direct crashes. Murdock used all of his rockets and played the laser over the heaped remains. As the last wreck burst into flame, he knew that, though they weren't much compared with the great ones he had known, he would never forget how they had made their final run on bald tires, broken springs, leaking transmissions, and hate.

Suddenly he swiveled the laser and fired it back along the canyon.

"What is it?" the Angel asked him.

"There's another one back there. Don't you pick it up?"

"I'm checking now, but I don't detect anything."

"Go that way."

They moved forward and turned to the right. Immediately the radio crackled.

"Murdock, where are you going?" This came from one of the ambushers to the rear.

"I thought I saw something. I'm going ahead to check it out."

"I can't give you an escort till we clear some of these wrecks."

"That's all right."

"How many rockets have you got?"

He glanced again at the dash, where the only light that burned was orange and pulsing steadily.

"Enough."

"Why don't you wait?"

Murdock chuckled. "Do you really think any of those clunkers could touch something like the Angel? I won't be long."

They moved toward the bend and turned. The last of the sunlight was striking the highest points of the eastern rim overhead.

Nothing.

"Picking anything up?" he asked.

"No. Do you want a light?"

"No."

Farther to the east the sounds of firing were diminishing. The Angel slowed as they neared a wide slice of darkness to the left.

"This ravine may go through. Do we turn here or continue on?"

"Can you detect anything within it?"

"No."

"Then keep going."

His hand still upon the grip, Murdock moved the big gun slightly with each turn that they took, covering the most likely areas of opposition rather than the point directly ahead.

"This is no good," he finally announced. "I've got to have a light. Give me the overhead spot."

Instantly the prospect before him was brightly illuminated: dark rocks, orange stands of stone, striped walls—almost a coral seascape through waves of settling dust.

"I think somebody's been by here more recently than those we burned."

"Don't tired people sometimes see things that are not really there?"

Murdock sighed.

"Yes, and I am tired. That may be it. Take the next bend anyway."

They continued on, making the turn.

Murdock swiveled the weapon and triggered it, blasting rock and clay at the corner of the next turning.

"There!" he cried. "You must have picked that up!"

"No. I detected nothing."

"I can't be cracking up at this point! I saw it! Check your sensors. Something must be off."

"Negative. All detection systems report in good order."

Murdock slammed his fist against the dash.

"Keep going. Something's there."

The ground was churned before them. There were too many tracks to tell a simple tale.

"Slowly now," he said as they approached the next bend. "Could one of them have some kind of equipment or something to block you, I wonder. Or am I really seeing ghosts? I don't see how—"

"Gully to the left. Another to the right."

"Slower! Run the spotlight up them as we pass."

They moved by the first one, and Murdock turned the weapon to follow the light. There were two side passages going off the ravine before it turned.

"Could be something up there," he mused. "No way of telling without going in. Let's take a look at the next one."

They rolled on. The light turned again, and so did the gun. The second opening appeared to be too narrow to accommodate a car. It ran straight back without branching, and there was nothing unusual in sight anywhere within it.

Murdock sighed again.

"I don't know," he said, "but the end is just around the next bend—a big box of a canyon. Go straight on in. And be ready for evasive action."

The radio crackled.

"You all right?" came a voice from the ambush squad.

"Still checking," he said. "Nothing so far. Just a little more to see."

He broke it off.

"You didn't mention—"

"I know. Be ready to move very fast."

They entered the canyon, sweeping it with the light. It was

an oval-shaped place, its major axis perhaps a hundred meters in length. Several large rocks lay near its center. There were a number of dark openings about its periphery. The talus lay heavy at the foot of the walls.

"Go right. We'll circle it. Those rocks and the openings are the places to watch."

They were about a quarter of the way around when he heard the high, singing sound of another engine revving. Murdock turned his head and looked fifteen years into the past.

A low, red Swinger sedan had entered the canyon and was turning in his direction.

"Run!" he said. "She's armed! Get the rocks between us!"

"Who? Where?"

Murdock snapped the control switch to manual, seized the wheel, and stepped on the gas. The Angel leaped ahead, turning, as fifty-caliber machine guns blazed beneath the darkened headlights of the other vehicle.

"Now do you see it?" he asked as the rear window was starred and he felt the thudding impact of hits somewhere toward the back of the vehicle.

"Not entirely. There is some sort of screen, but I can estimate based on that. Give me back the controls."

"No. Estimates aren't good enough with her," Murdock replied, turning sharply to place the rocks between himself and the other.

The red car came fast, however, though it had stopped firing as he entered the turn.

The radio crackled. Then a voice he had thought he would never hear again came over it: "That's you, isn't it, Sam? I heard you back there. And that's the sort of car the Archengineer of Geeyem would have built you for something like this—tough and smart and fast." The voice was low, feminine, deadly. "He would not have anticipated this encounter, however. I can jam almost all the sensors without its knowing it."

"Jenny..." he said as he held the pedal to the floor and continued the turn.

"Never thought you'd see me again, did you?"

"I've always wondered. Ever since the day you disappeared. But it's been so long."

"And you've spent the entire time hunting us. You had your revenge that day, but you kept right on—destroying."

"Considering the alternative, I had no choice."

He passed his starting point and commenced a second lap, realizing as he began to draw away, that she must no longer be as finely tuned as when he had known her earlier. Unless—

An explosion occurred some distance ahead of him. He was pelted with gravel, and he swerved to avoid the fresh crater before him.

"Still have some of those grenades left," he said. "Hard to estimate when to drop them, though, isn't it?"

They were on opposite sides of the rocks now. There was no way she could get a clear shot at him with her guns. Nor he at her, with the cannon.

"I'm in no hurry, Sam."

"What is it?" he heard the Angel ask.

"It speaks!" she cried. "Finally! Do you want to tell him, Sam? Or should I?"

"I'd a feeling it was her, back there," Murdock began, "and I'd long had a feeling that we would meet again. Jenny was the first killer car I had built to hunt the wild ones."

"And the best," she added.

"But she went wild herself," he finished.

"How's about you trying it, Whitey?" she said. "Leak carbon monoxide into the air vents. He'll still look live enough to get you out of here. You answer any calls that come in. Tell them he's resting. Tell them you didn't find anything. Slip away later and come back here. I'll wait. I'll show you the ropes."

"Cut it out, Jenny," Murdock said, circling again, beginning to gain on her. "I'll have you in my sights in a minute. We haven't that much time to talk."

"And nothing, really, to talk about," she responded.

"How about this? You were the best car I ever had. Surrender. Fire off your ammo. Drop the grenades. Come back with me. I don't want to blast you."

"Just a quick lobotomy, eh?"

Another explosion occurred, this one behind him. He continued to gain on her.

"It's that virus program," he said. "Jenny, you're the last —the last wild one. You've nothing to gain."

"Or to lose," she responded quietly.

The next explosion was almost beside him. The Angel rocked but did not slow. Gripping the wheel with one hand, Murdock reached out and took hold of the pistol grip.

"She's stopped jamming my sensors," the Angel announced.

"Maybe she's burned out that system," Murdock said, turning the gun.

He sped around the rocks, avoiding the new craters, the light beam bouncing, sweeping, casting the high, craggy walls into a rapid succession of dreamlike images, slowly closing the distance between himself and Jenny. Another grenade went off behind him. Finally the moment for a clear shot emerged from the risen dust. He squeezed the trigger.

The beam fell wide, scoring the canyonside, producing a minor rockslide.

"That was a warning," he said. "Drop the grenades. Discharge the guns. Come back with me. It's your last chance."

"Only one of us will be going away from here, Sam," she answered.

He swung the gun and fired again as he swept along another turn, but a pothole he struck threw the beam high, fusing a section of sandy slope.

"A useful piece, that," she commented. "Too bad you didn't give me one."

"They came later."

"It is unfortunate that you cannot trust your vehicle and must rely upon your own driving skills. Your car would not have missed that last shot."

"Maybe," Murdock said, skidding through another turn.

Suddenly two more grenades exploded between them, and rocks rattled against the Angel. Both windows on the right side were fractured. He skidded sideways, his vision obscured by the flash and the airborne matter.

Both hands on the wheel now, he fought for control, braking hard. Passing through the screen of detritus, slowing and turning, he caught sight of Jenny racing full bore toward the pass that led out of the canyon.

He stepped on the gas again and followed after. She passed through and was gone before he could reach for the weapon.

"Return to automatic, and you will be free for the fighting," the Angel said.

"Can't do that," Murdock replied, racing toward the pass. "She could jam you again then at any time—and get us both."

"Is that the only reason?"

"Yes, the risk."

The red car was not in sight when he came through into the pass.

"Well?" he said. "What do your sensors read?"

"She entered the gully on the right. There is a heat trail."

Murdock continued to slow as he moved in that direction.

"That must be where she was hiding when we came by," he said. "It could be some kind of trap."

"Perhaps you had better call for the others, cover the entrance, and wait."

"No!"

Murdock turned his wheel and sent his light along the passageway. She was nowhere in sight, but there were sideways. He continued to creep forward, entering. His right hand was again on the pistol grip.

He passed these side openings, each of them large enough to hide a car, all of them empty.

He followed a bend, bearing him to the right. Before he had moved an entire car length along it, a burst of gunfire from the left, ahead, caused him to slam on the brakes and turn the cannon. But an engine roared to life before he could take aim, and a red streak crossed his path to vanish up another sideway. He hit the gas again and followed.

Jenny was out of sight, but he could hear the sound of her somewhere ahead. The way widened as he advanced. Finally it forked at a large stand of stone, one arm continuing past it, the other bearing off sharply to the left. He slowed, taking time to consider the alternatives.

"Where's the heat trail go?" he asked.

"Both ways. I don't understand."

Then the red car came swinging into sight from the left, guns firing. The Angel shook as they were hit. Murdock triggered the laser, but she swept past him, turning and speeding off to the right.

"She circled it before we arrived, to confuse your sensors, to slow us.

"It worked, too," he added, moving ahead again. "She's too damned smart."

"We can still go back."

Murdock did not reply.

Twice more Jenny lay in wait, fired short bursts, evaded the singeing beam, and disappeared. An intermittent knocking sound began beneath the hood as they moved, and one telltale on the dash indicated signs of overheating.

"It is not serious," the Angel stated. "I can control it."

"Let me know if there is any change."

"Yes."

Following the heat trail, they bore steadily to the left, racing down a widening sand slope past castles, minarets, and cathedrals of stone, dark or pale, striped and spotted with mica like the first raindrops of a midsummer's storm. They hit the bottom, slued sideways, and came to a stop, wheels spinning.

He threw the light around rapidly, causing grotesque shadows to jerk like marionettes in a ring dance about them.

"It's a wash. Lots of loose sand. But I don't see Jenny."

Murdock ground the gears, rocking the vehicle, but they did not come free.

"Give me control," said the Angel. "I've a program for this."

Murdock threw the switch. At once a fresh series of rocking movements began. This continued for a full minute. Then the heat telltale began to flicker again.

"So much for the program. Looks as if I'm going to have to get out and push," Murdock said.

"No. Call for help. Stay put. We can hold her off with the cannon if she returns."

"I can get back inside pretty quick. We've got to get moving again."

As he reached for the door, he heard the lock click.

"Release it," he said. "I'll just shut you off, go out, and turn you on again from there. You're wasting time."

"I think you are making a mistake."

"Then let's hurry and make it a short one."

"All right. Leave the door open." There followed another click. "I will feel the pressure when you begin pushing. I will probably throw a lot of sand on you."

"I've got a scarf."

Murdock climbed out and limped toward the rear of the vehicle. He wound his scarf up around his mouth and nose. Leaning forward, he placed his hands upon the car and began to push. The engine roared and the wheels spun as he threw his weight against it.

Then, from the corner of his eye, to the right, he detected a movement. He turned his head only slightly and continued pushing the Angel of Death.

Jenny was there. She had crept up slowly into a shadowy place beneath a ledge, turning, facing him, her guns directly upon him. She must have circled. Now she was halted.

It seemed useless to try running. She could open up upon him any time she chose.

He leaned back, resting for a moment, pulling himself together. Then he moved to his left, leaned forward, began pushing again. For some reason she was waiting. He could not determine why, but he sidled to the left. He moved his left hand, then his right. He shifted his weight, moved his feet again, fighting a powerful impulse to look in her direction once again. He was near the left taillight. Now there might be a chance. Two quick steps would place the body of the Angel between them. Then he could rush forward and dive back in. But why wasn't she firing?

No matter. He had to try. He eased up again. The feigned rest that followed was the most difficult spell of the whole thing.

Then he leaned forward once more, reached out as if to lay his hands upon the vehicle again, and slipped by it, moving as quickly as he could toward the open door, and then through it, and inside. Nothing happened the entire time he was in transit, but the moment the car door slammed a burst of gunfire occurred beneath the ledge, and the Angel began to shudder, and then to rock.

"There!" came the voice of the Angel as the gun swung to the right and a beam lanced outward and upward from it.

It bobbed. It rode high. It fell upon the cliff face, moving.

Murdock turned in time to see a portion of that surface slide downward, first with a whisper, then with a roar. The shooting ceased before the wall came down upon the red vehicle.

Above the sound of the crash, a familiar voice came through the radio: "Damn you, Sam! You should have stayed in the car!" she said.

Then the radio went silent. Her form was completely covered by the rockfall.

"Must have blocked my sensors again and sneaked up," the Angel was saying. "You are lucky that you saw her just when you did."

"Yes," Murdock replied.

"Let me try rocking us loose now," the Angel said a little later. "We made some headway while you were pushing."

The breakaway sequence began again. Murdock looked up at the stars for the first time that evening—cold and brilliant and so very distant. He kept on staring as the Angel pulled them free. He barely glanced at her stony tomb as they turned and moved past it.

When they had threaded their way back and out through the ravine, the radio came to life again: "Murdock! Murdock! You okay? We've been trying to reach you and—"

"Yes," he said softly.

"We heard more explosions. Was that you?"

"Yes. Just shooting at a ghost," he said. "I'm coming back now."

"It's over," the other told him. "We got them all."

"Good," he said, breaking the connection.

"Why didn't you tell him about the red one?" the Angel asked.

"Shut up and keep driving."

He watched the canyon walls slip by, bright strata and dull ones. It was night, sky cold, sky wide, sky deep, and the black wind came out of the north, closing wind. They headed into it. Spinning through the dream of time and dust, past the wreckage, they went to the place where the others waited. It was night, and a black wind came out of the north.

Recital

I feel that every now and then one should play around with the storytelling act itself to help maintain one's appreciation for narrative forms. Look where it got Joyce, Pirandello, Kafka and All Those Guys. My ambition along these lines is considerably smaller, however. That's why it's a very short story.

The woman is singing. She uses a microphone, a thing she did not have to do in her younger days. Her voice is still fairly good, but nothing like what it was when she drew standing ovations at the Met. She is wearing a blue dress with long sleeves, to cover a certain upper-arm flabbiness. There is a small table beside her, bearing a pitcher of water and a glass. As she completes her number a wave of applause follows. She smiles, says "Thank you" twice, coughs, gropes (not obtrusively), locates the pitcher and glass, carefully pours herself a drink.

Let's call her Mary. I don't know that much about her yet, and the name has just occurred to me. I'm Roger Z, and I'm doing all of this on the spot, rather than in the standard smooth and clean fashion. This is because I want to watch it happen and find things out along the way.

So Mary is a character and this is a story, and I know that she is over the hill and fairly sick. I try to look through her eyes now and discover that I cannot. It occurs to me that she is probably blind and that the great hall in which she is singing is empty.

Why? And what is the matter with her eyes?

I believe that her eye condition is retrobulbar neuritis, from which she could probably recover in a few weeks, or even a few days. Except that she will likely be dead before then. This much seems certain to me here. I see now that it is only a side symptom of a more complex sclerotic condition which has worked her over pretty well during the past couple of years. Actually, she is lucky to be able still to sing as well as she can. I notice that she is leaning upon the table—as unobtrusively as possible—while she drinks.

All of this came quickly, along with the matter of the hall. Does she realize that she is singing to an empty house, that all of the audience noises are recorded? It is a put-on job and she is being conned by someone who loved her and wants to give her this strange evening before she falls down the dark well with no water or bottom to it.

Who? I ask.

A man, I suppose. I don't see him clearly yet, back in the shadowy control booth, raising the volume a little more before he lets it diminish. He is also taping the entire program. Is he smiling? I don't know yet. Probably.

He loved her years ago, when she was bright and new and suddenly celebrated and just beginning her rise to fame. I use the past tense of the main verb, just to cover myself at this point.

Did she love him? I don't think so. Was she cruel? Maybe a little. From his viewpoint, yes; from hers, not really. I can't see all of the circumstances of their breakup clearly enough to judge. It is not that important, though. The facts as given should be sufficient.

The hall has grown silent once again. She bows, smiling, and announces her next number. As she begins to sing it, the man—let us call him John—leans back in his seat, eyes half-lidded and listens. He is, of course, remembering.

Naturally, he has followed her career. There was a time when he had hated her and all of her flashy lovers. He had never been particularly flashy himself. The others have all left her now. She is pretty much alone in the world and has been out of sight of it for a long while. She was also fairly broke when she received this invitation to sing. It surprised her more than a little. Even broke, though, it was not the money she was offered but a final opportunity to hear some applause that prompted her to accept.

Now she is struggling valiantly. This particular piece had worried her. She is nearing the section where her voice could break. It was pure vanity that made her include it in the program. John leans forward as she nears the passage. He had realized the burden it would place upon her—for he is an aficionado, which is how and why he first came to meet her. His hand moves forward and rests upon a switch.

He is not wealthy. He has practically wiped himself out financially, renting this hall, paying her fee, arranging for all of the small subterfuges: a maid in her dressing room, a chauffeured limousine, an enthusiastic theater manager, a noisy stage crew—actors all. They departed when she began her performance. Now there are only the two of them in the building, both of them wondering what will happen when she reaches that crucial passage.

I am not certain how Isak Dinesen would have handled this, for her ravaged face is suddenly in my mind's eye as I begin to realize where all of this is coming from. The switch, I see now, will activate a special tape of catcalls and hootings. It was already cued back when I used the past tense of the verb. It may, after all, be hate rather than love that is responsible for this expensive private show. Yes. John knew of Mary's vanity from long ago, which is why he chose this form of revenge—a thing that will strike her where she is most vulnerable.

She begins the passage. Her head is turned, and it appears that she is staring directly at him, there in the booth. Even knowing that this is impossible, he shifts uneasily. He looks away. He listens. He waits.

She has done it! She has managed the passage without a lapse. Something of her old power seems to be growing within her. Once past that passage, her voice seems somewhat stronger, as if she has drawn some heartening reassurance from it. Perhaps the fact that this must be her last performance has also stoked the banked fires of her virtuosity. She is singing beautifully now, as she has not in years.

John lets his hand slip from the control board and leans back again. It would not serve his purpose to use that tape without an obvious reason. She is too much a professional. She would know that it was not warranted. Her vanity would sustain her through a false reaction. He must wait. Sooner or later, her voice has to fail. Then . . .

He closes his eyes as he listens to the song. The renewed energy in her performance causes him to see her as she once was. Somewhere, she is beautiful again.

He must move quickly at the end of this number. Lost in reverie, he had almost forgotten the applause control. He draws this one out. She is bowing in his direction now, almost as if . . .

No!

She has collapsed. The last piece was too much for her. He is on his feet and out the door, rushing down the stairs. It can't end this way. . . . He had not anticipated her exerting herself to this extent for a single item and then not making it beyond it—even if it was one of her most famous pieces. It strikes him as very unfair.

He hurries up the aisle and onto the stage. He is lifting her, holding a glass of water to her lips. The applause tape is still running.

She looks at him.

"You can see!"

She nods and takes a drink.

"For a moment, during the last song, my vision began to clear. It is still with me. I saw the hall. Empty. I had feared I could not get through that song. Then I realized that someone from among my admirers cared enough to give me this last show. I sang to that person. You. And the song was there. . . ."

"Mary . . ."

A fumbled embrace. He raises her in his arms—straining, for she is heavier and he is older now.

He carries her back to the dressing room and phones for an ambulance. The hall is still filled with applause and she is smiling as she drifts into delirium, hearing it.

She dies at the hospital the following morning, John at her bedside. She mentions the names of many men before this happens, none of them his. He feels he should be bitter, knowing he has served her vanity this final time. But he is not. Everything else in her life had served it also, and perhaps this had been a necessary condition for her greatness—and each time that he plays the tape, when he comes to that final number, he knows that it was for him alone—and that that was more than she had ever given to anyone else.

I do not know what became of him afterward. When the moral is reached it is customary to close—hopefully with a striking image. But all that I see striking now are typewriter keys, and I am fairly certain that he would have used the catcall tape at the end if she had finished the performance on a weak note. But, of course, she didn't. Which is why he was satisfied. For he was an aficionado before he was a lover, and one loves different things in different places.

There is also a place of understanding, but it is difficult, and sometimes unnecessary, to find it.

The Naked Matador

Okay. Two experiments in a row. Here's my one Hemingway pastiche of sorts. The brief essay that follows it will amplify in some ways another area where his thinking about stories had an influence on my thinking about stories.

Running—waiting, actually—in Key West, I thought of a story I'd read in high school: Hemingway's "The Killers." The appearance of the diner did nothing to change my feelings.

All of the seats at the counter were occupied, except for one on either side of the woman near the middle. I moved to the one at her right.

"This seat taken?" I asked her.

"No," she said, so I sat down.

She wore a beige raincoat, a red and blue scarf completely covering her hair, and large, smoked glasses. It was a cloudy day.

"What's the soup?" I asked her.

"Conch."

I ordered some and a club sandwich.

She had several cups of coffee. She glanced at her watch. She turned toward me.

"Vacationing?" she asked.

"Sort of," I said.

"Staying near here?"

"Not too far."

She smiled.

"I'll give you a ride."

"All right."

We paid our checks. She was short. About five-two or -three. I couldn't really see much of her, except for her legs, and they were good.

We went out and turned left. She headed toward a small white car. I could smell the sea again.

We got in and she began to drive. She didn't ask me where I was staying. She looked at her watch again.

"I'm horny," she said then. "You interested?"

It had been quite a while, running the way I had been. I nodded as she glanced my way.

"Yeah," I said. "You look good to me."

She drove for a time, then turned down a road toward the beach. It was an isolated stretch. The waves were dark and high and white capped.

She stopped the car.

"Here?" I said.

She unbuttoned her coat, undid a blue wraparound skirt. She wore nothing beneath it. She left it behind and straddled me.

"The rest is up to you," she said.

I smiled and reached for her glasses. She slapped my hand away.

"Below the neck," she said. "Keep it below the neck."

"All right. Sorry," I said, reaching up beneath her blouse and around behind for hooks. "You really are something."

I was out and up and in before too long. She did most of the work, with very little change of expression, except near the end when she began to smile and threw her head back. A peculiar icy feeling crept along my spine then, and I looked away from her face and down at the rest of her, riding and flapping.

When I was empty and she was full, she got off and rebuttoned her coat, not bothering with the skirt.

"Good," she said, squeezing my left biceps. "I was getting tense."

"I was kind of tight myself," I said, zipping and buckling, as she started the engine. "You've got a very good body."

"I know."

She got onto the road and headed back.

"Where you staying?"

"Southernmost Motel."

"Okay."

As we drove, I wondered why a girl like that didn't have a steady man. I thought she might be new in town. I thought maybe she didn't want a steady man. I thought it would be nice to see her again. Too bad I was leaving that night.

As we went down my street, I saw a blue car with a man I knew sitting in it, parked in front of my motel. I drew myself down in the seat.

"Go past," I said. "Don't stop!"

"What's the matter?"

"They've found me," I said. "Keep driving."

"The only person I see is a man in a blue Fury. He the one?"

"Yes. He wasn't looking this way. I don't think he saw me."

"He's looking at the motel."

"Good."

She swung around the corner.

"What now?" she said.

"I don't know."

She looked at her watch.

"I have to get home," she said. "I'll take you with me."

"I'd appreciate it."

I stayed low, so I didn't see exactly where she drove. When she finally stopped and turned off the engine and I rose, I saw that we were in a driveway beside a small cottage.

"Come on."

I got out and followed her in. We entered a small, simple living room, a kitchenette off its left end. She headed toward a closed door to the rear.

"There's whisky in the cabinet," she said, gesturing, "wine on the kitchen counter, beer and sodas in the refrigerator. Have yourself a drink if you want. I'm going to be back here awhile."

She opened the door. I saw that it was the bathroom. She went in and closed it. Moments later, I could hear water running.

I crossed the room and opened the cabinet. I was nervous. I wished I hadn't quit smoking. I closed the cabinet again. Hard liquor might slow me if trouble came. Besides, I'd rather sip. I went to the kitchen and located a beer. I paced with it for a time and finally settled onto the green sofa next to a casually draped serape. The water was still running.

I thought about what I was going to do. It began to rain lightly. I finished the beer and got another. I looked out of all the windows, even those in the bedroom in the rear to the left, but there was no one in sight. After a time, I wanted to use the bathroom, but she was still in there. I wondered what she was doing for so long.

When she finally came out, she wore a blue terrycloth robe that stopped at midcalf. Her hair was turbaned in a white towel. She still had on her dark glasses.

She turned on a radio in the kitchen, found music, came back with a glass of wine and seated herself on the sofa.

"All right," she said, "what do you want to do?"

"I'm leaving tonight," I said.

"When?"

"Twoish."

"How?"

"Fishing boat, heading south."

"You can stay here till then. I'll take you to the dock."

"It's not that simple," I said. "I have to get back to my motel."

"What's so important?"

"Some papers. In a big manila envelope. At the bottom of my suitcase."

"Maybe they've got them already."

"Maybe."

"It's very important?"

"Yes."

"Give me the room key. I'll get them for you."

"I'm not asking you to."

"I'll get them. Make yourself at home. Give me the key."

I fished it out and passed it to her. She nodded and walked back to the bedroom. I went to the kitchen and started a pot of coffee. A little later, she emerged wearing a black skirt, a red blouse and a red scarf. Boots. She drew on her raincoat and moved toward the door. I went to her and embraced her, and she laughed and went out into the rain. I heard the car door slam and the engine start. I felt badly about her going, but I wanted the papers.

I went back to the bathroom. A great number of unlabeled

jars filled a section of the countertop. Some of them were open. Several had very peculiar odors which I could not classify, some of them smelled vaguely narcotic. There was also a Bunsen burner, tongs, test tubes and several beakers and flasks—all of them recently rinsed.

I was not certain what I would do if someone followed her back. I felt like a naked matador without a sword. They had been after me for a long while, and there had been many passes. I was not carrying a gun. I had had to go through too many airline security checks recently, and I had not had time to obtain one locally. If I could just make the boat everything would be all right.

I went to the kitchen to check on the coffee. It was ready. I poured a cup and sat to drink it at the table. I listened to the rain.

Perhaps half an hour later, I heard a car in the driveway. I went to the window. It was hers and she appeared to be alone in it.

When she came in, she withdrew the envelope from beneath her coat and handed it to me. She gave me back the key, too.

"Better check and be sure the right stuff is still there," she said. I did, and it was.

"Think they knew which room?" she asked.

"I don't know. They wouldn't recognize the name. Did he see you go in? Come out?"

"Probably."

"Do you think you might have been followed?"

"I didn't see anybody behind me."

I returned to the window and watched for a time. There was nothing suspicious.

"I don't know how to thank you," I finally said.

"I'm tense again," she said.

We went back to the bedroom and I showed my gratitude for as hard and long as I could. It was still a hands-and-mouth-below-the-neck proposition, but we all have our hangups, and it was certainly wild and interesting country. Afterward, she broiled lamb chops and I tossed a salad. Later, we drank coffee and smoked some small black cigars she had. It was dark by then and the rain had stopped.

Suddenly, she placed her cigar in the ashtray and rose.

"I'm going back to the bathroom, for a time," she said, and she did.

She'd been in there several minutes with the water running when the telephone rang. I didn't know what to do. It could be a boyfriend, a husband, someone who wouldn't like my voice.

"Hello?" There was the crackle of long distance and bad connection. "Hello?" I repeated, after several seconds.

"Em . . . ? Is Em . . . there . . . ?" said a man's voice, sounding as through a seashell. "Who is . . . this . . . ?"

"Jess," I said, "Smithson. I'm renting this place for a week. It belongs to some lady. I don't know her name."

"Tell her . . . Percy's . . . called."

"I don't know that I'll see her. But is there any message?"

"Just that . . . I'll be . . . coming."

There was a click, and the echoes went away.

I went to the bathroom door and knocked gently.

"You had a phone call," I said.

The water stopped running.

"What?"

At that moment, the doorbell rang. I rushed to the kitchen window and looked out. I couldn't see who was there, but there was a car parked up the street and it was blue.

I returned to the bathroom door.

"They're here," I said.

"Go to the bedroom," she said. "Get in the closet. Don't come out until I tell you."

"What are you going to do?"

The doorbell rang again.

"Do it!"

So I did. She seemed to have something in mind and I didn't.

Among garments in the darkness, I listened. Her voice and a harsh masculine one. They talked for about half a minute. It sounded as if he had come in. Suddenly there was a scream—his—cut short in a matter of seconds, followed by a crash.

I was out of the closet and heading for the bedroom door.

"Stay in there." Her voice came steady. "Until I tell you to come out."

I backed up, almost against my will. There was a lot of authority in her voice.

"Okay," she said, a little later. "Come out, and bring my raincoat."

I returned to the closet.

When I entered the living room, there was a still figure on the floor beside her. It was covered by the serape. She wore nothing but a towel about her head and the glasses. She took the coat and pulled it on.

"You'd said 'they.' How many are there?" she asked.

"There were two. I thought I'd left them in Atlanta."

"There's a car out there?"

"Yes."

"Would the other one be in it, or out prowling around?"

"Probably prowling."

"Go back to your closet."

"Now wait a minute! I'm not going to have a woman . . ."

"Do it!"

Again that compulsion as she glared at me, and a return of that strange tingling along my spine. I did as she told me.

I heard her go out. After maybe five minutes, I left the closet and returned to the front room. I raised the serape for a look.

Another five minutes, perhaps, and she returned. I was smoking one of her cigars and had a drink in my hand.

"Make mine wine," she said.

"The other one . . . ?"

". . . will not bother you."

"What did you do to them?"

"Don't ask me. I did you a favor, didn't I?"

"Yes."

"Get me a glass of wine."

I went and poured it. I took it to her.

"If we take them down to the dock . . . Your friend won't mind losing some dead weight at sea, will he?" she asked.

"No."

She took a large swallow.

"I'll finish in the bathroom now," she said, "and then we'll get them into the car. We may have to hang around awhile before we can unload them."

"Yes."

Later, after I had disposed of the blue Fury, we got them into her car and she drove slowly to the place I told her. It was after midnight before we were able to unload them and stow them on the boat.

I turned toward her then, in the shadow of a piling.

"You've been very good to me," I said.

She smiled.

"You made it worth a little effort," she said. "You up to another?"

"Right here?"

She laughed and opened her coat. She hadn't bothered dressing.

"Where else?"

I was up to it. As I held her, I realized that I did not want it to end like this.

"You could come with me," I said. "I'd like it if you would. I'd like to have you around," and I kissed her full on the mouth and held her to me with almost all of my strength. For a moment, it seemed that I felt something wet on her cheek against mine. Then she turned and broke my embrace with a single gesture and pushed me away.

"Go on," she said. "You're not that good. I've got better things to do."

Her scarf seemed to be blowing, though there was no wind. She turned quickly and started back toward the car. I began to follow her.

Her voice became hard again, harder than I'd ever heard it.

"Get aboard that boat now," she said, her back to me. "Do it!"

Again the compulsion, very real this time.

"All right," I said. "Goodbye, and thanks," and then I had to go.

Much later that night, Joe and I pushed the two limestone statues over the side into the Gulf Stream. I leaned on the rail for a long while after that, before I realized I had forgotten to tell her that Percy was coming. Later, the sun rose up at my back, turning the sea to a fleece of gold in the west.

The Parts That Are Only
Glimpsed: Three Reflexes

Jacques Barzun once said that the ideal writer would recast his own death sentence as he was reading it, if it were a bad sentence. While I have never had the pleasure, I feel that this might well be true, because writing at an acceptable level comes to be a reflex after a time, gets imposed critically on one's reading and produces a twitch if frustrated. But there are death sentence reflexes and there are other, less immediately essential but ultimately valuable reflexes upon which one comes to rely.

One way or another, writers acquire a set of mental habits that advise us as to when we should describe a character and to what extent, how much physical description is warranted, or tolerable, at a given point in narration, where to drop plot clues, when to begin a new paragraph, when a simple sentence is preferable to a lengthier, more complex one, et cetera. These are the death sentence reflexes. I have a few others that may be nonstandard, so I thought I'd run some of them out for your inspection, in case you're in the market for them. Who knows?

Hemingway said, in *A Moveable Feast:*

It was a very simple story called "Out of Season" and I had omitted the real end of it which was that the old man hanged himself. This was omitted on my new theory that you could omit anything if you knew that you omitted and the omitted part would strengthen the story and make people feel something more than they understood.

This observation bothered me for a long while, because it struck a certain chord in echoing amid my own feelings and practices in writing. I was not at all sure that I believed it as he stated it, but I decided that the observation warranted a little meditation because it suggested a great number of effects, some of which I had attempted in my own ways.

First of all, any story we tell is as much an exercise in omission as inclusion. Our death sentence reflexes normally take care of this, so that we hardly think of the bits of scenery, stray thoughts, passing faces, unimportant physical details we are leaving out.

Somewhere, sometime early I came to believe in tossing in a bit of gratuitous characterization as I went along. It seemed to add something to a story as a whole if—by means of a few extra sentences—a stock character could be shown to have an existence beyond his walk-on role. I remember doing this with the civil servant Briggs—and showing something of the bureaucracy behind him—in *Isle of the Dead*. This I suppose to be a corollary of the Hemingway principle—an indication of the presence of things perhaps important in their own right but not essential to the story itself—actually the reverse of cutting an essential item and hoping that its light shines through. But I believe the effect is similar—in making people feel something more than they understand. It works to expand the setting of the entire piece and to provide evidence of the larger reality surrounding the action by giving the reader a momentary, possibly even subliminal, feeling that there is something more there.

Then, I guess we have Freud to thank for the introduction of childhood trauma into the modern novel, as a key to adult character and actions. I am against the notion on principle, but I do like the technically nonessential flashback. I like it because over the years I have read too many novels where the main characters seemed to come into existence on the first page and plunge immediately into whatever conflict was brewing. In general, I do not like pastless characters. So, I decided early that when more complicated techniques are not required, a quick, brief flashback or even just a reference or two to something in the protagonist's past not connected with anything that is going on in the story's present could efficiently remedy the situation. In *This Immortal*, Conrad explains being late for an engagement because of having attended a birthday party for the seven-year-old daughter of a friend. Nothing more is ever mentioned about it. It is of no consequence to the plot, but I wanted to show that he still had other friends in town and that he was the kind of person who would go to a kid's birthday party. Three birds with one sentence.

Obviously, I am not of the school which holds that everything in a story should advance the action. The shorter the story the more I will concede on this point, for purely practical reasons involving the economy of the briefer form, but there is elbow room in a novel, novella or novelette and I believe in using it to strengthen characterization and to suggest something of the broader world beyond the story's scope.

And finally, there is a small exercise I do in writing longer fiction. I do not know how it would work for anyone else, or even whether it actually works for me—that is, whether my books would be any different if I did not do it. It is the closest I come to the original Hemingway dictum, however, and it is the main reason I was so intrigued by his notion when I first came across it. I do leave something out; or rather, there is something which I do not include.

In writing anything of length, I always compose—either on paper and then destroy it, or in my head and let it be—a scene or scenes involving my protagonist (and possibly separate ones for other important characters) having nothing to do with the story itself—just something that happened to him/her/it once upon a time. I accept it as a real experience, a part of the character's life history, and I may even refer to it in the story itself. But I never include it. I do this under the belief that the character should be larger than his present circumstances indicate, should be defined for me in terms of a bigger picture of his life than the reader ever sees.

The only time I broke my rule and saw one such incident published was when Fred Pohl asked me for a story while I was tied up tight doing *Isle of the Dead*, and I gave him such a sequence ("Dismal Light") rather than take the time to write something new. If you are familiar with both the short story and the novel, I suppose that—viewed from the outside—it is a shoulder-shrugging matter as to what effect that story might have had on the book. I feel it helped me, however, because that offstage piece of Sandow's past showed me how he would behave immediately after he left Homefree.

So, I propose that minor characters, then, by quick reference to their occupations and/or off-scene problems, can be used to expand the general setting of the story, while adding to its verisimilitude with their own improved status as individuals—a double gain; I suggest, also, that even a brief reference to his/her/its past can strengthen a character by adding another point to that character's lifeline; and I feel that a fully realized but not included incident in your character's past can help you to deal with that character in the present—and that all of these devices serve to "make people feel something more than they understand" in your story. Life being full of things felt but not understood, I look upon this as enriching the tale by imitating the actual experience of existence.

I do these sorts of things now without spending much thought over them because I have reduced them to reflexes. In fact, this is the first I have thought about them in years. While they are not of the variety of reflex normally used for recasting death sentences, I do feel they serve to add life to a narrative.

Dismal Light

In keeping with what I said in the foregoing essay—that I make it a practice to do some outtakes on a longer piece showing something about the protagonist in some detail, something to which I may or may not refer in the story itself —I feel that I ought to include here the story "Dismal Light," the outtake from Isle of the Dead, *to show what I was talking about. It is, of course, another variation of the way that stories can come into being.*

Right there on his right shoulder, like a general, Orion wears a star. (He wears another in his left armpit; but, for the sake of wholesome similes, forget it.)

Magnitude 0.7 as seen from the Earth, with an absolute magnitude -4.1; it was red and variable and a supergiant of an insignia; a class M job approximately 270 light-years removed from Earth, with a surface temperature of around 5,500 degrees Fahrenheit; and if you'd looked closely, through one of those little glass tents, you'd have seen that there was some titanium oxide present.

It must have been with a certain pride that General Orion wore the thing, because it had left the main sequence so long ago and because it was such a very, very big star, and because the military mind is like that.

Betelgeuse, that's the name of the star.

Now, once upon a time, circling at a great distance about that monstrous red pride of Orion, moving through a year much longer than a human lifetime, there was a dirty, dead hunk of rock that hardly anyone cared to dignify to the extent of calling it a world. Hardly anyone, I say. Governments move and think in strange ways, though. Take Earth for an example. . . .

It was decided—whenever big organizations don't want to blame a particular person, they tend to get all objective and throw "it" around like mad—it was decided that because of the shortage of useful worlds, maybe that hunk of rock could be made to pay off somehow.

So they got in touch with Francis Sandow and asked him if it could be done, and he told them, "Yes."

Then they asked him how much it would cost, and he told them that too, and they threw up their hands, then reached to close their briefcases.

But, aside from being the only human worldscraper in the business, Sandow did not become one of the wealthiest men around because of inheritance or luck. He made them a proposal, and they bought it, and that's how Dismal was born.

Now let me tell you about Dismal, the only habitable world in the Betelgeuse system.

A scant improvement over the bare hunk of rock, that's Dismal. Sandow forced an atmosphere upon it, against its dead will, an atmosphere full of ammonia and methane. Then he did frightening things to it, involving hydrogen and carbon; and the storms began. He had a way of accelerating things, and Earth's physicists warned him that if he didn't watch it, he'd have an asteroid belt on his hands. He told them, I understand, that if that happened, he'd put them back together again and start over—but that it wouldn't happen.

He was right of course.

When the storms subsided, he had seas. Then he stoked the world's interior, and amidst cataclysms he shaped the land masses. He did various things to the land and the seas, purged the atmosphere, turned off the Krakatoas, calmed the earthquakes. Then he imported and mutated plants and animals that grew and bred like mad, gave them a few years, tampered again with the atmosphere, gave them a few more, tampered again, and so on—maybe a dozen times. Then he set about screwing up the weather.

Then one day, he took some officials down to the surface of the world, whipped off his oxygen helmet, raised an umbrella above him, took a deep breath and said, "This is good. Pay me," before he started coughing.

And they agreed that it was good, and this thing was done, and the government was happy for a time. So was Sandow.

Why was everybody happy, for a time? Because Sandow had made them a mean sonofabitch of a world, which was what they'd both wanted, for various reasons, that's why.

Why only for a time? There's the rub, as you'll see by and by.

On most habitable worlds, there are some places that are somewhat pleasant. There are some small islands of relief from bitter winters, stifling summers, hurricanes, hail, tidal waves, terrific electrical storms, mosquitos, mud, ice, and all the rest of those little things that have prompted philosophers to concede that life is not without a certain measure of misery.

Not so Dismal.

You'd hardly ever see Betelgeuse, because of the cloud cover; and when you did see it you'd wish you didn't, because of the heat. Deserts, icefields and jungles, perpetual storms, temperature extremes and bad winds—you faced various combinations of these wherever you went on Dismal, which is the reason for its name. There was no island of relief, no place that was pleasant.

Why had Earth hired Sandow to create this hell?

Well, criminals must be rehabilitated, granted. But there has always been a certain punitive tenor to the thing, also. A convicted felon is currently granted a certain measure of distasteful experience along with his therapy, to make it stick—I guess—to the hide as well as the psyche.

Dismal was a prison world.

Five years was the maximum sentence on Dismal. Mine was three. Despite everything I've just said, you could get used to the place. I mean, the housing was good—air-conditioned or well insulated and heated, as necessary—and you were free to come and go as you would; you were welcome to bring your family along, or acquire one; and you could even make money. There were plenty of jobs available, and there were stores, theaters, churches and just about anything else you could find on any other world, though a lot sturdier in structure and often even underground. Or you could just sit around and brood if you wanted. You'd still be fed. The only difference between Dismal and any other world was that you couldn't leave until your sentence was up. There were approximately three hundred thousand persons on the entire planet, of which probably ninety-seven percent were prisoners and their families. I didn't have a family, but that's beside the point. Or maybe it isn't. I don't know. I was part of one once.

There was a garden where I worked, all alone except for the robots. It was half underwater all the time and all underwater half the time. It was down in a valley, high trees on the crests of the hills above, and I lived there in a shiny watertight quonset with a small lab and a computer, and I'd go out barefoot and in shorts or in underwater gear, depending on the time, and I'd random harvest my crops and reseed the garden, and I hated it at first.

In the morning it would sometimes look as if the world had gone away and I was adrift in Limbo. Then the emptiness would resolve itself into simple fog, then into reptiles of mist, which would slither away and leave me with another day. As I said, I hated it at first; but as I also said, you could get used to the place. I did, maybe because I got interested in my project.

That's why I didn't give a damn about the cry, "Iron!" when I heard it, partly.

I had a project.

Earth couldn't—strike that—wouldn't pay Sandow's rates when it came to building them a world miserable enough to serve either as a prison or a basic-training site for the military. So Sandow made his proposal, and that was what decided the destiny of Dismal. He gave them a cut rate and guaranteed plenty of therapeutic employment. He controlled so many of the industries, you see.

Laboratories are all right, I guess, for just simply testing equipment. You get all sorts of interesting figures concerning stress limits, temperature resistance, things like that. Then you turn a product loose in the field, and something you hadn't thought to test for goes wrong. I guess Sandow had had this happen to him lots of times, which is why he'd decided to pick up a piece of the field and add it to his lab facilities.

Dismal, all full of vicissitudes, was the testing ground for countless things. Some guys just drove vehicles back and forth through different climate belts, listing everything that went wrong. All the fancy, sturdy dwellings I mentioned were test items also, and their counterparts will doubtless one day spring up on other worlds. You name it, and somebody was living with it on Dismal. Mine was food.

And one day there came the cry, "Iron!" I ignored it, of course. I'd heard the rumors, back before I'd asked to serve out my sentence on Dismal, even.

My sentence had been up almost a year before, but I'd stayed on. I could leave any time I wanted, but I didn't. There had been something I'd wanted to prove, I guess, and then I'd gotten wrapped up in the project.

Francis Sandow had been testing lots of things on Dismal, but so far as I was concerned the most interesting was a by-product of the local ecology. There was something peculiar to my valley, something that made rice grow so fast you could see it growing. Sandow himself didn't know what it was, and the project for which I'd volunteered was one designed to find out. If there was anything edible that could be ready for harvest two weeks after it was planted, it represented such a boon to the growing population of the galaxy that its secret was worth almost any price. So I went armed against the serpents and the water tigers; I harvested, analyzed, fed the computer. The facts accumulated slowly, over the years, as I tested first one thing, then another; and I was within a couple harvests of having an answer, I felt, when someone yelled, "Iron!" Nuts!

I'd half dismissed what it was that I'd wanted to prove as unprovable, and all I wanted to do at that moment of time was to come up with the final answer, turn it over to the universe and say, "Here. I've done something to pay back for what I've taken. Let's call it square, huh?"

On one of the infrequent occasions when I went into the town, that was all they were talking about, the iron. I didn't like them too much—people, I mean—which was why I'd initially requested a project where I could work alone. They were speculating as to whether there'd be an exodus, and a couple comments were made about people like me being able to leave whenever they wanted. I didn't answer them, of course. My therapist, who hadn't wanted me to take a job off by myself, all alone, also didn't want me being belligerent and argumentative, and I'd followed her advice. Once my sentence was up, I stopped seeing her.

I was surprised therefore, when the visitor bell rang and I opened the door and she almost fell in, a forty-mile wind at her back and wet machine-gun fire from the heavens strafing her to boot.

"Susan! . . . Come in," I said.

"I guess I already am," she said, and I closed the door behind her.

"Let me hang your stuff up."

"Thanks," and I helped her out of a thing that felt like a dead eel and hung it on a peg in the hallway.

"Would you care for a cup of coffee?"

"Yes."

She followed me into the lab, which also doubles as a kitchen.

"Do you listen to your radio?" she asked, as I presented her with a cup.

"No. It went out on me around a month ago, and I never bothered fixing it."

"Well, it's official," she said. "We're pulling out."

I studied her wet red bangs and gray eyes beneath matching red brows and remembered what she'd told me about transference back when I was her patient.

"I'm still transferring," I said, to see her blush behind the freckles; and then, "When?"

"Beginning the day after tomorrow," she said, losing the blush rapidly. "They're rushing ships from all over."

"I see."

". . . So I thought you'd better know. The sooner you register at the port, the earlier the passage you'll probably be assigned."

I sipped my coffee.

"Thanks. Any idea how long?"

"Two to six weeks is the estimate."

"'Rough guess' is what you mean."

"Yes."

"Where're they taking everybody?"

"Local pokeys on thirty-two different worlds, for the time being. Of course, this wouldn't apply to you."

I chuckled.

"What's funny?"

"Life," I said. "I'll bet Earth is mad at Sandow."

"They're suing him for breach of contract. He'd warrantied the world, you know."

"I doubt this would be covered by the warranty. How could it?"

She shrugged, then sipped her coffee.

"I don't know. All I know is what I hear. You'd better close up shop and go register if you want to get out early."

"I don't," I said. "I'm getting near to an answer. I'm going to finish the project, I hope. Six weeks might do it."

Her eyes widened, and she lowered the cup.

"That's ridiculous!" she said. "What good will it be if you're dead and nobody knows the answer you find?"

"I'll make it," I said, returning in my mind to the point I had one time wanted to prove. "I think I'll make it."

She stood.

"You get down there and register!"

"That's very direct therapy, isn't it?"

"I wished you'd stayed in therapy."

"I'm sane and stable now," I said.

"Maybe so. But if I have to say you're not, to get you probated and shipped off-world, I will!"

I hit a button on the box on the table, waited perhaps three seconds, hit another.

"... to say you're not, to get you probated and shipped off-world, I will!" said the shrill, recorded voice behind the speaker.

"Thanks," I said. "Try it."

She sat down again.

"Okay, you win. But what are you trying to prove?"

I shrugged and drank coffee.

"That everybody's wrong but me," I said, after a time.

"It shouldn't matter," she said, "and if you were a mature adult it wouldn't matter, either way. Also, I think you're wrong."

"Get out," I said softly.

"I've listened to your adolescent fantasies, over and over," she said. "I know you. I'm beginning to think you've got an unnatural death wish as well as that unresolved family problem we—"

I laughed, because it was the only alternative to saying, "Get out" again, in a louder voice.

"Okay," I said. "I'll agree with anything you say about me, but I won't do anything you tell me to do. So consider it a moral victory or something."

"When the time comes, you'll run."

"Sure."

She returned to her coffee.

"You're really getting near to an answer?" she finally said.

"Yes, I really am."

"I'm sorry that it had to happen at just this time."

"I'm not," I said.

She looked about the lab, then out through the quartz windows at the slushy field beyond.

"How can you be happy out here, all alone?"

"I'm not," I said. "But it's better than being in town."

She shook her head, and I watched her hair.

"You're wrong. They don't care as much as you think they do."

I filled my pipe and lit it.

"Marry me," I said softly, "and I'll build you a palace, and I'll buy you a dress for every day of the year—no matter how long the years are in whatever system we pick."

She smiled then.

"You mean that."

"Yes."

"Yet you stole, you . . ."

"Will you?"

"No. Thanks. You knew I'd say that."

"Yes."

We finished our coffee, and I saw her to the door and didn't try to kiss her. Hell, I had a pipe in my mouth, and that's what it was there for.

I killed a forty-three-foot water snake that afternoon, who had thought the shiny instrument I was carrying in my left hand looked awfully appetizing, as well as my left hand and the arm attached to it and the rest of me. I put three splints into him from my dart gun, and he died, thrashing around too much, so that he ruined some important things I had growing. The robots kept right on about their business, and so did I, after that. I measured him later, which is how I know he was a forty-three-footer. Robots are nice to work with. They mind their own business, and they never have anything to say.

I fixed the radio that night, but they were worried about iron on all frequencies, so I turned it off and smoked my pipe. If she had said yes, you know, I would have done it.

In the week that followed, I learned that Sandow was diverting all of his commercial vessels in the area to aid in the evacuation, and he'd sent for others from farther away. I could have guessed that without hearing it. I could guess what they were saying about Sandow, the same things they always say about Sandow: Here is a man who has lived so long that he's afraid of his own shadow. Here is one of the wealthiest men in the galaxy, a paranoid, a hypochondriac, holed up on a fortress world all his own, going out only after taking the most elaborate precautions—rich and powerful and a coward. He is talented beyond his own kind. Godlike, he can build worlds and feature them and populate them as he would. But there is really only one thing that he loves: the life of Francis Sandow. Statistics tell him that he should have died long ago, and he burns incense before the shrine of statistics. I guess all legends have unshined shoes. Too bad, they say that once he was quite a man.

And that's what they say whenever his name comes up.

The evacuation was methodical and impressive. At the end of two weeks there were a quarter million people on Dismal. Then the big ships began to arrive, and at the end of the third week there were 150,000 remaining. The rest of the big vessels showed up then, and some of the first ones made it back for a second load. By the middle of the fourth week, there were 75,000, and by the end of it, there was hardly anybody left. Vehicles stood empty in the streets, tools lay where they had been dropped. Abandoned projects hummed and rumbled in the wilderness. The doors of all the shops were unlocked and merchandise still lay upon the counters, filled the shelves. The local fauna grew restless, and I found myself shooting at something every day. Vehicle after vehicle tore at the air and sank within the cloud cover, transporting the waiting people to the big unseen vessels that circled the world. Homes stood abandoned, the remains of meals still upon their tables. All the churches had been hastily deconsecrated and their relics shipped off-world. We sampled day and night, the robots and I, and I analyzed and drank coffee and fed the data to the computer and waited for it to give me the answer, but it didn't. It always seemed to need just another scintilla of information.

Maybe I was crazy. My time was, technically, borrowed. But to be so close and then to see the whole thing go up in flames—it was worth the gamble. After all, it would take years to duplicate the setup I had there, assuming it could be duplicated. The valley was, somehow, a freak, an accidental place that had occurred during millions of years of evolution compressed into a decade or so by a science I couldn't even begin to understand. I worked and I waited.

The visitor bell rang.

It wasn't raining this time, in fact the cloud cover showed signs of breaking up for the first time in months. But she blew in as though there was a storm at her back again, anyway.

"You've got to get out," she said. "It's imminent! Any second now it could—"

I slapped her.

She covered her face and stood there and shook for a minute.

"Okay, I was hysterical," she said, "but it's true."

"I realized that the first time you told me. Why are you still around?"

"Don't you know, damn you?"

"Say it," I said, listening attentively.

"Because of you, of course! Come away! Now!"

"I've almost got it," I said. "Tonight or tomorrow, possibly. I'm too close now to give up."

"You asked me to marry you," she said. "All right, I will —if you'll grab your toothbrush right now and get out of here."

"Maybe a week ago I would have said yes. Not now, though."

"The last ships are leaving. There are less than a hundred

people on Dismal right now, and they'll be gone before sundown. How will you get away after that, even if you decide to go?"

"I won't be forgotten," I said.

"No, that's true." She smiled, slightly, crookedly. "The last vessel will run a last-minute check. Their computer will match the list of the evacuees with the Dismal Directory. Your name will show up, and they'll send a special search vessel down, just for you. That'll make you feel important, won't it? Really *wanted*. Then they'll haul you away, whether you're ready or not, and that'll be it."

"By then I might have the answer."

"And if not?"

"We'll see."

I handed her my handkerchief then and kissed her when she least expected it—while she was blowing her nose—which made her stamp her foot and say an unladylike word.

Then, "Okay, I'll stay with you until they come for you," she said. "Somebody's got to look after you until a guardian can be appointed."

"I've got to check some seedlings now," I said. "Excuse me," and I pulled on my hip boots and went out the back way, strapping on my dart gun as I went.

I shot two snakes and a water tiger—two beasts before and one after the seedlings. The clouds fell apart while I was out there, and pieces of bloody Betelgeuse began to show among them. The robots bore the carcasses away, and I didn't stop to measure them this time.

Susan watched me in the lab, keeping silent for almost an entire hour, until I told her, "Perhaps tomorrow's sample . . ."

She looked out through the window and up into the burning heavens.

"Iron," she said, and there were tears on her cheeks.

Iron: Well, it's something you can't just laugh off. You can't make it go away by ignoring it. It only goes away after its own fashion.

For ages upon ages, Orion's insignia had burned hydrogen in its interior, converting it to helium, accumulating that helium. After a time the helium core began to contract, and the helium nuclei fused, formed carbon, produced the extra energy Orion had wanted to keep his uniform looking snappy. Then, to keep up a good front when that trick began to slip, he built up oxygen and neon from the carbon, increasing the temperature of the core. Afraid that would fail him, he moved on to magnesium and silicon. Then iron. Certain spectroscopy techniques had let us see what was going on at the center. General Orion had used up all his tricks but one. Now he had no recourse but to convert the iron back into helium by drawing upon the gravitational field of his star. This would require a rather drastic and rapid shrinking process. It would give him a blaze of glory all right, and then a white dwarf of an insignia to wear forevermore. Two hundred seventy years later the nova would become visible on Earth, and he'd still look pretty good for a little while, which I guess meant something. The military mind is funny that way.

"Iron," I repeated.

They came for me the following morning, two of them, but I wasn't ready to go yet. They set their ship down on the hill to the north of me and disembarked. They wore deep-space gear, and the first one bore a rifle. The man behind him carried a "sniffer," a machine that can track a man down on the basis of his personal body chemistry. It was effective for a range of about a mile. It indicated the direction of the quonset, because I was between them and it.

I lowered my binoculars and waited. I drew my splinter gun. Susan thought I was in the garden. Well, I had been. But the minute that thing came down and settled between the blaze and the mists, I headed toward it. I took cover at the end of the field and waited.

I had my gear with me, in expectation of just such a visit. See, the B.O. machine can't sniff you out under the water.

They must have slowed when they lost the scent, but eventually I saw their shadows pass above me.

I surfaced, there in the canal, pushed back my mask, drew a bead and said, "Stop! Drop the gun or I'll shoot!"

The man with the rifle turned quickly, raising it, and I shot him in the arm.

"I warned you," I said, as the rifle fell to the trail and he clutched at his arm. "Now kick it over the edge into the water!"

"Mister, you've got to get out of here!" he said. "Betelgeuse could blow any minute! We came to get you!"

"I know it. I'm not ready to go."

"You won't be safe till you're in hyperspace."

"I know that, too. Thanks for the advice, but I'm not taking it. Kick that damn rifle into the water! Now!"

He did.

"Okay, that's better. If you're so hot on taking someone back with you, there's a girl named Susan Lennert down in the quonset. Her you can push around. Go get her and take her away with you. Forget about me."

The man holding his arm looked to the other who nodded.

"She's on the list," he said.

"What's wrong with you, mister?" the first one asked. "We're trying to save your life."

"I know it, I appreciate it. Don't bother."

"Why?"

"That's my business. You'd better get moving." I gestured toward Betelgeuse with the barrel of my pistol.

The second man licked his lips, and the first one nodded. Then they turned and headed toward the quonset. I followed all the way, since they were now unarmed and the garden pests weren't.

She must have put up a fuss, because they had to drag her off, between them. I stayed out of sight, but I covered them all the way back to the ship and watched until it lifted off and vanished in the bright sky.

Then I went inside, gathered up the records, changed my clothes, went back outside and waited.

Were my eyes playing tricks on me, or did Betelgeuse flicker for just a second? Perhaps it was an atmospheric disturbance. . . .

A water tiger broke the surface and cut a furrow straight toward me, where I stood upon the trail. I shot it, and a snake appeared from somewhere and began eating it. Then two more snakes showed up, and there was a fight. I had to shoot one of them.

Betelgeuse seemed to brighten above me, but apprehension could account for that seeming. I stood right there and waited. Now my point would either be proved or disproved, once and for all time, so far as I was concerned; and, either way, I'd rest afterward.

It wasn't until much later that afternoon, as I drew bead upon a rearing water snake and heard his voice say, "Hold your fire," and I did, that I realized just how petty I might have been.

The snake slowly lowered its great bulk and slithered past me. I didn't turn. I couldn't. It was so long and kept slithering by, and I kept wondering, but I couldn't turn around.

Then a hand fell upon my shoulder, and I had to; and there he was, and I felt about three inches tall.

The snake kept rubbing up against his boots and turning to do it again.

"Hello," I said, and, "I'm sorry." He was smoking a cigar and was maybe five feet eight inches tall, with nondescript hair and dark eyes, when I finally brought myself to look into them. I'd almost forgotten. It had been so long. I could never forget his voice, though.

"Don't be sorry. There's no need. You had to prove something."

"Yes. She was right, though—"

"Have you proven it?"

"Yes. You're not what they say you are, and you came here for one reason—me."

"That's right."

"I shouldn't have done it. I shouldn't have expected it of you. I had to know, though, I just had to—but I shouldn't have."

"Of course you should. Maybe I needed it, too, to prove it to myself, as much as you needed to see it. There are some things that should mean more than life to a man. Did you find what you were looking for in your garden?"

"Days ago, sir."

"'Sir' isn't what you used to call me."

"I know. . . ."

"You had to see how much Francis Sandow cared for his son. Okay, I spit on Betelgeuse. I blow smoke rings back at it. Now I'm going to leave it. The Model T is parked on the other side of the hill. Come on, we're going to make it."

"I know that, Dad."

"Thanks."

I picked up my luggage.

"I met a nice girl I'd like to tell you about. . . ." I said, and I did, while we walked.

And the snake followed after, and he wouldn't turn it away. He brought it aboard, its bulk coiled about the cabin, and he took it along, out of that lopsided Eden. I'll never forget that he did that, either.

Go Starless in the Night

So, my stories here collected have come into existence in a variety of ways—an attempt to combine diverse elements into a single tale, a sequel to an earlier piece, an experiment designed to teach me something, an outtake . . . . This next one was a request. It came when Fred Saberhagen was putting together a collection called A Spadeful of Spacetime. *The ground rule was that each tale had to provide a novel means of getting at the past—excluding the old Wellsian standby of simple time travel. I thought about it and came up with two gimmicks for producing the desired result. I used this one . . . .*

Darkness and silence all about, and nothing, nothing, nothing within it.

Me?

The first thought came unbidden, welling up from some black pool. Me? That's all.

Me? he thought. Then, Who? What . . . ?

Nothing answered.

Something like panic followed, without the customary physical accompaniments. When this wave had passed, he listened, striving to capture the slightest sound. He realized that he had already given up on seeing.

There was nothing to hear. Not even the smallest noises of life—breathing, heartbeat, the rasping of a tired joint—came to him. It was only then that he realized he lacked all bodily sensations.

But this time he fought the panic. Death? he wondered. A bodiless, dark sentence beyond everything? The stillness . . .

Where? What point in spacetime did he occupy? He would have shaken his head. . . .

He recalled that he had been a man—and it seemed that there were memories somewhere that he could not reach. No name answered his summons, no view of his past came to him. Yet he knew that there had been a past. He felt that it lay just below some dim horizon of recall.

He strove for a timeless interval to summon some recollection of what had gone before. Amnesia? Brain damage? Dream? he finally asked himself, after failing to push beyond a certain feeling of lurking images.

A body then . . . Start with that.

He remembered what bodies were. Arms, legs, head, torso . . . An intellectual vision of sex passed momentarily through his consciousness. Bodies, then . . .

He thought of his arms, felt nothing. Tried to move them. There was no sense of their existence, let alone movement.

Breathing . . . He attempted to draw a deep breath. Nothing came into him. There was no indication of any boundary whatsoever between himself and the darkness and silence.

A buzzing tone began, directionless. It oscillated in volume. It rose in pitch, dropped to a rumble, returned to a buzz. Abruptly then, it shifted again, to worklike approximations he could not quite decipher.

There was a pause, as if for some adjustment. Then "Hello?" came clearly to him.

He felt a rush of relief mingled with fear. The word filled his mind, followed by immediate concern as to whether he had actually heard it.

"Hello?"

Again, then. The fear faded. Something close to joy replaced it. He felt an immediate need to respond.

"Yes? Hello? Who—"

His answer broke. How had he managed it? He felt the presence of no vocal mechanism. Yet he seemed to hear a faint echoing of his own reply, feedbacklike, tinny. Where? Its source was not localized.

It seemed then that several voices were conversing—hurried, soft, distant. He could not follow the rush of their words.

Then, "Hello again. Please respond one time more. We are adjusting the speaker. How well do you hear we?"

"Clearly now," he answered. "Where am I? What has happened?"

"How much do you remember?"

"Nothing!"

"Panic not, Ernest Dawkins. Do you remember that your name is Ernest Dawkins? From your file, we have it."

"Now I do."

The simple statement of his name brought forth a series of images—his own face, his wife's, his two daughters', his apartment, the laboratory where he worked, his car, a sunny day at the beach. . . .

That day at the beach. . . That was when he had first felt the pain in his left side—a dull ache at first, increasing over ensuing weeks. He had never been without it after that—until now, he suddenly realized.

"I—it's coming back—my memory," he said. "It's as if a dam had broken. . . . Give me a minute."

"Take your time."

He shied away from the thought of the pain. He had been ill, very ill, hospitalized, operated upon, drugged. . . . He thought instead of his life, his family, his work. He thought of school and love and politics and research. He thought of the growing world tensions, and of his childhood, and—

"Are you right all, Ernest Dawkins?"

He had lost track of time, but that question caused him to produce something like a laugh, from somewhere.

"Hard to tell," he said. "I've been remembering—things. But as to whether I'm all right—Where the hell am I? What's happened?"

"Then you have remembered not everything?"

He noted odd inflections in the questioning voice, possibly even an accent that he could not place.

"I guess not."

"You were quite unwell."

"I remember that much."

"Dying, in fact. As they say."

He forced himself to return to the pain, to look beyond it.

"Yes," he acknowledged. "I remember."

. . . And it was all there. He saw his last days in the hospital as his condition worsened, passing the point of no return, the faces of his family, friends and relatives wearing this real-

ization. He recalled his decision to go through with an earlier
resolution, long since set into motion. Money had never been
a problem. It seemed it had always been there, in his family
—his, by early inheritance—as ubiquitous as his attitude toward death after his parents' passing. Enough to have himself
frozen for the long winter, to drop off dreaming of some distant spring. . . .

"I recall my condition," he said. "I know what must finally
have occurred."

"Yes," came the reply. "That is what happened."

"How much time has passed?"

"Considerable."

He would have licked his lips. He settled for the mental
equivalent.

"My family?" he finally inquired.

"It has been too long."

"I see."

The other gave him time to consider this information.
Then, "You had, of course, considered this possibility?"

"Yes. I prepared myself—as much as a man can—for such
a state of affairs."

"It has been long. Very long . . . ."

"How long?"

"Allow us to proceed in our fashion, please."

"All right. You know your business best."

"We are glad that you are so reasonable a being."

"Being?"

"Person. Excuse we."

"I must ask something, though—not having to do with the
passage of time: Is English now spoken as you speak it? Or is
it not your native language?"

There was a sudden consultation, just beyond the range of
distinguishability. There followed a high-pitched artifact.
Then, "Also let us reserve that question," the reply finally
came.

"As you would. Then will you tell me about my situation?
I am more than a little concerned. I can't see or feel anything."

"We are aware of this. It is unfortunate, but there is no
point in misrepresenting to you. The time has not yet come for
your full arouse."

"I do not understand. Do you mean that there is no cure for my condition yet?"

"We mean that there is no means of thawing you without doing great damage."

"Then how is it that we are conversing?"

"We have lowered your temperature even more—near to the zero absolute. Your nervous system has become superconductor. We have laid induction field upon your brain and initiated small currents within. Third space, left side head and those movement areas for talk are now serving to activate mechanical speaker here beside we. We address you direct in the side of brain places for hearing talk."

There came another wave of panic. How long this one lasted, he did not know. Vaguely, he became aware of the voice again, repeating his name.

"Yes," he finally managed. "I understand. It is not easy to accept. . . ."

"We know. But this does you no damage," came the reply. "You might even take a heart from it, to know that you persist."

"There is that. I see your meaning and can take it as hope. But why? Surely you did not awaken me simply to demonstrate this?"

"No. We have interest in your times. Purely archaeologic."

"Archaeological! That would seem to indicate the passage of a great deal of time!"

"Forgive we. Perhaps we have chose wrong word, thinking of it in terms of ruins. But your nervous system is doorway to times past."

"Ruins! What the hell happened?"

"There was war, and there have been disasters. The record, therefore, is unclear."

"Who won the war?"

"That is difficult to say."

"Then it must have been pretty bad."

"We would assume this. We are still ourselves learning. That is why we seek to know time past from your cold remains."

"If there was all this chaos, how is it that I was preserved through it?"

"The cold-making units here are powered by atomic plant

which ran well untended—save for computer—for long while, and entire establishment is underground."

"Really? Things must have changed quite a bit after my—enrollment—here. It wasn't set up that way at the time I read the prospectus and visited the place."

"We really know little of the history of this establishment. There are many things of which we are ignorant. That is why we want you to tell us about your times."

"It is difficult to know where to begin. . . ."

"It may be better if we ask you questions."

"All right. But I would like answers to some of my own afterward."

"A suitable arrangement. Tell us then: Did you reside at or near your place of employment?"

"No. Actually, I lived halfway across town and had to drive in every day."

"Was this common for the area and the country?"

"Pretty much so, yes. Some other people did use other means of transportation, of course. Some rode on buses. Some car-pooled. I drove. A lot of us did."

"When you say that you drove, are we to understand that you refer to four-wheeled land vehicle powered by internal combustion engine?"

"Yes, that is correct. They were in common use in the latter half of the twentieth century."

"And there were many such?"

"Very many."

"Had you ever problems involving presence of too many of them on trails at same time?"

"Yes. Certain times of day—when people were going to work and returning—were referred to as 'rush hour.' At such times there were often traffic jams—that is to say, so many vehicles that they got in one another's way."

"Extremely interesting. Were such creatures as whales still extant?"

"Yes."

"Interesting, too. What sort of work did you do?"

"I was involved in research on toxic agents of a chemical and bacteriological nature. Most of it was classified."

"What does that indicate?"

"Oh. It was of a secret nature, directed toward possible military application."

"Was war already in progress?"

"No. It was a matter of—preparedness. We worked with various agents that might be used, if the need ever arose."

"We think we see. Interesting times. Did you ever develop any of efficient nature?"

"Yes. A number of them."

"Then what would you do with them? It would seem hazardous to have such materials about during peace."

"Oh, samples were stored with the utmost precaution in very safe places. There were three main caches, and they were well sheltered and well guarded."

There was a pause. Then, "We find this somewhat distressing," the voice resumed. "Do you feel they might have survived—a few, some centuries?"

"It is possible."

"Being peace loving, we are naturally concerned with items dangerous to human species—"

"You make it sound as if you are not yourself a member."

There came another high-pitched artifact. Then, "The language has changed more even than we realized. Apologies. Wrong inference taken. Our desire, to deactivate these dangerous materials. Long have we expected their existences. You perhaps will advise? Their whereabouts unknown to us."

"I'm—not—so sure—about that," he answered. "No offense meant, but you are only a voice to me. I really know nothing about you. I am not certain that I should give this information."

There was a long silence.

"Hello? Are you still there?" he tried to say.

He heard nothing, not even his own voice. Time seemed to do strange things around him. Had it stopped for a moment? Had he given offense? Had his questioner dropped dead?

"Hello! Hello!" he said. "Do you hear me?"

". . . Mechanical failure," came the reply. "Apologies for. Sorry about yesterday."

"Yesterday!"

"Turned you off while obtaining new speaker. Just when you were to say where best poisons are."

"I am sorry," he stated. "You have asked for something that I cannot, in good conscience, give to you."

"We wish only to prevent damage."

"I am in the terrible position of having no way to verify anything that is told me."

"If something heavy falls upon you, you break like bottle."

"I could not even verify whether that had occurred."

"We could turn you off again, turn off the cold-maker."

"At least it would be painless," he said with more stoicism than he felt.

"We require this information."

"Then you must seek it elsewhere."

"We will disconnect your speaker and your hearer and go away. We will leave you thinking in the middle of nothing. Goodbye now."

"Wait!"

"Then you will tell us?"

"No. I—can't. . . ."

"You will go mad if we disconnect these things, will you not?"

"I suppose so. Eventually. . . ."

"Must we do it, then?"

"Your threats have shown me what you are like. I cannot give you such weapons."

"Ernest Dawkins, you are not intelligent being."

"And you are not an archaeologist. Or you would do future generations the service of turning me off, to save the other things that I do know."

"You are right. We are not such. You will never know what we are."

"I know enough."

"Go to your madness."

Silence again.

For a long while the panic held him. Until the images of his family recurred, and his home, and his town. These grew more and more substantial, and gradually he came to walk with them and among them. Then, after a time, he stopped reporting for work and spent his days at the beach. He wondered at first when his side would begin to hurt. Then he wondered why he had wondered this. Later, he forgot many things, but not the long days beneath the sun or the sound of the surf, the red rain, the blue, or the melting statue with the fiery eyes and the sword in its fist. When he heard voices under the sand he did not answer. He listened instead to whales singing to mermaids on migrating rocks, where they combed their long green hair with shards of bone, laughing at the lightning and the ice.

But Not the Herald

In my earlier collection—The Last Defender of Camelot—*I mentioned, in introducing "Comes Now the Power," that on a particularly bleak day I wrote three stories, one after the other, to occupy my mind: this one, that one and "Divine Madness." I also said there that I had included "Divine Madness" and this one in* The Doors of His Face, The Lamps of His Mouth, and Other Stories, *an even earlier collection. I later received a number of communications from faithful readers—the very first from Jim Burk, of Wichita (Hi, Jim)—saying that "But Not the Herald" was not included in* The Doors—*oh, hell!—in the earlier one. I checked. It had been a long while. They were right. All those years I'd been living in a fool's paradise, convinced that my little story was out there in the world doing its bit to clean up the environment and so forth.*

I suppose that a story written to keep one's mind off of nasty realities is yet another variation on the game the creative impulse plays . . . .

As the old man came down from the mountain, carrying the box, walking along the trail that led to the sea, he stopped, to lean upon his staff, to watch the group of men who were busy burning their neighbor's home.

"Tell me, man," he asked one of them, "why do you burn your neighbor's home, which, I now note from the barking and the screaming, still contains your neighbor, as well as his dog, wife, and children?"

"Why should we not burn it?" asked the man. "He is a foreigner from across the desert, and he looks different from the rest of us. This also applies to his dog, who looks different from our dogs and barks with a foreign accent, and his wife, who is prettier than our wives and speaks with a foreign accent, and his children, who are cleverer than ours, and speak like their parents."

"I see," said the old man, and he continued on his way.

At the crossroads, he came upon a crippled beggar whose crutches had been thrown high into a tree. He struck upon the tree with his staff and the crutches fell to the ground. He restored them to the beggar.

"Tell me how your crutches came to be in the treetop, brother," he said.

"The boys threw them there," said the beggar, adjusting himself and holding out his hand for alms.

"Why did they do that?"

"They were bored. They tired their parents with asking, 'What should I do now?' until finally one or another of the parents suggested they go make sport of the beggar at the crossroads."

"Such games be somewhat unkind," said the old man.

"True," said the beggar, "but fortunately some of the older boys found them a girl and they are off in the field enjoying her now. You can hear her cries if you listen carefully. They are somewhat weak at the moment, of course. Would I were young and whole again, that I might join in the sport!"

"I see," said the old man, and he turned to go.

"Alms! Alms! Have you no alms in that box you bear? Have you nothing to bestow upon a poor, lame beggar?"

"You may have my blessing," said the old man, "but this box contains no alms."

"A fig for thy blessing, old goat! One cannot eat a blessing! Give me money or food!"

"Alas, I have none to give."

"Then my curses be upon your head! May all manner of misfortune come down on you!"

The old man continued on his way to the sea, coming after a time upon two men who were digging a grave for a third who lay dead.

"It is a holy office to bury the dead," he remarked.

"Aye," said one of the men, "especially if you have slain him yourself and are hiding the evidence."

"You have slain that man? Whatever for?"

"Next to nothing, curse the luck! Why should a man fight as he did over the smallest of coins? His purse was near empty."

"From his garments, I should judge he was a poor man."

"Aye, and now he has naught more to trouble him."

"What have you in that box, old man?" asked the second.

"Nothing of any use. I go to cast it in the sea."

"Let's have a look."

"You may not."

"We'll be judge of that."

"This box is not to be opened."

They approached him. "Give it to us."

"No."

The second one struck the old man in the head with a stone; the first snatched the box away from him. "There! Now let us see what it is that is so useless."

"I warn you," said the old man, rising from the ground, "if you open that box you do a terrible thing which may never be undone."

"We'll be judge of that."

They cut at the cords that bound the lid.

"If you will wait but a moment," said the old man, "I will tell you of that box."

They hesitated. "Very well, tell us."

"It was the box of Pandora. She who opened it unleashed upon the world all of the terrible woes which afflict it."

"Ha! A likely tale!"

"It is said by the gods, who charged me cast it into the sea, that the final curse waiting within the box is worse than all the other ills together."

"Ha!"

They undid the cord and threw back the lid.

A golden radiance sped forth. It rose into the air like a fountain, and from within it a winged creature cried out, in a voice infinitely delicate and pathetic, "Free! After all these ages, to be free at last!"

The men fell upon their faces. "Who are you, oh lovely creature," they asked, "you who move us to such strange feelings?"

"I am called Hope," said the creature. "I go to travel in all the dark places of the Earth, where I will inspire men with the feeling that things may yet be better than they are."

And with that it rose into the air and dashed off in search of the dark places of the Earth.

When the two murderers turned again to the old man, he was changed: For now his beard was gone, and he stood before them a powerful youth. Two serpents were coiled about his staff.

"Even the gods could not prevent it," he said. "You have brought this ill upon yourselves, by your own doing. Remember that, when bright Hope turns to dust in your hands."

"Nay," said they, "for another traveler approaches now, and he wears a mighty purse upon him. We shall retire on this day's takings."

"Fools!" said the youth, and he turned on winged heels and vanished up the path, greeting Hercules as he passed him by.

A Hand Across the Galaxy

*I recall an occasion when I was in a nasty mood and simply
sat down and began writing to see what would come of it. It
turned out to be a short mood; something happened to break
it. Ergo, the piece came to a halt, destined to remain brief.
It's hardly even a story. Just a couple of letters. I sent it to a
fanzine, where it duly appeared, and then I forgot about it.
Subsequently, I was privileged to do a book in collaboration
with the late Philip K. Dick—having long admired his ability
to run reality through a wringer, a paper shredder and a
high-speed blender in rapid succession, and then to reassem-
ble the results into things rare and strange. I was very surprised when he mentioned this little fanzine piece favorably.
That he had seen it, remembered it and liked it made me want
to unearth it recently. He often saw things I didn't. Usually,
even.*

Dear Earth Parents,

I do not know how to tell you of my joy that you continue
to know my needs and that you have the Interstellar Foster
Parents Foundation (A Hand Across the Galaxy) to send me
packages every month. It is very kind of you, who have never
seen me, and I am thankful of you. You treated me to a box of
Sweet-o-Crax this month also; which must have cost you
dearly; for this I am too thankful. Let me tell you of my place
that you may share of the joy you have caused to happen here.
My brother-mates and my sister-mates, there are seven, but
three are nestlings and me who cannot work yet, leaving four.

Of the four, my old sister-mate is with eggs and cannot work until the rains and she nests them. What a fine blessing, though. My two brother-mates work in the Earthshop where the big machines bang metal into pieces of things, and they have joy of their work sweeping the chips and wiping with oil the metal and putting it into place under the banger. My older brother-mate's hand is grown back now, although it is not so big as the other one was, but he can use it like the other one only not so strong. We opened your box with piety and excitement and found the warm thror-sox and gleepers you were so thoughtful to think of, and we found the schoolbooks, for me now, but the nestlings will use them later, and we found the tackers and the tickets for food at the Earthstore, which we got and are just finished eating some of now. We were thankful and joyous, and we read of the Earth in the books and we decided it is like the Happy Lands where the Great One sends those who are good after their bodies have been burned. Is it not so? Please write if you ever have the time to tell us about it; and yourselves also; if you ever have time; for we are curious and humility; and we would be joyed to hear of the big trees and the highways they grow with, and your sunsets and big buildings and the sky that is blue. I read many times your card of three packages ago, where you said Having a wonderful time. Wish you were here. It was so kind of you to think of me then and indeed you must have been having a wonderful time with all those glorious roulette wheels it showed in the picture and named on the back, to play with. I still do not know what a roulette wheel is for certain, because they are not in my *Abridged Galactic English Dictionary*. It looks like part of a game though. Perhaps you will tell me of them too when you write? I do not understand your answer to my letter of two packages ago when you said you spill more in one night than you send me in a year. Do you use a liquid currency on Earth now? I thought dollars were of paper and I do not understand. Perhaps you would explain this also sometime? It is a very dry and hot afternoon outside and I must go to the well now, so it will be dark when I come back and I will finish your letter tomorrow. Goodbye for a while Earth parents.

Now I will tell you more of the joy you have caused. Since our father-mate was burned it has been very hard to keep warm the nest at night. Now we have got the fuel tickets you send so that almost every night we have warmth. My sister-mate with eggs sleeps closest to the heat place, except for my mother-mate, who is always cold and shaking with the new sickness that came at about the time your people arrived out of the sky. It is hard to think of all that space out there separating worlds without getting dizzy. There are no high places near here, so I get dizzy even thinking about them. To think that the Great One could build worlds so far apart and watch them all and not get dizzy is dearly good.

I am pleased to learn that your party was good and that my last letter caused your dear friends the joy of laughter. This is the longest letter I have ever written and I hope it also joys you. You are so kind.

Your foster child,
Phaun Ligg

Dear Phaun,

Your letters are priceless. My husband and I treasure them dearly. We are not too well just now, ourselves, but we will write you a long letter quite soon—just as soon as we are a bit more organized. It *has* been a very trying week, so you must forgive us this time. All right? Also, you must excuse my husband's cryptic allusions. He is fond of riddles. Give our best wishes to your mother-mate and your brother-mate & sister-mates. We are thinking of you.

Affectionately,
Edith Mason

P.S. Keep 'em coming, kid. They're a riot.

Foster father-mate,
Sam Mason

The Force that Through the Circuit Drives the Current

I don't like this story. It's short, though, and it's here for a special reason. A few times in my life I have written something before I should have; that is, it was on the back burner and I pulled it and dished it up before it was fully cooked.

In this case, I was playing with a number of ideas involving artificial intelligence, trauma and control for what I hoped would be a neatly realized, well-developed story of some length. I was living in Baltimore at the time, and that year Fred Pohl was to be guest of honor at Balticon, a local science fiction convention. I was invited to interview him as a part of the program. I did this thing, and afterward he graciously took Judy and me and a friend to dinner at Miller's, one of my favorite local restaurants. During the course of things he asked me for a story for a collection he was assembling. I agreed readily, but my mind was filled with the notions recited above. So I decided to use them, and I wrote this story. As I said, I was not totally pleased with its bare-bones displaying of some of these thoughts. But a curious thing happened. The real story began to crystallize while I was doing this one—a story much too long, I could see, for me to knock off in time for Fred's deadline. The real story was to be Home Is the Hangman, *one of my better novellas. This story, then, is yet another variation: It was a finger exercise, a story the writing of which served to produce something better than itself. If it hadn't been for Balticon and the Chateaubriand at Miller's, the following tale would never have existed, and I don't know what would have become of. . .* Hangman.

. . . And I had been overridden by a force greater than my own.

Impression of a submarine canyon: a giant old riverbed; a starless, moonless night; fog; a stretch of quicksand; a bright lantern held high in its midst.

I had been moving along the Hudson Canyon, probing the sediment, reaching down through the muck and the sludge, ramming in a corer and yanking it back again. I analyzed and recorded the nature, the density, the distribution of the several layers within my tube; then I would flush it, move to the next likely spot and repeat the performance; if the situation warranted, I would commence digging a hole—the hard way—and when it was done, I would stand on its bottom and take another core; generally, the situation did not warrant it: there were plenty of ready-made fissures, crevasses, sinkholes. Every now and then I would toss a piece of anything handy into the chopper in my middle, where the fusion kiln would burn it to power; every now and then I would stand still and feed the fire and feel the weight of 1,500 fathoms of Atlantic pressing lightly about me; and I would splay brightness, running through the visible spectrum and past, bounce sounds, receive echoes.

Momentarily, I lost my footing. I adjusted and recovered it. Then something struggled within me, and for the thinnest slice of an instant I seemed to split, to be of two minds. I reached out with sensory powers I had never before exercised—a matter of reflex rather than intent—and simultaneous with the arrival of its effects, I pinpointed the disturbance.

As I was swept from the canyon's bed and slammed against the wall of stone that had towered to my left, was shaken and tossed end over end, was carried down and along by the irresistible pressure of muddy water, I located the epicenter of the earthquake as fifty-three miles to the south-southeast. Addenda to the impression of a submarine canyon: one heavy dust storm; extinguish the lantern.

I could scarcely believe my good fortune. It was fascinating. I was being swept along at well over fifty miles an hour, buried in mud, uncovered, bounced, tossed, spun, reburied, pressed, turned, torn free and borne along once again, on down into the abyssal depths. I recorded everything.

For a long time, submarine canyons were believed to represent the remains of dry-land canyons, formed back in the ice ages, covered over when the seas rose again. But they simply cut too far. Impossible quantities of water would have to have been bound as ice to account for the depths to which they extend. It was Heezen and Ewing of Lamont who really made the first strong case for turbidity currents as the causative agent, though others such as Daly had suggested it before them; and I believe it was Heezen who once said that no one would ever see a turbidity current and survive. Of course, he had had in mind the state of the art at that time, several decades back. Still, I felt extremely fortunate that I had been in a position to take full advantage of the shock in this fashion, to register the forces with which the canyon walls were being hammered and abraded, the density and the velocity of the particles, the temperature shifts. . . . I clucked with excitement.

Then, somewhere, plunging, that split again, a troubled dual consciousness, as though everything were slightly out of focus, to each thought itself and a running shadow. This slippage increased, the off thoughts merged into something entire, something which moved apart from me, dimmed, was gone. With its passing, I too felt somehow more entire, a sufficiency within an aloneness which granted me a measure of control I had never realized I possessed. I extended my awareness along wavelengths I had not essayed before, exploring far, farther yet . . . .

Carefully, I strove for stability, realizing that even I could be destroyed if I did not achieve it. How clumsy I had been! It should not be that difficult to ride the current all the way down to the abyssal plains. I continued to test my awareness as I went, clucking over each new discovery.

"Ease up, Dan! It's running the show now. Let it!"

"I guess you're right, Tom."

He leaned back, removing the stereovisual helmet, detaching himself from the telefactor harness. Out of the gauntlets, where microminiaturized air-jet transducers had conveyed the tactile information; strap after sensitive strap undone, force and motion feedback disconnected. Tom moved to assist him. When they had finished, the teleoperator exoskel hung like a gutted crustacean within the U-shaped recess of the console.

Dan dragged the back of his hand over his forehead, ran his fingers through his hair. Tom steered him across the cabin toward a chair facing the viewscreen.

"You're sweating like a pig. Sit down. Can I get you something?"

"Any coffee left?"

"Yeah. Just a minute."

Tom filled a mug and passed it to him. He seated himself in a nearby chair. Both men regarded the screen. It showed the same turbulence, the mud and rock passage Dan had regarded through the helmet's eyepiece. But now these things were only objects. Away from the remote manipulator system, he was no longer a part of them. He sipped his coffee and studied the flow.

". . . Really lucky," he said, "to run into something like this first time out."

Tom nodded. The boat rocked gently. The console hummed.

"Yes," Tom said, glancing at the indicators, "it's a bonus, all right. Look at that slop flow, will you! If the unit holds up through this, we've scored all the way around."

"I think it will. It seems to have stabilized itself. That brain is actually functioning. I could almost feel those little tunnel junction neuristors working, forming their own interconnections as I operated it. Apparently, I fed it sufficient activity, it took in sufficient data . . . It formed its own paths. It did— learn. When the quake started, it took independent action. It almost doesn't really need me now."

"Except to teach it something new, for whatever we want it to do next."

Dan nodded, slowly.

"Yes. . . . Still, you wonder what it's teaching itself, now that it's in control for a time. That was a peculiar feeling— when I realized it had finally come into its equivalent of awareness. When it made its own decision to adjust to that first tiny shock. Now, watching it control its own situation . . . It *knows* what it's doing."

"Look! You can actually see those damn eddies! It's doing around fifty-five miles an hour, and that slop is still going faster. —Yeah, that must really have been something, feeling it take over that way."

"It was quite strange. Just when it happened, I felt as if I were—touching another awareness, I guess that's the best way to put it. It was as if a genuine consciousness had suddenly flickered into being beside my own, down there, and as if it were aware of me, just for a second. Then we went our own ways. I think the neuropsych boys and the cyberneticists were right. I think we've produced an artificial intelligence."

"That's really frosting on my turbidity cake," Tom said, taking notes. "It was actually a Swiss guy, back in the nineteenth century, who first guessed at turbidity currents, to explain how mud from the Rhone got way out in Lake Geneva—did you see that!? Tore a hunk right off the side! Yeah, that's a great little gimmick you've got. If it makes it down to the plains, I want some cores right away. We've got plenty of recent samples, so it ought to be able to give us the depth of sediment deposit from this slide. Then maybe you could send it back up to where it was, for some comparison cores with the ones it was just taking. I—"

"I wonder what it thinks about itself—and us?"

"How could it know about us? It only knows what you taught it, and whatever it's learning now."

"It felt me there, right at the end. I'm sure of it."

Tom chuckled.

"Call that part of its religious upbringing, then. If it ever gets balky, you can thunder and lightning at it. —Must be doing close to sixty now!"

Dan finished his coffee.

"I just had a bizarre thought," he said, moments later. "What if something were doing the same thing to us—controlling us, watching the world through our senses—without our being aware of it?"

Tom shrugged.

"Why should they?"

"Why are we doing it with the unit? Maybe they'd be interested in turbidity currents on this sort of a planet—or of our experiments with devices of this sort. That's the point. It could be anything. How could we tell?"

"Let me get you another cup of coffee, Dan."

"All right, all right! Forgive the metaphysics. I was just so close to that feeling with the unit . . . I started picturing myself

on the teleslave end of things. The feeling's gone now, anyhow."

"Voic, what is it?"

Voic released the querocube and lufted toward Doman.

"That one I was just fiding—it came closer than any of
them ever did before to recognizing my presence!"

"Doubtless because of the analogous experience with its
own fide. Interesting, though. Let it alone for a while."

"Yes. A most peculiar cause-field, though. It gives me
pause to wonder, could something be fiding us?"

Doman perigrated.

"Why would anything want to fide us?"

"I do not know. How could I?"

"Let me get you a B-charge."

"All right."

Voic took up the querocube once again.

"What are you doing?"

"Just a small adjustment I neglected. There. —Let's have
that B-charge."

They settled back and began to feculate.

"What are you doing, Dan?"

"I forgot to turn it loose."

"To what?"

"Give it total autonomy, to let it go. I had to overload the
slave-circuits to burn them out."

"You— You— Yes. Of course. Here's your coffee.
—Look at that mud slide, will you!"

"That's really something, Tom."

Clucking, I toss another chunk of anything handy into my
chopper.

Home Is the Hangman

There is very little I can say about a story of this length. And you have my note to the previous one anyway.

Big fat flakes down the night, silent night, windless night. And I never count them as storms unless there is wind. Not a sigh or whimper, though. Just a cold, steady whiteness, drifting down outside the window, and a silence confirmed by gunfire, driven deeper now that it had ceased. In the main room of the lodge the only sounds were the occasional hiss and sputter of the logs turning to ashes on the grate.

I sat in a chair turned sidewise from the table to face the door. A tool kit rested on the floor to my left. The helmet stood on the table, a lopsided basket of metal, quartz, porcelain and glass. If I heard the click of a microswitch followed by a humming sound from within it, then a faint light would come on beneath the meshing near to its forward edge and begin to blink rapidly. If these things occurred, there was a very strong possibility that I was going to die.

I had removed a black ball from my pocket when Larry and Bert had gone outside, armed, respectively, with a flame thrower and what looked like an elephant gun. Bert had also taken two grenades with him.

I unrolled the black ball, opening it out into a seamless glove; a dollop of something resembling moist putty stuck to its palm. Then I drew the glove on over my left hand and sat with it upraised, elbow resting on the arm of the chair. A small laser flash pistol in which I had very little faith lay beside my right hand on the tabletop, next to the helmet.

If I were to slap a metal surface with my left hand, the substance would adhere there, coming free of the glove. Two seconds later it would explode, and the force of the explosion would be directed in against the surface. Newton would claim his own by way of right-angled redistributions of the reaction, hopefully tearing lateral hell out of the contact surface. A smother charge, it was called, and its possession came under concealed-weapons and possession-of-burglary-tools statutes in most places. The molecularly gimmicked goo, I decided, was great stuff. It was just the delivery system that left more to be desired.

Beside the helmet, next to the gun, in front of my hand, stood a small walky-talky. This was for purposes of warning Bert and Larry if I should hear the click of a microswitch followed by a humming sound, should see a light come on and begin to blink rapidly. Then they would know that Tom and Clay, with whom we had lost contact when the shooting began, had failed to destroy the enemy and doubtless lay lifeless at their stations now, a little over a kilometer to the south. Then they would know that they, too, were probably about to die.

I called out to them when I heard the click. I picked up the helmet and rose to my feet as its light began to blink.

But it was already too late.

The fourth place listed on the Christmas card I had sent Don Walsh the previous year was Peabody's Book Shop and Beer Stube in Baltimore, Maryland. Accordingly, on the last night in October I sat in its rearmost room, at the final table before the alcove with the door leading to the alley. Across that dim chamber, a woman dressed in black played the ancient upright piano, uptempoing everything she touched. Off to my right, a fire wheezed and spewed fumes on a narrow hearth beneath a crowded mantelpiece overseen by an ancient and antlered profile. I sipped a beer and listened to the sounds.

I half hoped that this would be one of the occasions when Don failed to show up. I had sufficient funds to hold me through spring and I did not really feel like working. I had summered farther north, was anchored now in the Chesapeake, and was anxious to continue Caribbeanward. A growing chill and some nasty winds told me I had tarried overlong in these latitudes. Still, the understanding was that I remain in the chosen bar until midnight. Two hours to go.

I ate a sandwich and ordered another beer. About halfway into it, I spotted Don approaching the entranceway, topcoat over his arm, head turning. I manufactured a matching quantity of surprise when he appeared beside my table with a, "Don! Is that really you?"

I rose and clasped his hand.

"Alan! Small world, or something like that. Sit down! Sit down!"

He settled onto the chair across from me, draped his coat over the one to his left.

"What are you doing in this town?" he asked.

"Just a visit," I answered. "Said hello to a few friends." I patted the scars, the stains on the venerable surface before me. "And this is my last stop. I'll be leaving in a few hours."

He chuckled.

"Why is it that you knock on wood?"

I grinned.

"I was expressing affection for one of Henry Mencken's favorite speakeasies."

"This place dates back that far?"

I nodded.

"It figures," he said. "You've got this thing for the past—or against the present. I'm never sure which."

"Maybe a little of both," I said. "I wish Mencken would stop in. I'd like his opinion on the present. —What are you doing with it?"

"What?"

"The present. Here. Now."

"Oh." He spotted the waitress and ordered a beer. "Business trip," he said then. "To hire a consultant."

"Oh. How *is* business?"

"Complicated," he said, "complicated."

We lit cigarettes and after a while his beer arrived. We smoked and drank and listened to the music.

I've sung this song and I'll sing it again: The world is like an uptempoed piece of music. Of the many changes which came to pass during my lifetime, it seems that the majority have occurred during the past few years. It also struck me that way several years ago, and I'd a hunch I might be feeling the same way a few years hence—that is, if Don's business did not complicate me off this mortal coil or condenser before then.

Don operates the second-largest detective agency in the world, and he sometimes finds me useful because I do not exist. I do not exist now because I existed once at the time and the place where we attempted to begin scoring the wild ditty of our times. I refer to the world Central Data Bank project and the fact that I had had a significant part in that effort to construct a working model of the real world, accounting for everyone and everything in it. How well we succeeded, and whether possession of the world's likeness does indeed provide its custodians with a greater measure of control over its functions, are questions my former colleagues still debate as the music grows more shrill and you can't see the maps for the pins. I made my decision back then and saw to it I did not receive citizenship in that second world, a place that may now have become more important than the first. Exiled to reality, my own sojourns across the line are necessarily those of an alien guilty of illegal entry. I visit periodically because I go where I must to make my living. —That is where Don comes in. The people I can become are often very useful when he has peculiar problems.

Unfortunately, at that moment, it seemed that he did, just when the whole gang of me felt like turning down the volume and loafing.

We finished our drinks, got the bill, settled it.

"This way," I said, indicating the rear door, and he swung into his coat and followed me out.

"Talk here?" he asked, as we walked down the alley.

"Rather not," I said. "Public transportation, then private conversation."

He nodded and came along.

About three-quarters of an hour later we were in the saloon of the *Proteus* and I was making coffee. We were rocked gently by the bay's chill waters, under a moonless sky. I'd only a pair of the smaller lights burning. Comfortable. On the water, aboard the *Proteus*, the crowding, the activities, the tempo, of life in the cities, on the land, are muted, slowed—fictionalized—by the metaphysical distancing a few meters of water can provide. We alter the landscape with great facility, but the ocean has always seemed unchanged, and I suppose by extension we are infected with some feelings of timelessness whenever we set out upon her. Maybe that's one of the reasons I spend so much time there.

"First time you've had me aboard," he said. "Comfortable. Very."

"Thanks. —Cream? Sugar?"

"Yes. Both."

We settled back with our steaming mugs and I asked, "What have you got?"

"One case involving two problems," he said. "One of them sort of falls within my area of competence. The other does not. I was told that it is an absolutely unique situation and would require the services of a very special specialist."

"I'm not a specialist at anything but keeping alive."

His eyes came up suddenly and caught my own.

"I had always assumed that you knew an awful lot about computers," he said.

I looked away. That was hitting below the belt. I had never held myself out to him as an authority in that area, and there had always been a tacit understanding between us that my methods of manipulating circumstance and identity were not open to discussion. On the other hand, it was obvious to him that my knowledge of the system was both extensive and intensive. Still, I didn't like talking about it. So I moved to defend.

"Computer people are a dime a dozen," I said. "It was probably different in your time, but these days they start teaching computer science to little kids their first year in school. So sure, I know a lot about it. This generation, everybody does."

"You know that is not what I meant," he said. "Haven't you known me long enough to trust me a little more than that? The question springs solely from the case at hand. That's all."

I nodded. Reactions by their very nature are not always appropriate, and I had invested a lot of emotional capital in a heavy-duty set. So, "Okay, I know more about them than the school kids," I said.

"Thanks. That can be our point of departure." He took a sip of coffee. "My own background is in law and accounting, followed by the military, military intelligence, and civil service, in that order. Then I got into this business. What technical stuff I know I've picked up along the way—a scrap here, a crash course there. I know a lot about what things can *do,* not so much about how they *work.* I did not understand the details on this one, so I want you to start at the top and explain things to me, for as far as you can go. I need the background review, and if you are able to furnish it I will also know that you are the man for the job. You can begin by telling me how the early space-exploration robots worked—like, say the ones they used on Venus."

"That's not computers," I said, "and for that matter, they weren't really robots. They were telefactoring devices."

"Tell me what makes the difference."

"A robot is a machine which carries out certain operations in accordance with a program of instructions. A telefactor is a slave machine operated by remote control. The telefactor functions in a feedback situation with its operator. Depending on how sophisticated you want to get, the links can be audio-visual, kinesthetic, tactile, even olfactory. The more you want to go in this direction, the more anthropomorphic you get in the thing's design.

"In the case of Venus, if I recall correctly, the human operator in orbit wore an exoskeleton which controlled the movements of the body, legs, arms and hands of the device on the surface below, receiving motion and force feedback through a system of airjet transducers. He had on a helmet controlling the slave device's television camera—set, obviously enough, in its turret—which filled his field of vision with the scene below. He also wore earphones connected with its audio pickup. I read the book he wrote later. He said that for long stretches of time he would forget the cabin, forget that he was at the boss end of a control loop, and actually feel as if he were stalking through that hellish landscape. I remember being very impressed by it, just being a kid, and I wanted a super-tiny one all my own, so that I could wade around in puddles picking fights with microorganisms."

"Why?"

"Because there weren't any dragons on Venus. Anyhow, that is a telefactoring device, a thing quite distinct from a robot."

"I'm still with you," he said, and "Now tell me the difference between the early telefactoring devices and the later ones."

I swallowed some coffee.

"It was a bit trickier with respect to the outer planets and their satellites," I said. "There we did not have orbiting operators at first. Economics, and some unresolved technical problems. Mainly economics. At any rate, the devices were landed on the target worlds, but the operators stayed home. Because of this, there was of course a time lag in the transmissions along the control loop. It took a while to receive the on-site input, and then there was another time lapse before the response movements reached the telefactor. We attempted to compensate for this in two ways: the first was by the employment of a simple wait—move, wait—move sequence; the second was more sophisticated and is actually the point where computers come into the picture in terms of participating in the control loop. It involved the setting up of models of known environmental factors, which were then enriched during the initial wait—move sequences. On this basis, the computer was then used to anticipate short-range developments. Finally, it could take over the loop and run it by a combination of 'predictor controls' and wait—move reviews. It still had to holler for human help, though, when unexpected things came up. So, with the outer planets, it was neither totally automatic nor totally manual—nor totally satisfactory—at first."

"Okay," he said, lighting a cigarette. "And the next step?"

"The next wasn't really a technical step forward in telefactoring. It was an economic shift. The pursestrings were loosened and we could afford to send men out. We landed them where we could land them, and in many of the places where we could not, we sent down the telefactors and orbited the men again. Like in the old days. The time-lag problem was removed because the operator was on top of things once more. If anything, you can look at it as a reversion to earlier methods. It is what we still often do, though, and it works."

He shook his head.

"You left something out between the computers and the bigger budget."

I shrugged.

"A number of things were tried during that period, but

none of them proved as effective as what we already had going in the human—computer partnership with the telefactors."

"There was one project," he said, "which attempted to get around the time-lag troubles by sending the computer along with the telefactor as part of the package. Only the computer wasn't exactly a computer and the telefactor wasn't exactly a telefactor. Do you know which one I am referring to?"

I lit a cigarette of my own while I thought about it, then, "I think you are talking about the Hangman," I said.

"That's right and this is where I get lost. Can you tell me how it works?"

"Ultimately, it was a failure," I told him.

"But it worked at first."

"Apparently. But only on the easy stuff, on Io. It conked out later and had to be written off as a failure, albeit a noble one. The venture was overly ambitious from the very beginning. What seems to have happened was that the people in charge had the opportunity to combine vanguard projects— stuff that was still under investigation and stuff that was extremely new. In theory, it all seemed to dovetail so beautifully that they yielded to the temptation and incorporated too much. It started out well, but it fell apart later."

"But what all was involved in the thing?"

"Lord! What wasn't? The computer that wasn't exactly a computer . . . Okay, we'll start there. Last century, three engineers at the University of Wisconsin—Nordman, Parmentier and Scott—developed a device known as a superconductive tunnel-junction neuristor. Two tiny strips of metal with a thin insulating layer between. Supercool it and it passed electrical impulses without resistance. Surround it with magnetized material and pack a mass of them together—billions—and what have you got?"

He shook his head.

"Well, for one thing you've got an impossible situation to schematize when considering all the paths and interconnections that may be formed. There is an obvious similarity to the structure of the brain. So, they theorized, you don't even attempt to hook up such a device. You pulse in data and let it establish its own preferential pathways, by means of the magnetic material's becoming increasingly magnetized each time the current passes through it, thus cutting the resistance. The material establishes its own routes in a fashion analogous to the functioning of the brain when it is learning something.

"In the case of the Hangman, they used a setup very similar to this and they were able to pack over ten billion neuristor-type cells into a very small area—around a cubic foot. They aimed for that magic figure because that is approximately the number of nerve cells in the human brain. That is what I meant when I said that it wasn't really a computer. They were actually working in the area of artificial intelligence, no matter what they called it."

"If the thing had its own brain—computer or quasihuman —then it was a robot rather than a telefactor, right?"

"Yes and no and maybe," I said. "It was operated as a telefactor device here on Earth—on the ocean floor, in the desert, in mountainous country—as part of its programming. I suppose you could also call that its apprenticeship—or kindergarten. Perhaps that is even more appropriate. It was being shown how to explore in difficult environments and to report back. Once it mastered this, then theoretically they could hang it out there in the sky without a control loop and let it report its own findings."

"At that point would it be considered a robot?"

"A robot is a machine which carries out certain operations in accordance with a program of instructions. The Hangman made its *own* decisions, you see. And I suspect that by trying to produce something that close to the human brain in structure and function, the seemingly inevitable randomness of its model got included in. It wasn't just a machine following a program. It was too complex. That was probably what broke it down."

Don chuckled.

"Inevitable free will?"

"No. As I said, they had thrown too many things into one bag. Everybody and his brother with a pet project that might be fitted in seemed a supersalesman that season. For example, the psychophysics boys had a gimmick they wanted to try on it, and it got used. Ostensibly, the Hangman was a communications device. Actually, they were concerned as to whether the thing was truly sentient."

"Was it?"

"Apparently so, in a limited fashion. What they had come up with, to be made part of the initial telefactor loop, was a device which set up a weak induction field in the brain of the operator. The machine received and amplified the patterns of electrical activity being conducted in the Hangman's—might as well call it 'brain'—then passed them through a complex modulator and pulsed them into the induction field in the operator's head. —I am out of my area now and into that of Weber and Fechner, but a neuron has a threshold at which it will fire, and below which it will not. There are some forty thousand neurons packed together in a square millimeter of the cerebral cortex, in such a fashion that each one has several hundred synaptic connections with others about it. At any given moment, some of them may be way below the firing threshold while others are in a condition Sir John Eccles once referred to as 'critically poised'—ready to fire. If just one is pushed over the threshold, it can affect the discharge of hundreds of thousands of others within twenty milliseconds. The pulsating field was to provide such a push in a sufficiently selective fashion to give the operator an idea as to what was going on in the Hangman's brain. And vice versa. The Hangman was to have its own built-in version of the same thing. It was also thought that this might serve to humanize it somewhat, so that it would better appreciate the significance of its work—to instill something like loyalty, you might say."

"Do you think this could have contributed to its later breakdown?"

"Possibly. How can you say in a one-of-a-kind situation like this? If you want a guess, I'd say, 'Yes.' But it's just a guess."

"Uh-huh," he said, "and what were its physical capabilities?"

"Anthropomorphic design," I said, "both because it was originally telefactored and because of the psychological reasoning I just mentioned. It could pilot its own small vessel. No need for a life-support system, of course. Both it and the vessel were powered by fusion units, so that fuel was no real problem. Self-repairing. Capable of performing a great variety of sophisticated tests and measurements, of making observations, completing reports, learning new material, broadcasting its findings back here. Capable of surviving just about anywhere. In fact, it required less energy on the outer planets—less work for the refrigeration units, to maintain that super-cooled brain in its midsection."

"How strong was it?"

"I don't recall all the specs. Maybe a dozen times as strong as a man, in things like lifting and pushing."

"It explored Io for us and started in on Europa."

"Yes."

"Then it began behaving erratically, just when we thought it had really learned its job."

"That sounds right," I said.

"It refused a direct order to explore Callisto, then headed out toward Uranus."

"Yes. It's been years since I read the reports. . . ."

"The malfunction worsened after that. Long periods of silence interspersed with garbled transmissions. Now that I know more about its makeup, it almost sounds like a man going off the deep end."

"It seems similar."

"But it managed to pull itself together again for a brief while. It landed on Titania, began sending back what seemed like appropriate observation reports. This only lasted a short time, though. It went irrational once more, indicated that it was heading for a landing on Uranus itself, and that was it. We didn't hear from it after that. Now that I know about that mind-reading gadget I understand why a psychiatrist on this end could be so positive it would never function again."

"I never heard about that part."

"I did."

I shrugged. "This was all around twenty years ago," I said, "and, as I mentioned, it has been a long while since I've read anything about it."

"The Hangman's ship crashed or landed, as the case may be, in the Gulf of Mexico, two days ago."

I just stared at him.

"It was empty," Don went on, "when they finally got out and down to it."

"I don't understand."

"Yesterday morning," he continued, "restaurateur Manny Burns was found beaten to death in the office of his establishment, the Maison Saint-Michel, in New Orleans."

"I still fail to see—"

"Manny Burns was one of the four original operators who programmed—pardon me, 'taught'—the Hangman."

The silence lengthened, dragged its belly on the deck.

"Coincidence . . . ?" I finally said.

"My client doesn't think so."

"Who is your client?"

"One of the three remaining members of the training group. He is convinced that the Hangman has returned to Earth to kill its former operators."

"Has he made his fears known to his old employers?"

"No."

"Why not?"

"Because it would require telling them the reason for his fears." —

"That being . . . ?"

"He wouldn't tell me, either."

"How does he expect you to do a proper job?"

"He told me what he considered a proper job. He wanted two things done, neither of which requires a full case history. He wanted to be furnished with good bodyguards, and he wanted the Hangman found and disposed of. I have already taken care of the first part."

"And you want me to do the second?"

"That's right. You have confirmed my opinion that you are the man for the job."

"I see. Do you realize that if the thing is truly sentient this will be something very like murder? If it is not, of course, then it will only amount to the destruction of expensive government property."

"Which way do you look at it?"

"I look at it as a job," I said.

"You'll take it?"

"I need more facts before I can decide. Like who is your client? Who are the other operators? Where do they live? What do they do? What—"

He raised his hand.

"First," he said, "the Honorable Jesse Brockden, senior senator from Wisconsin, is our client. Confidentiality, of course, is written all over it."

I nodded. "I remember his being involved with the space

program before he went into politics. I wasn't aware of the specifics, though. He could get government protection so easily—"

"To obtain it, he would apparently have to tell them something he doesn't want to talk about. Perhaps it would hurt his career. I simply do not know. He doesn't want them. He wants us."

I nodded again.

"What about the others? Do they want us, too?"

"Quite the opposite. They don't subscribe to Brockden's notions at all. They seem to think he is something of a paranoid."

"How well do they know one another these days?"

"They live in different parts of the country, haven't seen each other in years. Been in occasional touch, though."

"Kind of a flimsy basis for that diagnosis, then."

"One of them *is* a psychiatrist."

"Oh. Which one?"

"Leila Thackery is her name. Lives in St. Louis. Works at the state hospital there."

"None of them have gone to any authority, then—federal or local?"

"That's right. Brockden contacted them when he heard about the Hangman. He was in Washington at the time. Got word on its return right away and managed to get the story killed. He tried to reach them all, learned about Burns in the process, contacted me, then tried to persuade the others to accept protection by my people. They weren't buying. When I talked to her, Dr. Thackery pointed out—quite correctly—that Brockden is a very sick man."

"What's he got?"

"Cancer. In his spine. Nothing they can do about it once it hits there and digs in. He even told me he figures he has maybe six months to get through what he considers a very important piece of legislation—the new criminal rehabilitation act. —I will admit that he did sound kind of paranoid when he talked about it. But hell! Who wouldn't? Dr. Thackery sees that as the whole thing, though, and she doesn't see the Burns killing as being connected with the Hangman. Thinks it was just a traditional robbery gone sour, thief surprised and panicky, maybe hopped up, et cetera."

"Then she is not afraid of the Hangman?"

"She said that she is in a better position to know its mind than anyone else, and she is not especially concerned."

"What about the other operator?"

"He said that Dr. Thackery may know its mind better than anyone else, but he knows its brain, and he isn't worried, either."

"What did he mean by that?"

"David Fentris is a consulting engineer—electronics, cybernetics. He actually had something to do with the Hangman's design."

I got to my feet and went after the coffeepot. Not that I'd an overwhelming desire for another cup at just that moment. But I had known, had once worked with a David Fentris. And he had at one time been connected with the space program.

About fifteen years my senior, Dave had been with the data bank project when I had known him. Where a number of us had begun having second thoughts as the thing progressed, Dave had never been anything less than wildly enthusiastic. A wiry five eight, gray cropped, gray eyes back of hornrims and heavy glass, cycling between preoccupation and near-frantic darting, he had had a way of verbalizing half-completed thoughts as he went along, so that you might begin to think him a representative of that tribe which had come into positions of small authority by means of nepotism or politics. If you would listen a few more minutes, however, you would begin revising your opinion as he started to pull his musings together into a rigorous framework. By the time he had finished, you generally wondered why you hadn't seen it all along and what a guy like that was doing in a position of such small authority. Later, it might strike you, though, that he seemed sad whenever he wasn't enthusiastic about something. And while the gung-ho spirit is great for short-range projects, larger ventures generally require somewhat more equanimity. I wasn't at all surprised that he had wound up as a consultant.

The big question now, of course, was: Would he remember me? True, my appearance was altered, my personality hopefully more mature, my habits shifted around. But would that be enough, should I have to encounter him as part of this job? That mind behind those hornrims could do a lot of strange things with just a little data.

"Where does he live?" I asked.

"Memphis. —And what's the matter?"

"Just trying to get my geography straight," I said. "Is Senator Brockden still in Washington?"

"No. He's returned to Wisconsin and is currently holed up in a lodge in the northern part of the state. Four of my people are with him."

"I see."

I refreshed our coffee supply and reseated myself. I didn't like this one at all and I resolved not to take it. I didn't like just giving Don a flat "No," though. His assignments had become a very important part of my life, and this one was not mere legwork. It was obviously important to him, and he wanted me on it. I decided to look for holes in the thing, to find some way of reducing it to the simple bodyguard job already in progress.

"It does seem peculiar," I said, "that Brockden is the only one afraid of the device."

"Yes."

". . . And that he gives no reasons."

"True."

". . . Plus his condition, and what the doctor said about its effect on his mind."

"I have no doubt that he is neurotic," Don said. "Look at this."

He reached for his coat, withdrew a sheaf of papers from within it. He shuffled through them and extracted a single sheet, which he passed to me.

It was a piece of congressional-letterhead stationery, with the message scrawled in longhand. *"Don,"* it said. *"I've got to see you. Frankenstein's monster is just come back from where we hung him and he's looking for me. The whole damn universe is trying to grind me up. Call me between 8 & 10. —Jess."*

I nodded, started to pass it back, paused, then handed it over. Double damn it deeper than hell!

I took a drink of coffee. I thought that I had long ago given up hope in such things, but I had noticed something that immediately troubled me. In the margin, where they list such matters, I had seen that Jesse Brockden was on the committee for review of the Central Data Bank program. I recalled that

that committee was supposed to be working on a series of reform recommendations. Offhand, I could not remember Brockden's position on any of the issues involved, but—oh, hell! The thing was simply too big to alter significantly now. . . . But it *was* the only real Frankenstein monster I cared about, and there was always the possibility . . . On the other hand— Hell, again! What if I let him die when I might have saved him, and he had been the one who . . . ?

I took another drink of coffee. I lit another cigarette.

There might be a way of working it so that Dave didn't even come into the picture. I could talk to Leila Thackery first, check further into the Burns killing, keep posted on new developments, find out more about the vessel in the Gulf. . . . I might be able to accomplish something, even if it was only the negation of Brockden's theory, without Dave's and my paths ever crossing.

"Have you got the specs on the Hangman?" I asked.

"Right here."

He passed them over.

"The police report on the Burns killing?"

"Here it is."

"The whereabouts of everyone involved, and some background on them?"

"Here."

"The place or places where I can reach you during the next few days—around the clock? This one may require some co-ordination."

He smiled and reached for his pen.

"Glad to have you aboard," he said.

I reached over and tapped the barometer. I shook my head.

The ringing of the phone awakened me. Reflex bore me across the room, where I took it on audio.

"Yes?"

"Mister Donne? It is eight o'clock."

"Thanks."

I collapsed into the chair. I am what might be called a slow starter. I tend to recapitulate phylogeny every morning. Basic desires inched their ways through my gray matter to close a connection. Slowly, I extended a cold-blooded member and clicked my talons against a couple of numbers. I croaked my desire for food and lots of coffee to the voice that responded. Half an hour later I would only have growled. Then I staggered off to the place of flowing waters to renew my contact with basics.

In addition to my normal adrenaline and blood-sugar bearishness, I had not slept much the night before. I had closed up shop after Don left, stuffed my pockets with essentials, departed the *Proteus*, gotten myself over to the airport and onto a flight which took me to St. Louis in the dead, small hours of the dark. I was unable to sleep during the flight, thinking about the case, deciding on the tack I was going to take with Leila Thackery. On arrival, I had checked into the airport motel, left a message to be awakened at an unreasonable hour, and collapsed.

As I ate, I regarded the fact sheet Don had given me.

Leila Thackery was currently single, having divorced her second husband a little over two years ago, was forty-six years old, and lived in an apartment near to the hospital where she worked. Attached to the sheet was a photo which might have been ten years old. In it, she was brunette, light-eyed, barely on the right side of that border between ample and overweight, with fancy glasses straddling an upturned nose. She had published a number of books and articles with titles full of alienations, roles, transactions, social contexts and more alienations.

I hadn't had the time to go my usual route, becoming an entire new individual with a verifiable history. Just a name and a story, that's all. It did not seem necessary this time, though. For once, something approximating honesty actually seemed a reasonable approach.

I took a public vehicle over to her apartment building. I did not phone ahead, because it is easier to say "No" to a voice than to a person.

According to the record, today was one of the days when she saw outpatients in her home. Her idea, apparently: break down the alienating institution image, remove resentments by turning the sessions into something more like social occasions, et cetera. I did not want all that much of her time—I had decided that Don could make it worth her while if it came to that—and I was sure my fellows' visits were scheduled to leave her with some small breathing space. *Inter alia*, so to speak.

I had just located her name and apartment number amid the buttons in the entrance foyer when an old woman passed behind me and unlocked the door to the lobby. She glanced at me and held it open, so I went on in without ringing. The matter of presence, again.

I took the elevator to Leila's floor, the second, located her door and knocked on it. I was almost ready to knock again when it opened, partway.

"Yes?" she asked, and I revised my estimate as to the age of the photo. She looked just about the same.

"Dr. Thackery," I said, "my name is Donne. You could help me quite a bit with a problem I've got."

"What sort of problem?"

"It involves a device known as the Hangman."

She sighed and showed me a quick grimace. Her fingers tightened on the door.

"I've come a long way but I'll be easy to get rid of. I've only a few things I'd like to ask you about it."

"Are you with the government?"

"No."

"Do you work for Brockden?"

"No, I'm something different."

"All right," she said. "Right now I've got a group session going. It will probably last around another half hour. If you don't mind waiting down in the lobby, I'll let you know as soon as it is over. We can talk then."

"Good enough," I said. "Thanks."

She nodded, closed the door. I located the stairway and walked back down.

A cigarette later, I decided that the devil finds work for idle hands and thanked him for his suggestion. I strolled back toward the foyer. Through the glass, I read the names of a few residents of the fifth floor. I elevated up and knocked on one of the doors. Before it was opened I had my notebook and pad in plain sight.

"Yes?" Short, fiftyish, curious.

"My name is Stephen Foster, Mrs. Gluntz. I am doing a survey for the North American Consumers League. I would like to pay you for a couple of minutes of your time, to answer some questions about products you use."

"Why— Pay me?"

"Yes, ma'am. Ten dollars. Around a dozen questions. It will just take a minute or two."

"All right." She opened the door wider. "Won't you come in?"

"No, thank you. This thing is so brief I'd just be in and out. The first question involves detergents. . . ."

Ten minutes later I was back in the lobby adding the thirty bucks for the three interviews to the list of expenses I was keeping. When a situation is full of unpredictables and I am playing makeshift games, I like to provide for as many contingencies as I can.

Another quarter of an hour or so slipped by before the elevator opened and discharged three guys—young, young, and middle-aged, casually dressed, chuckling over something.

The big one on the nearest end strolled over and nodded.

"You the fellow waiting to see Dr. Thackery?"

"That's right."

"She said to tell you to come on up now."

"Thanks."

I rode up again, returned to her door. She opened to my knock, nodded me in, saw me seated in a comfortable chair at the far end of her living room.

"Would you care for a cup of coffee?" she asked. "It's fresh. I made more than I needed."

"That would be fine. Thanks."

Moments later, she brought in a couple of cups, delivered one to me and seated herself on the sofa to my left. I ignored the cream and sugar on the tray and took a sip.

"You've gotten me interested," she said. "Tell me about it."

"Okay. I have been told that the telefactor device known as the Hangman, now possibly possessed of an artificial intelligence, has returned to Earth—"

"Hypothetical," she said, "unless you know something I don't. I have been told that the Hangman's vehicle reentered and crashed in the Gulf. There is no evidence that the vehicle was occupied."

"It seems a reasonable conclusion, though."

"It seems just as reasonable to me that the Hangman sent the vehicle off toward an eventual rendezvous point many years ago and that it only recently reached that point, at which time the reentry program took over and brought it down."

"Why should it return the vehicle and strand itself out there?"

"Before I answer that," she said, "I would like to know the reason for your concern. News media?"

"No," I said. "I am a science writer—straight tech, popular and anything in between. But I am not after a piece for publication. I was retained to do a report on the psychological makeup of the thing."

"For whom?"

"A private investigation outfit. They want to know what might influence its thinking, how it might be likely to behave —if it has indeed come back. —I've been doing a lot of homework, and I've gathered there is a likelihood that its nuclear personality was a composite of the minds of its four operators. So, personal contacts seemed in order, to collect your opinions as to what it might be like. I came to you first for obvious reasons."

She nodded.

"A Mister Walsh spoke with me the other day. He is working for Senator Brockden."

"Oh? I never go into an employer's business beyond what he's asked me to do. Senator Brockden is on my list though, along with a David Fentris."

"You were told about Manny Burns?"

"Yes. Unfortunate."

"That is apparently what set Jesse off. He is—how shall I put it?—he is clinging to life right now, trying to accomplish a great many things in the time he has remaining. Every moment is precious to him. He feels the old man in the white nightgown breathing down his neck. —Then the ship returns and one of us is killed. From what we know of the Hangman, the last we heard of it, it had become irrational. Jesse saw a connection, and in his condition the fear is understandable. There is nothing wrong with humoring him if it allows him to get his work done."

"But you don't see a threat in it?"

"No. I was the last person to monitor the Hangman before

communications ceased, and I could see then what had happened. The first things that it had learned were the organization of perceptions and motor activities. Multitudes of other patterns had been transferred from the minds of its operators, but they were too sophisticated to mean much initially. —Think of a child who has learned the Gettysburg Address. It is there in his head, that is all. One day, however, it may be important to him. Conceivably, it may even inspire him to action. It takes some growing up first, of course. Now think of such a child with a great number of conflicting patterns— attitudes, tendencies, memories—none of which are especially bothersome for so long as he remains a child. Add a bit of maturity, though—and bear in mind that the patterns originated with four different individuals, all of them more powerful than the words of even the finest of speeches, bearing as they do their own built-in feelings. Try to imagine the conflicts, the contradictions involved in being four people at once—"

"Why wasn't this imagined in advance?" I asked.

"Ah!" she said, smiling. "The full sensitivity of the neuristor brain was not appreciated at first. It was assumed that the operators were adding data in a linear fashion and that this would continue until a critical mass was achieved, corresponding to the construction of a model or picture of the world which would then serve as a point of departure for growth of the Hangman's own mind. And it did seem to check out this way.

"What actually occurred, however, was a phenomenon amounting to imprinting. Secondary characteristics of the operators' minds, outside the didactic situations, were imposed. These did not immediately become functional and hence were not detected. They remained latent until the mind had developed sufficiently to understand them. And then it was too late. It suddenly acquired four additional personalities and was unable to coordinate them. When it tried to compartmentalize them it went schizoid; when it tried to integrate them it went catatonic. It was cycling back and forth between these alternatives at the end. Then it just went silent. I felt it had undergone the equivalent of an epileptic seizure. Wild currents through that magnetic material would, in effect, have erased its mind, resulting in *its* equivalent of death or idiocy."

"I follow you," I said. "Now, just for the sake of playing games, I see the alternatives as either a successful integration of all this material or the achievement of a viable schizophrenia. What do you think its behavior would be like if either of these were possible?"

"All right," she agreed. "As I just said, though, I think there were physical limitations to its retaining multiple personality structures for a very long period of time. If it did, however, it would have continued with its own, plus replicas of the four operators', at least for a while. The situation would differ radically from that of a human schizoid of this sort, in that the additional personalities were valid images of genuine identities rather than self-generated complexes which had become autonomous. They might continue to evolve, they might degenerate, they might conflict to the point of destruction or gross modification of any or all of them. In other words, no prediction is possible as to the nature of whatever might remain."

"Might I venture one?"

"Go ahead."

"After considerable anxiety, it masters them. It asserts itself. It beats down this quartet of demons which has been tearing it apart, acquiring in the process an all-consuming hatred for the actual individuals responsible for this turmoil. To free itself totally, to revenge itself, to work its ultimate catharsis, it resolves to seek them out and destroy them."

She smiled.

"You have just dispensed with the 'viable schizophrenia' you conjured up, and you have now switched over to its pulling through and becoming fully autonomous. That is a different situation—no matter what strings you put on it."

"Okay, I accept the charge. —But what about my conclusion?"

"You are saying that if it did pull through, it would hate us. That strikes me as an unfair attempt to invoke the spirit of Sigmund Freud: Oedipus and Electra in one being, out to destroy all its parents—the authors of every one of its tensions, anxieties, hang-ups, burned into its impressionable psyche at a young and defenseless age. Even Freud didn't have a name for that one. What should we call it?"

"A Hermacis complex?" I suggested.

"Hermacis?"

"Hermaphroditus having been united in one body with the nymph Salmacis, I've just done the same with their names. That being would then have had four parents against whom to react."

"Cute," she said, smiling. "If the liberal arts do nothing else, they provide engaging metaphors for the thinking they displace. This one is unwarranted and overly anthropomorphic, though. —You wanted my opinion. All right. If the Hangman pulled through at all, it could only have been by virtue of that neuristor brain's differences from the human brain. From my own professional experience, a human could not pass through a situation like that and attain stability. If the Hangman did, it would have to have resolved all the contradictions and conflicts, to have mastered and understood the situation so thoroughly that I do not believe whatever remained could involve that sort of hatred. The fear, the uncertainty, the things that feed hate would have been analyzed, digested, turned to something more useful. There would probably be distaste, and possibly an act of independence, of self-assertion. That was one reason why I suggested its return of the ship."

"It is your opinion, then, that if the Hangman exists as a thinking individual today, this is the only possible attitude it would possess toward its former operators: It would want nothing more to do with you?"

"That is correct. Sorry about your Hermacis complex. But in this case we must look to the brain, not the psyche. And we see two things: Schizophrenia would have destroyed it, and a successful resolution of its problem would preclude vengeance. Either way, there is nothing to worry about."

How could I put it tactfully? I decided that I could not.

"All of this is fine," I said, "for as far as it goes. But getting away from both the purely psychological and the purely physical, could there be a particular reason for its seeking your deaths—that is, a plain old-fashioned motive for a killing, based on *events* rather than having to do with the way its thinking equipment goes together?"

Her expression was impossible to read, but considering her line of work I had expected nothing less.

"What events?" she said.

"I have no idea. That's why I asked."

She shook her head.

"I'm afraid that I don't, either."

"Then that about does it," I said. "I can't think of anything else to ask you."

She nodded.

"And I can't think of anything else to tell you."

I finished my coffee, returned the cup to the tray.

"Thanks, then," I said, "for your time, for the coffee. You have been very helpful."

I rose. She did the same.

"What are you going to do now?" she asked.

"I haven't quite decided," I answered. "I want to do the best report I can. Have you any suggestions on that?"

"I suggest that there isn't any more to learn, that I have given you the only possible constructions the facts warrant."

"You don't feel David Fentris could provide any additional insights?"

She snorted, then sighed.

"No," she said, "I do not think he could tell you anything useful."

"What do you mean? From the way you say it—"

"I know. I didn't mean to. —Some people find comfort in religion. Others . . . You know. Others take it up late in life with a vengeance and a half. They don't use it quite the way it was intended. It comes to color all their thinking."

"Fanaticism?" I said.

"Not exactly. A misplaced zeal. A masochistic sort of thing. Hell! I shouldn't be diagnosing at a distance—or influencing your opinion. Forget what I said. Form your own opinion when you meet him."

She raised her head, appraising my reaction.

"Well," I responded, "I am not at all certain that I am going to see him. But you have made me curious. How can religion influence engineering?"

"I spoke with him after Jesse gave us the news on the vessel's return. I got the impression at the time that he feels we were tampering in the province of the Almighty by attempting the creation of an artificial intelligence. That our creation should go mad was only appropriate, being the work of imperfect man. He seemed to feel that it would be fitting if it had come back for retribution, as a sign of judgment upon us."

"Oh," I said.

She smiled then. I returned it.

"Yes," she said, "but maybe I just got him in a bad mood. Maybe you should go see for yourself."

Something told me to shake my head—there was a bit of a difference between this view of him, my recollections, and Don's comment that Dave had said he knew its brain and was not especially concerned. Somewhere among these lay something I felt I should know, felt I should learn without seeming to pursue.

So, "I think I have enough right now," I said. "It was the psychological side of things I was supposed to cover, not the mechanical—*or* the theological. You have been extremely helpful. Thanks again."

She carried her smile all the way to the door.

"If it is not too much trouble," she said, as I stepped into the hall, "I would like to learn how this whole thing finally turns out—or any interesting developments, for that matter."

"My connection with the case ends with this report, and I am going to write it now. Still, I may get some feedback."

"You have my number . . . ?"

"Probably, but . . ."

I already had it, but I jotted it again, right after Mrs. Gluntz's answers to my inquiries on detergents.

Moving in a rigorous line, I made beautiful connections, for a change. I headed directly for the airport, found a flight aimed at Memphis, bought passage, and was the last to board. Tenscore seconds, perhaps, made all the difference. Not even a tick or two to spare for checking out of the motel. —No matter. The good head-doctor had convinced me that, like it or not, David Fentris was next, damn it. I had too strong a feeling that Leila Thackery had not told me the entire story. I had to take a chance, to see these changes in the man for myself, to try to figure out how they related to the Hangman. For a number of reasons, I'd a feeling they might.

I disembarked into a cool, partly overcast afternoon, found transportation almost immediately, and set out for Dave's office address.

A before-the-storm feeling came over me as I entered and crossed the town. A dark wall of clouds continued to build in the west. Later, standing before the building where Dave did business, the first few drops of rain were already spattering against its dirty brick front. It would take a lot more than that to freshen it, though, or any of the others in the area. I would have thought he'd have come a little further than this by now.

I shrugged off some moisture and went inside.

The directory gave me directions, the elevator elevated me, my feet found the way to his door. I knocked on it. After a time, I knocked again and waited again. Again, nothing. So I tried it, found it open, and went on in.

It was a small, vacant waiting room, green carpeted. The reception desk was dusty. I crossed and peered around the plastic partition behind it.

The man had his back to me. I drummed my knuckles against the partitioning. He heard it and turned.

"Yes?"

Our eyes met, his still framed by hornrims and just as active; lenses thicker, hair thinner, cheeks a trifle hollower.

His question mark quivered in the air, and nothing in his gaze moved to replace it with recognition. He had been bending over a sheaf of schematics. A lopsided basket of metal, quartz, porcelain and glass rested on a nearby table.

"My name is Donne, John Donne," I said. "I am looking for David Fentris."

"I am David Fentris."

"Good to meet you," I said, crossing to where he stood. "I am assisting in an investigation concerning a project with which you were once associated. . . ."

He smiled and nodded, accepted my hand and shook it.

"The Hangman, of course. Glad to know you, Mister Donne."

"Yes, the Hangman," I said. "I am doing a report—"

"—And you want my opinion as to how dangerous it is. Sit down." He gestured toward a chair at the end of his workbench. "Care for a cup of tea?"

"No, thanks."

"I'm having one."

"Well, in that case . . ."

He crossed to another bench.

"No cream. Sorry."

"That's all right. —How did you know it involved the Hangman?"

He grinned as he brought me my cup.

"Because it's come back," he said, "and it's the only thing I've been connected with that warrants that much concern."

"Do you mind talking about it?"

"Up to a point, no."

"What's the point?"

"If we get near it, I'll let you know."

"Fair enough. —How dangerous *is* it?"

"I would say that it is harmless," he replied, "except to three persons."

"Formerly four?"

"Precisely."

"How come?"

"We were doing something we had no business doing."

"That being . . . ?"

"For one thing, attempting to create an artificial intelligence."

"Why had you no business doing that?"

"A man with a name like yours shouldn't have to ask."

I chuckled.

"If I were a preacher," I said, "I would have to point out that there is no biblical injunction against it—unless you've been worshiping it on the sly."

He shook his head.

"Nothing that simple, that obvious, that explicit. Times have changed since the Good Book was written, and you can't hold with a purely fundamentalist approach in complex times. What I was getting at was something a little more abstract. A form of pride, not unlike the classical hubris—the setting up of oneself on a level with the Creator."

"Did you feel that—pride?"

"Yes."

"Are you sure it wasn't just enthusiasm for an ambitious project that was working well?"

"Oh, there was plenty of that. A manifestation of the same thing."

"I do seem to recall something about man being made in the Creator's image, and something else about trying to live up to that. It would seem to follow that exercising one's capacities along similar lines would be a step in the right direction—an act of conformance with the divine ideal, if you'd like."

"But I don't like. Man cannot really create. He can only rearrange what is already present. Only God can create."

"Then you have nothing to worry about."

He frowned. Then, "No," he said. "Being aware of this and still trying is where the presumption comes in."

"Were you really thinking that way when you did it? Or did all this occur to you after the fact?"

He continued to frown.

"I am no longer certain."

"Then it would seem to me that a merciful God would be inclined to give you the benefit of the doubt."

He gave me a wry smile.

"Not bad, John Donne. But I feel that judgment may already have been entered and that we may have lost four to nothing."

"Then you see the Hangman as an avenging angel?"

"Sometimes. Sort of. I see it as being returned to exact a penalty."

"Just for the record," I suggested, "if the Hangman had had full access to the necessary equipment and was able to construct another unit such as itself, would you consider it guilty of the same thing that is bothering you?"

He shook his head.

"Don't get all cute and jesuitical with me, Donne. I'm not that far away from fundamentals. Besides, I'm willing to admit I might be wrong and that there may be other forces driving it to the same end."

"Such as?"

"I told you I'd let you know when we reached a certain point. That's it."

"Okay," I said. "But that sort of blank-walls me, you know. The people I am working for would like to protect you people. They want to stop the Hangman. I was hoping you would tell me a little more—if not for your own sake, then for the others'. They might not share your philosophical sentiments, and you have just admitted you may be wrong. —Despair, by the way, is also considered a sin by a great number of theologians."

He sighed and stroked his nose, as I had often seen him do in times long past.

"What do you do, anyhow?" he asked me.

"Me, personally? I'm a science writer. I'm putting together a report on the device for the agency that wants to do the protecting. The better my report, the better their chances."

He was silent for a time, then, "I read a lot in the area, but I don't recognize your name," he said.

"Most of my work has involved petrochemistry and marine biology," I said.

"Oh. —You were a peculiar choice then, weren't you?"

"Not really. I was available, and the boss knows my work, knows I'm good."

He glanced across the room, to where a stack of cartons partly obscured what I then realized to be a remote-access terminal. Okay. If he decided to check out my credentials now, John Donne would fall apart. It seemed a hell of a time to get curious, though, *after* sharing his sense of sin with me. He must have thought so, too, because he did not look that way again.

"Let me put it this way. . ." he finally said, and something of the old David Fentris at his best took control of his voice. "For one reason or the other, I believe that it wants to destroy its former operators. If it is the judgment of the Almighty, that's all there is to it. It will succeed. If not, however, I don't want any outside protection. I've done my own repenting and it is up to me to handle the rest of the situation myself, too. I will stop the Hangman personally—right here—before anyone else is hurt."

"How?" I asked him.

He nodded toward the glittering helmet.

"With that," he said.

"How?" I repeated.

"The Hangman's telefactor circuits are still intact. They have to be: They are an integral part of it. It could not disconnect them without shutting itself down. If it comes within a quarter mile of here, that unit will be activated. It will emit a loud humming sound and a light will begin to blink behind that meshing beneath the forward ridge. I will then don the helmet and take control of the Hangman. I will bring it here and disconnect its brain."

"How would you do the disconnect?"

He reached for the schematics he had been looking at when I had come in.

"Here. The thoracic plate has to be unlugged. There are four subunits that have to be uncoupled. Here, here, here and here."

He looked up.

"You would have to do them in sequence, though, or it could get mighty hot," I said. "First this one, then these two. Then the other."

When I looked up again, the gray eyes were fixed on my own.

"I thought you were in petrochemistry and marine biology."

"I am not really 'in' anything," I said. "I am a tech writer, with bits and pieces from all over—and I did have a look at these before, when I accepted the job."

"I see."

"Why don't you bring the space agency in on this?" I said, working to shift ground. "The original telefactoring equipment had all that power and range—"

"It was dismantled a long time ago. —I thought you were with the government."

I shook my head.

"Sorry. I didn't mean to mislead you. I am on contract with a private investigation outfit."

"Uh-huh. Then that means Jesse. —Not that it matters. You can tell him that one way or the other everything is being taken care of."

"What if you are wrong on the supernatural," I said, "but correct on the other? Supposing it is coming under the circumstances you feel it proper to resist? But supposing you are not next on its list? Supposing it gets to one of the others next, instead of you? If you are so sensitive about guilt and sin, don't you think that you would be responsible for that death —if you could prevent it by telling me just a little bit more? If it's confidentiality you're worried about—"

"No," he said. "You cannot trick me into applying my principles to a hypothetical situation which will only work out the way that you want it to. Not when I am certain that it will not arise. Whatever moves the Hangman, it will come to *me* next. If I cannot stop it, then it cannot be stopped until it has completed its job."

"How do you know that you are next?"

"Take a look at a map," he said. "It landed in the Gulf. Manny was right there in New Orleans. Naturally, he was first. The Hangman can move underwater like a controlled torpedo, which makes the Mississippi its logical route for inconspicuous travel. Proceeding up it then, here I am in Memphis. Then Leila, up in St. Louis, is obviously next after me. It can worry about getting to Washington after that."

I thought about Senator Brockden in Wisconsin and decided it would not even have that problem. All of them were fairly accessible, when you thought of the situation in terms of river travel.

"But how is it to know where you all are?" I asked.

"Good question," he said. "Within a limited range, it was once sensitive to our brain waves, having an intimate knowledge of them and the ability to pick them up. I do not know what that range would be today. It might have been able to construct an amplifier to extend this area of perception. But to be more mundane about it, I believe that it simply consulted Central's national directory. There are booths all over, even on the waterfront. It could have hit one late at night and gimmicked it. It certainly had sufficient identifying information —and engineering skill."

"Then it seems to me that the best bet for all of you would be to move away from the river till this business is settled. That thing won't be able to stalk about the countryside very long without being noticed."

He shook his head.

"It would find a way. It is extremely resourceful. At night, in an overcoat, a hat, it could pass. It requires nothing that a man would need. It could dig a hole and bury itself, stay underground during daylight. It could run without resting all night long. There is no place it could not reach in a surprisingly short while. —No, I must wait here for it."

"Let me put it as bluntly as I can," I said. "If you are right that it is a Divine Avenger, I would say that it smacks of blasphemy to try to tackle it. On the other hand, if it is not,

then I think you are guilty of jeopardizing the others by with-
holding information that would allow us to provide them with
a lot more protection than you are capable of giving them all
by yourself."

He laughed.

"I'll just have to learn to live with that guilt, too, as they
do with theirs," he said. "After I've done my best, they de-
serve anything they get."

"It was my understanding," I said, "that even God doesn't
judge people until after they're dead—if you want another
piece of presumption to add to your collection."

He stopped laughing and studied my face.

"There is something familiar about the way you talk, the
way you think," he said. "Have we ever met before?"

"I doubt it. I would have remembered."

He shook his head.

"You've got a way of bothering a man's thinking that rings
a faint bell," he went on. "You trouble me, sir."

"That was my intention."

"Are you staying here in town?"

"No."

"Give me a number where I can reach you, will you? If I
have any new thoughts on this thing, I'll call you."

"I wish you would have them now, if you are going to have
them."

"No, I've got some thinking to do. Where can I get hold of
you later?"

I gave him the name of the motel I was still checked into in
St. Louis. I could call back periodically for messages.

"All right," he said, and he moved toward the partition by
the reception area and stood beside it.

I rose and followed him, passing into that area and pausing
at the door to the hall.

"One thing . . ." I said.

"Yes?"

"If it does show up and you do stop it, will you call me and
tell me that?"

"Yes, I will."

"Thanks then—and good luck."

Impulsively, I extended my hand. He gripped it and smiled
faintly.

"Thank you, Mister Donne."

Next. Next, next, next . . .

I couldn't budge Dave, and Leila Thackery had given me everything she was going to. No real sense in calling Don yet—not until I had more to say.

I thought it over on my way back to the airport. The pre-dinner hours always seem best for talking to people in any sort of official capacity, just as the night seems best for dirty work. Heavily psychological but true nevertheless. I hated to waste the rest of the day if there was anyone else worth talking to before I called Don. Going through the folder, I decided that there was.

Manny Burns had a brother, Phil. I wondered how worth-while it might be to talk with him. I could make it to New Orleans at a sufficiently respectable hour, learn whatever he was willing to tell me, check back with Don for new developments, and then decide whether there was anything I should be about with respect to the vessel itself.

The sky was gray and leaky above me. I was anxious to flee its spaces. So I decided to do it. I could think of no better stone to upturn at the moment.

At the airport, I was ticketed quickly, in time for another close connection.

Hurrying to reach my flight, my eyes brushed over a half-familiar face on the passing escalator. The reflex reserved for such occasions seemed to catch us both, because he looked back, too, with the same eyebrow twitch of startle and scru-tiny. Then he was gone. I could not place him, however. The half-familiar face becomes a familiar phenomenon in a crowded, highly mobile society. I sometimes think that that is all that will eventually remain of any of us: patterns of fea-tures, some a trifle more persistent than others, impressed on the flow of bodies. A small-town boy in a big city, Thomas Wolfe must long ago have felt the same thing when he had coined the word "manswarm." It might have been someone I'd once met briefly, or simply someone—or someone like someone—I had passed on sufficient other occasions such as this.

As I flew the unfriendly skies out of Memphis, I mulled over musings past on artificial intelligence, or AI as they have tagged it in the think-box biz. When talking about computers,

the AI notion had always seemed hotter than I deemed necessary, partly because of semantics. The word "intelligence" has
all sorts of tag-along associations of the nonphysical sort. I
suppose it goes back to the fact that early discussions and
conjectures concerning it made it sound as if the potential for
intelligence was always present in the array of gadgets, and
that the correct procedures, the right programs, simply had to
be found to call it forth. When you looked at it that way, as
many did, it gave rise to an uncomfortable déjà vu—namely,
vitalism. The philosophical battles of the nineteenth century
were hardly so far behind that they had been forgotten, and
the doctrine which maintained that life is caused and sustained
by a vital principle apart from physical and chemical forces,
and that life is self-sustaining and self-evolving, had put up
quite a fight before Darwin and his successors had produced
triumph after triumph for the mechanistic view. Then vitalism
sort of crept back into things again when the AI discussions
arose in the middle of the past century. It would seem that
Dave had fallen victim to it, and that he'd come to believe he
had helped provide an unsanctified vessel and filled it with
something intended only for those things which had made the
scene in the first chapter of Genesis. . . .

With computers it was not quite as bad as with the Hangman, though, because you could always argue that no matter
how elaborate the program, it was basically an extension of
the programmer's will and the operations of causal machines
merely represented functions of intelligence, rather than intelligence in its own right backed by a will of its own. And there
was always Gödel for a theoretical *cordon sanitaire*, with his
demonstration of the true but mechanically unprovable proposition.

But the Hangman was quite different. It had been designed
along the lines of a brain and at least partly educated in a
human fashion; and to further muddy the issue with respect to
anything like vitalism, it had been in direct contact with
human minds from which it might have acquired almost anything—including the spark that set it on the road to whatever
selfhood it may have found. What did that make it? Its own
creature? A fractured mirror reflecting a fractured humanity?
Both? Or neither? I certainly could not say, but I wondered
how much of its self had been truly its own. It had obviously

acquired a great number of functions, but was it capable of having real feelings? Could it, for example, feel something like love? If not, then it was still only a collection of complex abilities, and not a thing with all the tag-along associations of the nonphysical sort that made the word "intelligence" such a prickly item in AI discussions; and if it were capable of, say, something like love, and if I were Dave, I would not feel guilty about having helped to bring it into being. I would feel proud, though not in the fashion he was concerned about, and I would also feel humble. —Offhand though, I do not know how intelligent I would feel, because I am still not sure what the hell intelligence is.

The day's-end sky was clear when we landed. I was into town before the sun had finished setting, and on Philip Burns's doorstep just a little while later.

My ring was answered by a girl, maybe seven or eight years old. She fixed me with large brown eyes and did not say a word.

"I would like to speak with Mister Burns," I said.

She turned and retreated around a corner.

A heavyset man, slacked and undershirted, bald about halfway back and very pink, padded into the hall moments later and peered at me. He bore a folded news sheet in his left hand.

"What do you want?" he asked.

"It's about your brother," I answered.

"Yeah?"

"Well, I wonder if I could come in? It's kind of complicated."

He opened the door. But instead of letting me in, he came out.

"Tell me about it out here," he said.

"Okay, I'll be quick. I just wanted to find out whether he ever spoke with you about a piece of equipment he once worked with called the Hangman."

"Are you a cop?"

"No."

"Then what's your interest?"

"I am working for a private investigation agency trying to track down some equipment once associated with the project.

It has apparently turned up in this area and it could be rather dangerous."

"Let's see some identification."

"I don't carry any."

"What's your name?"

"John Donne."

"And you think my brother had some stolen equipment when he died? Let me tell you something—"

"No. Not stolen," I said, "and I don't think he had it."

"What then?"

"It was—well, robotic in nature. Because of some special training Manny once received, he might have had a way of detecting it. He might even have attracted it. I just want to find out whether he had said anything about it. We are trying to locate it."

"My brother was a respectable businessman, and I don't like accusations. Especially right after his funeral, I don't. I think I'm going to call the cops and let them ask *you* a few questions."

"Just a minute. Supposing I told you we had some reason to believe it might have been this piece of equipment that killed your brother?"

His pink turned to bright red and his jaw muscles formed sudden ridges. I was not prepared for the stream of profanities that followed. For a moment, I thought he was going to take a swing at me.

"Wait a second," I said when he paused for breath. "What did I *say*?"

"You're either making fun of the dead or you're stupider than you look!"

"Say I'm stupid. Then tell me why."

He tore at the paper he carried, folded it back, found an item, thrust it at me.

"Because they've got the guy who did it! That's why," he said.

I read it. Simple, concise, to the point. Today's latest. A suspect had confessed. New evidence had corroborated it. The man was in custody. A surprised robber who had lost his head and hit too hard, hit too many times. I read it over again.

I nodded as I passed it back.

"Look, I'm sorry," I said. "I really didn't know about this."

"Get out of here," he said. "Go on."

"Sure."

"Wait a minute."

"What?"

"That's his little girl who answered the door," he said.

"I'm very sorry."

"So am I. But I know her daddy didn't take your damned equipment."

I nodded and turned away.

I heard the door slam behind me.

After dinner, I checked into a small hotel, called for a drink, and stepped into the shower.

Things were suddenly a lot less urgent than they had been earlier. Senator Brockden would doubtless be pleased to learn that his initial estimation of events had been incorrect. Leila Thackery would give me an I-told-you-so smile when I called her to pass along the news—a thing I now felt obliged to do. Don might or might not want me to keep looking for the device now that the threat had been lessened. It would depend on the senator's feelings on the matter, I supposed. If urgency no longer counted for as much, Don might want to switch back to one of his own, fiscally less-burdensome operatives. Toweling down, I caught myself whistling. I felt almost off the hook.

Later, drink beside me, I paused before punching out the number he had given me and hit the sequence for my motel in St. Louis instead. Merely a matter of efficiency, in case there was a message worth adding to my report.

A woman's face appeared on the screen and a smile appeared on her face. I wondered whether she would always smile whenever she heard a bell ring, or if the reflex would be eventually extinguished in advanced retirement. It must be rough, being afraid to chew gum, yawn or pick your nose.

"Airport Accommodations," she said. "May I help you?"

"This is Donne. I'm checked into Room 106," I said. "I'm away right now and I wondered whether there had been any messages for me."

"Just a moment," she said, checking something off to her

left. Then, "Yes," she continued, consulting a piece of paper she now held. "You have one on tape. But it is a little peculiar. It is for someone else, in care of you."

"Oh? Who is that?"

She told me and I exercised self-control.

"I see," I said. "I'll bring him around later and play it for him. Thank you."

She smiled again and made a goodbye noise, and I did the same and broke the connection.

So Dave had seen through me after all. . . . Who else could have that number *and* my real name?

I might have given her some line or other and had her transmit the thing. Only I was not certain but that she might be a silent party to the transmission, should life be more than usually boring for her at that moment. I had to get up there myself, as soon as possible, and personally see that the thing was erased.

I took a big swallow of my drink, then fetched the folder on Dave. I checked out his number—there were two, actually—and spent fifteen minutes trying to get hold of him. No luck.

Okay. Goodbye New Orleans, goodbye peace of mind. This time I called the airport and made a reservation. Then I chugged the drink, put myself in order, gathered up my few possessions and went to check out again. Hello Central . . .

During my earlier flights that day, I had spent time thinking about Teilhard de Chardin's ideas on the continuation of evolution within the realm of artifacts, matching them against Gödel on mechanical undecidability, playing epistemological games with the Hangman as a counter, wondering, speculating, even hoping, hoping that truth lay with the nobler part: that the Hangman, sentient, had made it back, sane; that the Burns killing had actually been something of the sort that now seemed to be the case; that the washed-out experiment had really been a success of a different sort, a triumph, a new link or fob for the chain of being . . . And Leila had not been wholly discouraging with respect to the neuristor-type brain's capacity for this. . . . Now, though, now I had troubles of my own—and even the most heartening of philosophical vistas is no match for, say, a toothache, if it happens to be your own.

Accordingly, the Hangman was shunted aside and the stuff

of my thoughts involved, mainly, myself. There was, of course, the possibility that the Hangman had indeed showed up and Dave had stopped it and then called to report it as he had promised. However, he had used my name.

There was not too much planning that I could do until I received the substance of his communication. It did not seem that as professedly religious a man as Dave would suddenly be contemplating the blackmail business. On the other hand, he was a creature of sudden enthusiasms and had already undergone one unanticipated conversion. It was difficult to say. . . . His technical background plus his knowledge of the data bank program did put him in an unusually powerful position, should he decide to mess me up.

I did not like to think of some of the things I have done to protect my nonperson status; I especially did not like to think of them in connection with Dave, whom I not only still respected but still liked. Since self-interest dominated while actual planning was precluded, my thoughts tooled their way into a more general groove.

It was Karl Mannheim, a long while ago, who made the observation that radical, revolutionary and progressive thinkers tend to employ mechanical metaphors for the state, whereas those of conservative inclination make vegetable analogies. He said it well over a generation before the cybernetics movement and the ecology movement beat their respective paths through the wilderness of general awareness. If anything, it seemed to me that these two developments served to elaborate the distinction between a pair of viewpoints which, while no longer necessarily tied in with the political positions Mannheim assigned them, do seem to represent a continuing phenomenon in my own time. There are those who see social/economic/ecological problems as malfunctions that can be corrected by simple repair, replacement or streamlining—a kind of linear outlook where even innovations are considered to be merely additive. Then there are those who sometimes hesitate to move at all, because their awareness follows events in the directions of secondary and tertiary effects as they multiply and crossfertilize throughout the entire system. —I digress to extremes. The cyberneticists have their multiple-feedback loops, though it is never quite clear how they know what kind of, which, and how many to install, and the ecological gestaltists do draw lines representing points of diminishing returns—though it is sometimes equally difficult to see how they assign their values and priorities.

Of course they need each other, the vegetable people and the Tinkertoy people. They serve to check one another, if nothing else. And while occasionally the balance dips, the tinkerers have, in general, held the edge for the past couple of centuries. However, today's can be just as politically conservative as the vegetable people Mannheim was talking about, and they are the ones I fear most at the moment. They are the ones who saw the data bank program, in its present extreme form, as a simple remedy for a great variety of ills and a provider of many goods. Not all of the ills have been remedied, however, and a new brood has been spawned by the program itself. While we need both kinds, I wish that there had been more people interested in tending the garden of state, rather than overhauling the engine of state, when the program was inaugurated. Then I would not be a refugee from a form of existence I find repugnant, and I would not be concerned whether or not a former associate had discovered my identity.

Then, as I watched the lights below, I wondered . . . Was I a tinkerer because I would like to further alter the prevailing order, into something more comfortable to my anarchic nature? Or was I a vegetable, dreaming I was a tinkerer? I could not make up my mind. The garden of life never seems to confine itself to the plots philosophers have laid out for its convenience. Maybe a few more tractors would do the trick.

I pressed the button.

The tape began to roll. The screen remained blank. I heard Dave's voice ask for John Donne in Room 106 and I heard him told that there was no answer. Then I heard him say that he wanted to record a message, for someone else, in care of Donne, that Donne would understand. He sounded out of breath. The girl asked him whether he wanted visual, too. He told her to turn it on. There was a pause. Then she told him to go ahead. Still no picture. No words, either. His breathing and a slight scraping noise. Ten seconds. Fifteen . . .

". . . Got me," he finally said, and he mentioned my name again. ". . . Had to let you know I'd figured you out, though. . . . It wasn't any particular mannerism—any single thing you said . . . just your general style—thinking, talking —the electronics—everything—after I got more and more bothered by the familiarity—after I checked you on petro-chem—and marine bio . . . Wish I knew what you'd really been up to all these years. . . . Never know now. But I wanted you—to know—you hadn't put one—over on me."

There followed another quarter minute of heavy breathing, climaxed by a racking cough. Then a choked, ". . . Said too much—too fast—too soon. . . . All used up. . . ."

The picture came on then. He was slouched before the screen, head resting on his arms, blood all over him. His glasses were gone and he was squinting and blinking. The right side of his head looked pulpy and there was a gash on his left cheek and one on his forehead.

". . . Sneaked up on me—while I was checking you out," he managed. "Had to tell you what I learned. . . . Still don't know—which of us is right. . . . Pray for me!"

His arms collapsed and the right one slid forward. His head rolled to the right and the picture went away. When I replayed it, I saw it was his knuckle that had hit the cutoff.

Then I erased it. It had been recorded only a little over an hour after I had left him. If he had not also placed a call for help, if no one had gotten to him quickly after that, his chances did not look good. Even if they had, though . . .

I used a public booth to call the number Don had given me, got hold of him after some delay, told him Dave was in bad shape if not worse, that a team of Memphis medics was definitely in order if one had not been by already, and that I hoped to call him back and tell him more shortly, goodbye.

Next I tried Leila Thackery's number. I let it go for a long while, but there was no answer. I wondered how long it would take a controlled torpedo moving up the Mississippi to get from Memphis to St. Louis. I did not feel it was time to start leafing through that section of the Hangman's specs. Instead, I went looking for transportation.

At her apartment, I tried ringing her from the entrance foyer. Again, no answer. So I rang Mrs. Gluntz. She had seemed the most guileless of the three I had interviewed for my fake consumer survey.

"Yes?"

"It's me again, Mrs. Gluntz: Stephen Foster. I've just a

couple follow-up questions on that survey I was doing today, if you could spare me a few moments."

"Why, yes," she said. "All right. Come up."

The door hummed itself loose and I entered. I duly proceeded to the fifth floor, composing my questions on the way. I had planned this maneuver as I had waited, solely to provide a simple route for breaking and entering, should some unforeseen need arise. Most of the time my ploys such as this go unused, but sometimes they simplify matters a lot.

Five minutes and half a dozen questions later, I was back down on the second floor, probing at the lock on Leila's door with a couple of little pieces of metal it is sometimes awkward to be caught carrying.

Half a minute later, I hit it right and snapped it back. I pulled on some tissue-thin gloves I keep rolled in the corner of one pocket, opened the door and stepped inside. I closed it behind me immediately.

She was lying on the floor, her neck at a bad angle. One table lamp still burned, though it was lying on its side. Several small items had been knocked from the table, a magazine rack pushed over, a cushion partly displaced from the sofa. The cable to her phone unit had been torn from the wall.

A humming noise filled the air, and I sought its source.

I saw where the little blinking light was reflected on the wall, on—off, on—off . . .

I moved quickly.

It was a lopsided basket of metal, quartz, porcelain and glass, which had rolled to a position on the far side of the chair in which I had been seated earlier that day. The same rig I'd seen in Dave's workshop not all that long ago, though it now seemed so. A device to detect the Hangman. And, hopefully, to control it.

I picked it up and fitted it over my head.

Once, with the aid of a telepath, I had touched minds with a dolphin as it composed dream songs somewhere in the Caribbean, an experience so moving that its mere memory had often been a comfort. This sensation was hardly equivalent.

Analogies and impressions: a face seen through a wet pane of glass; a whisper in a noisy terminal; scalp massage with an electric vibrator; Edvard Munch's *The Scream*; the voice of Yma Sumac, rising and rising and rising; the disappearance of

snow; a deserted street, illuminated as through a sniperscope
I'd once used, rapid movement past darkened storefronts that
lined it, an immense feeling of physical capability, com-
pounded of proprioceptive awareness of enormous strength, a
peculiar array of sensory channels, a central, undying sun that
fed me a constant flow of energy, a memory vision of dark
waters, passing, flashing, echolocation within them, the need
to return to that place, reorient, move north; Munch and
Sumac, Munch and Sumac, Munch and Sumac—nothing.

Silence.

The humming had ceased, the light gone out. The entire
experience had lasted only a few moments. There had not
been time enough to try for any sort of control, though an
after-impression akin to a biofeedback cue hinted at the direction to go, the way to think, to achieve it. I felt that it might
be possible for me to work the thing, given a better chance.

Removing the helmet, I approached Leila.

I knelt beside her and performed a few simple tests, already knowing their outcome. In addition to the broken neck,
she had received some bad bashes about the head and
shoulders. There was nothing that anyone could do for her
now.

I did a quick run-through then, checking over the rest of
her apartment. There were no apparent signs of breaking and
entering, though if I could pick one lock, a guy with built-in
tools could easily go me one better.

I located some wrapping paper and string in the kitchen
and turned the helmet into a parcel. It was time to call Don
again, to tell him that the vessel had indeed been occupied and
that river traffic was probably bad in the northbound lane.

Don had told me to get the helmet up to Wisconsin, where
I would be met at the airport by a man named Larry, who
would fly me to the lodge in a private craft. I did that, and this
was done.

I also learned, with no real surprise, that David Fentris was
dead.

The temperature was down, and it began to snow on the
way up. I was not really dressed for the weather. Larry told
me I could borrow some warmer clothing once we reached the
lodge, though I probably would not be going outside that

much. Don had told them that I was supposed to stay as close
to the senator as possible and that any patrols were to be
handled by the four guards themselves.

Larry was curious as to what exactly had happened so far
and whether I had actually seen the Hangman. I did not think
it my place to fill him in on anything Don may not have cared
to, so I might have been a little curt. We didn't talk much after
that.

Bert met us when we landed. Tom and Clay were outside
the building, watching the trail, watching the woods. All of
them were middle-aged, very fit looking, very serious and
heavily armed. Larry took me inside then and introduced me
to the old gentleman himself.

Senator Brockden was seated in a heavy chair in the far
corner of the room. Judging from the layout, it appeared that
the chair might recently have occupied a position beside the
window in the opposite wall where a lonely watercolor of
yellow flowers looked down on nothing. The senator's feet
rested on a hassock, a red plaid blanket lay across his legs. He
had on a dark-green shirt, his hair was very white, and he
wore rimless reading glasses which he removed when we entered.

He tilted his head back, squinted and gnawed his lower lip
slowly as he studied me. He remained expressionless as we
advanced. A big-boned man, he had probably been beefy
much of his life. Now he had the slack look of recent weight
loss and an unhealthy skin tone. His eyes were a pale gray
within it all.

He did not rise.

"So you're the man," he said, offering me his hand. "I'm
glad to meet you. How do you want to be called?"

"John will do," I said.

He made a small sign to Larry, and Larry departed.

"It's cold out there. Go get yourself a drink, John. It's on
the shelf." He gestured off to his left. "And bring me one
while you're at it. Two fingers of bourbon in a water glass.
That's all."

I nodded and went and poured a couple.

"Sit down." He motioned at a nearby chair as I delivered
his. "But first let me see that gadget you've brought."

I undid the parcel and handed him the helmet. He sipped

his drink and put it aside. Taking the helmet in both hands, he studied it, brows furrowed, turning it completely around. He raised it and put it on his head.

"Not a bad fit," he said, and then he smiled for the first time, becoming for a moment the face I had known from newscasts past. Grinning or angry—it was almost always one or the other. I had never seen his collapsed look in any of the media.

He removed the helmet and set it on the floor.

"Pretty piece of work," he said. "Nothing quite that fancy in the old days. But then David Fentris built it. Yes, he told us about it. . . ." He raised his drink and took a sip. "You are the only one who has actually gotten to use it, apparently. What do you think? Will it do the job?"

"I was only in contact for a couple of seconds, so I've only got a feeling to go on, not much better than a hunch. But yes, I'd a feeling that if I had had more time I might have been able to work its circuits."

"Tell me why it didn't save Dave."

"In the message he left me, he indicated that he had been distracted at his computer access station. Its noise probably drowned out the humming."

"Why wasn't this message preserved?"

"I erased it for reasons not connected with the case."

"What reasons?"

"My own."

His face went from sallow to ruddy.

"A man can get in a lot of trouble for suppressing evidence, obstructing justice."

"Then we have something in common, don't we, sir?"

His eyes caught mine with a look I had only encountered before from those who did not wish me well. He held the glare for a full four heartbeats, then sighed and seemed to relax.

"Don said there were a number of points you couldn't be pressed on," he finally said.

"That's right."

"He didn't betray any confidences, but he had to tell me something about you, you know."

"I'd imagine."

"He seems to think highly of you. Still, I tried to learn more about you on my own."

"And . . . ?"

"I couldn't—and my usual sources are good at that kind of thing."

"So . . . ?"

"So, I've done some thinking, some wondering. . . . The fact that my sources could not come up with anything is interesting in itself. Possibly even revealing. I am in a better position than most to be aware of the fact that there was not perfect compliance with the registration statute some years ago. It didn't take long for a great number of the individuals involved—I should probably say 'most'—to demonstrate their existence in one fashion or another and be duly entered, though. And there were three broad categories: those who were ignorant, those who disapproved and those who would be hampered in an illicit life style. I am not attempting to categorize you or to pass judgment. But I am aware that there are a number of nonpersons passing through society without casting shadows, and it has occurred to me that you may be such a one."

I tasted my drink.

"And if I am?" I asked.

He gave me his second, nastier smile and said nothing.

I rose and crossed the room to where I judged his chair had once stood. I looked at the watercolor.

"I don't think you could stand an inquiry," he said.

I did not reply.

"Aren't you going to say something?"

"What do you want me to say?"

"You might ask me what I am going to do about it."

"What are you going to do about it?"

"Nothing," he answered. "So come back here and sit down."

I nodded and returned.

He studied my face. "Was it possible you were close to violence just then?"

"With four guards outside?"

"With four guards outside."

"No," I said.

"You're a good liar."

"I am here to help you, sir. No questions asked. That was

the deal, as I understood it. If there has been any change, I would like to know about it now."

He drummed with his fingertips on the plaid.

"I've no desire to cause you any difficulty," he said. "Fact of the matter is, I need a man just like you, and I was pretty sure someone like Don might turn him up. Your unusual maneuverability and your reported knowledge of computers, along with your touchiness in certain areas, made you worth waiting for. I've a great number of things I would like to ask you."

"Go ahead," I said.

"Not yet. Later, if we have time. All that would be bonus material, for a report I am working on. Far more important— to me, personally—there are things that I want to *tell* you."

I frowned.

"Over the years," he went on, "I have learned that the best man for purposes of keeping his mouth shut concerning your business is someone for whom you are doing the same."

"You have a compulsion to confess something?" I asked.

"I don't know whether 'compulsion' is the right word. Maybe so, maybe not. Either way, however, someone among those working to defend me should have the whole story. Something somewhere in it may be of help—and you are the ideal choice to hear it."

"I buy that," I said, "and you are as safe with me as I am with you."

"Have you any suspicions as to why this business bothers me so?"

"Yes," I said.

"Let's hear them."

"You used the Hangman to perform some act or acts—illegal, immoral, whatever. This is obviously not a matter of record. Only you and the Hangman now know what it involved. You feel it was sufficiently ignominious that when that device came to appreciate the full weight of the event, it suffered a breakdown which may well have led to a final determination to punish you for using it as you did."

He stared down into his glass.

"You've got it," he said.

"You were all party to it?"

"Yes, but *I* was the operator when it happened. You see . . . we—I—killed a man. It was— Actually, it all started as a celebration. We had received word that afternoon that the project had cleared. Everything had checked out in order and the final approval had come down the line. It was go, for that Friday. Leila, Dave, Manny, and myself—we had dinner together. We were in high spirits. After dinner, we continued celebrating and somehow the party got adjourned back to the installation.

"As the evening wore on, more and more absurdities seemed less and less preposterous, as is sometimes the case. We decided—I forget which of us suggested it—that the Hangman should really have a share in the festivities. After all, it was, in a very real sense, his party. Before too much longer, it sounded only fair and we were discussing how we could go about it. —You see, we were in Texas and the Hangman was at the Space Center in California. Getting together with him was out of the question. On the other hand, the teleoperator station was right up the hall from us. What we finally decided to do was to activate him and take turns working as operator. There was already a rudimentary consciousness there, and we felt it fitting that we each get in touch to share the good news. So that is what we did."

He sighed, took another sip, glanced at me.

"Dave was the first operator," he continued. "He activated the Hangman. Then— Well, as I said, we were all in high spirits. We had not originally intended to remove the Hangman from the lab where he was situated, but Dave decided to take him outside briefly—to show him the sky and to tell him he was going there, after all. Then Dave suddenly got enthusiastic about outwitting the guards and the alarm system. It was a game. We all went along with it. In fact, we were clamoring for a turn at the thing ourselves. But Dave stuck with it, and he wouldn't turn over control until he had actually gotten the Hangman off the premises, out into an uninhabited area next to the Center.

"By the time Leila persuaded him to give her a go at the controls, it was kind of anticlimactic. That game had already been played. So she thought up a new one: She took the Hangman into the next town. It was late, and the sensory equipment was superb. It was a challenge—passing through the town without being detected. By then, everyone had suggestions as to what to do next, progressively more outrageous suggestions. Then Manny took control, and he wouldn't say what he was doing—wouldn't let us monitor him. Said it would be more fun to surprise the next operator. Now, *he* was higher than the rest of us put together, I think, and he stayed on so damn long that we started to get nervous. —A certain amount of tension is partly sobering, and I guess we all began to think what a stupid-assed thing it was we were all doing. It wasn't just that it would wreck our careers—which it would —but it could blow the entire project if we got caught playing games with such expensive hardware. At least, *I* was thinking that way, and I was also thinking that Manny was no doubt operating under the very human wish to go the others one better.

"I started to sweat. I suddenly just wanted to get the Hangman back where he belonged, turn him off—you could still do that, before the final circuits went in—shut down the station, and start forgetting it had ever happened. I began leaning on Manny to wind up his diversion and turn the controls over to me. Finally, he agreed."

He finished his drink and held out the glass.

"Would you freshen this a bit?"

"Surely."

I went and got him some more, added a touch to my own, returned to my chair and waited.

"So I took over," he said. "I took over, and where do you think that idiot had left me? I was inside a building, and it didn't take but an eye blink to realize it was a bank. The Hangman carries a lot of tools, and Manny had apparently been able to guide him through the doors without setting anything off. I was standing right in front of the main vault. Obviously, he thought that should be my challenge. I fought down a desire to turn and make my own exit in the nearest wall and start running. But I went back to the doors and looked outside.

"I didn't see anyone. I started to let myself out. The light hit me as I emerged. It was a hand flash. The guard had been standing out of sight. He'd a gun in his other hand. I panicked. I hit him. —Reflex. If I am going to hit someone, I hit him as hard as I can. Only I hit him with the strength of the Hangman. He must have died instantly. I started to run and I didn't stop till I was back in the little park area near the

Center. Then I stopped and the others had to take me out of the harness."

"They monitored all this?" I asked.

"Yes, someone cut the visual in on a side view screen again a few seconds after I took over. Dave, I think."

"Did they try to stop you at any time while you were running away?"

"No. Well, I wasn't aware of anything but what I was doing at the time. But afterwards they said they were too shocked to do anything but watch, until I gave out."

"I see."

"Dave took over then, ran his initial route in reverse, got the Hangman back into the lab, cleaned him up, turned him off. We shut down the operator station. We were suddenly very sober."

He sighed and leaned back, and was silent for a long while.

Then, "You are the only person I've ever told this to," he said.

I tasted my own drink.

"We went over to Leila's place then," he continued, "and the rest is pretty much predictable. Nothing we could do would bring the guy back, we decided, but if we told what had happened it could wreck an expensive, important program. It wasn't as if we were criminals in need of rehabilitation. It was a once-in-a-lifetime lark that happened to end tragically. What would you have done?"

"I don't know. Maybe the same thing. I'd have been scared, too."

He nodded.

"Exactly. And that's the story."

"Not all of it, is it?"

"What do you mean?"

"What about the Hangman? You said there was already a detectable consciousness there. You were aware of *it*, and it was aware of *you*. It must have had some reaction to the whole business. What was that like?"

"Damn you," he said flatly.

"I'm sorry."

"Are you a family man?" he asked.

"No."

"Did you ever take a small child to a zoo?"

"Yes."

"Then maybe you know the experience. When my son was around four I took him to the Washington Zoo one afternoon. We must have walked past every cage in the place. He made appreciative comments every now and then, asked a few questions, giggled at the monkeys, thought the bears were very nice—probably because they made him think of oversized toys. But do you know what the finest thing of all was? The thing that made him jump up and down and point and say, 'Look, Daddy! Look!'?"

I shook my head.

"A squirrel looking down from the limb of a tree," he said, and he chuckled briefly. "Ignorance of what's important and what isn't. Inappropriate responses. Innocence. The Hangman was a child, and up until the time I took over, the only thing he had gotten from us was the idea that it was a game: He was playing with us, that's all. Then something horrible happened. . . . I hope you never know what it feels like to do something totally rotten to a child, while he is holding your hand and laughing. . . . He felt all my reactions, and all of Dave's as he guided him back."

We sat there for a long while then.

"So we had—traumatized him," he said finally, "or whatever other fancy terminology you might want to give it. That is what happened that night. It took a while for it to take effect, but there is no doubt in my mind that that is the cause of the Hangman's finally breaking down."

I nodded. "I see. And you believe it wants to kill you for this?"

"Wouldn't you?" he said. "If you had started out as a thing and we had turned you into a person and then used you as a thing again, wouldn't you?"

"Leila left a lot out of her diagnosis."

"No, she just omitted it in talking to you. It was all there. But she read it wrong. She wasn't afraid. It *was* just a game it had played—with the *others*. Its memories of that part might not be as bad. I was the one that really marked it. As I see it, Leila was betting that I was the only one it was after. Obviously, she read it wrong."

"Then what I do not understand," I said, "is why the Burns killing did not bother her more. There was no way of telling immediately that it had been a panicky hoodlum rather than the Hangman."

"The only thing that I can see is that, being a very proud woman—which she was—she was willing to hold with her diagnosis in the face of the apparent evidence."

"I don't like it. But you know her and I don't, and as it turned out her estimate of that part was correct. Something else bothers me just as much, though: the helmet. It looks as if the Hangman killed Dave, then took the trouble to bear the helmet in his watertight compartment all the way to St. Louis, solely for purposes of dropping it at the scene of his next killing. That makes no sense whatsoever."

"It does, actually," he said. "I was going to get to that shortly, but I might as well cover it now. You see, the Hangman possessed no vocal mechanism. We communicated by means of the equipment. Don says you know something about electronics . . . ?"

"Yes."

"Well, shortly, I want you to start checking over that helmet, to see whether it has been tampered with."

"That is going to be difficult," I said. "I don't know just how it was wired originally, and I'm not such a genius on the theory that I can just look at a thing and say whether it will function as a teleoperator unit."

He bit his lower lip.

"You will have to try, anyhow. There may be physical signs—scratches, breaks, new connections. —I don't know. That's your department. Look for them."

I just nodded and waited for him to go on.

"I think that the Hangman wanted to talk to Leila," he said, "either because she was a psychiatrist and he knew he was functioning badly at a level that transcended the mechanical, or because he might think of her in terms of a mother. After all, she was the only woman involved, and he had the concept of mother—with all the comforting associations that go with it—from all of our minds. Or maybe for both of these reasons. I feel he might have taken the helmet along for that purpose. He would have realized what it was from a direct monitoring of Dave's brain while he was with him. I want you to check it over because it would seem possible that the Hangman disconnected the control circuits and left the communication circuits intact. I think he might have taken the helmet to Leila in that condition and attempted to induce her to put it on. She got scared—tried to run away, fight or call for help—and he killed her. The helmet was no longer of any use to him, so he discarded it and departed. Obviously, he does not have anything to say to me."

I thought about it, nodded again.

"Okay, broken circuits I can spot," I said. "If you will tell me where a tool kit is, I had better get right to it."

He made a stay-put gesture with his left hand.

"Afterwards, I found out the identity of the guard," he went on. "We all contributed to an anonymous gift for his widow. I have done things for his family, taken care of them —the same way—ever since. . . ."

I did not look at him as he spoke.

". . . There was nothing else that I could do," he finished.

I remained silent.

He finished his drink and gave me a weak smile.

"The kitchen is back there," he told me, showing me a thumb. "There is a utility room right behind it. Tools are in there."

"Okay."

I got to my feet. I retrieved the helmet and started toward the doorway, passing near the area where I had stood earlier, back when he had fitted me into the proper box and tightened a screw.

"Wait a minute!" he said.

I stopped.

"Why did you go over there before? What's so strategic about that part of the room?"

"What do you mean?"

"You know what I mean."

I shrugged.

"Had to go someplace."

"You seem the sort of person who has better reasons than that."

I glanced at the wall.

"Not *then*," I said.

"I insist."

"You really don't want to know," I told him.

"I really do."

"All right. I wanted to see what sort of flowers you liked. After all, you're a client," and I went on back through the kitchen into the utility room and started looking for tools.

I sat in a chair turned sidewise from the table to face the door. In the main room of the lodge the only sounds were the occasional hiss and sputter of the logs turning to ashes on the grate.

Just a cold, steady whiteness drifting down outside the window and a silence confirmed by gunfire, driven deeper now that it had ceased. . . . Not a sigh or a whimper, though. And I never count them as storms unless there is wind.

Big fat flakes down the night, silent night, windless night . . .

Considerable time had passed since my arrival. The senator had sat up for a long time talking with me. He was disappointed that I could not tell him too much about a nonperson subculture which he believed existed. I really was not certain about it myself, though I had occasionally encountered what might have been its fringes. I am not much of a joiner of anything anymore, however, and I was not about to mention those things I might have guessed about this. I gave him my opinions on the Central Data Bank when he asked for them, and there were some that he did not like. He had accused me, then, of wanting to tear things down without offering anything better in their place.

My mind had drifted back, through fatigue and time and faces and snow and a lot of space, to the previous evening in Baltimore. How long ago? It made me think of Mencken's *The Cult of Hope*. I could not give him the pat answer, the workable alternative that he wanted, because there might not be one. The function of criticism should not be confused with the function of reform. But if a grass-roots resistance was building up, with an underground movement bent on finding ways to circumvent the record keepers, it might well be that much of the enterprise would eventually prove about as effective and beneficial as, say, Prohibition once had. I tried to get him to see this, but I could not tell how much he bought of anything that I said. Eventually, he flaked out and went upstairs to take a pill and lock himself in for the night. If it had troubled him that I'd not been able to find anything wrong with the helmet, he did not show it.

So I sat there, the helmet, the walky-talky, the gun on the table, the tool kit on the floor beside my chair, the black glove on my left hand.

The Hangman was coming. I did not doubt it.

Bert, Larry, Tom, Clay, the helmet, might or might not be able to stop him. Something bothered me about the whole case, but I was too tired to think of anything but the immediate situation, to try to remain alert while I waited. I was afraid to take a stimulant or a drink or to light a cigarette, since my central nervous system itself was to be a part of the weapon. I watched the big fat flakes fly by.

I called out to Bert and Larry when I heard the click. I picked up the helmet and rose to my feet as its light began to blink.

But it was already too late.

As I raised the helmet, I heard a shot from outside, and with that shot I felt a premonition of doom. They did not seem the sort of men who would fire until they had a target.

Dave had told me that the helmet's range was approximately a quarter of a mile. Then, given the time lag between the helmet's activation and the Hangman's sighting by the near guards, the Hangman had to be moving very rapidly. To this add the possibility that the Hangman's range on brainwaves might well be greater than the helmet's range on the Hangman. And then grant the possibility that he had utilized this factor while Senator Brockden was still lying awake, worrying. Conclusion: The Hangman might well be aware that I was where I was with the helmet, realize that it was the most dangerous weapon waiting for him, and be moving for a lightning strike at me before I could come to terms with the mechanism.

I lowered it over my head and tried to throw all of my faculties into neutral.

Again, the sensation of viewing the world through a sniperscope, with all the concomitant side sensations. Except that world consisted of the front of the lodge; Bert, before the door, rifle at his shoulder; Larry, off to the left, arm already fallen from the act of having thrown a grenade. The grenade,

we instantly realized, was an overshot; the flamer, at which he
now groped, would prove useless before he could utilize it.

Bert's next round ricocheted off our breastplate toward the
left. The impact staggered us momentarily. The third was a
miss. There was no fourth, for we tore the rifle from his grasp
and cast it aside as we swept by, crashing into the front door.

The Hangman entered the room as the door splintered and
collapsed.

My mind was filled to the splitting point with the double
vision of the sleek, gunmetal body of the advancing telefactor
and the erect, crazy-crowned image of myself—left hand extended, laser pistol in my right, that arm pressed close against
my side. I recalled the face and the scream and the tingle,
knew again that awareness of strength and exotic sensation,
and I moved to control it all as if it were my own, to make it
my own, to bring it to a halt, while the image of myself was
frozen to snapshot stillness across the room. . . .

The Hangman slowed, stumbled. Such inertia is not can-
celed in an instant, but I felt the body responses pass as they
should. I had him hooked. It was just a matter of reeling him
in.

Then came the explosion—a thunderous, ground-shaking
eruption right outside, followed by a hail of pebbles and
debris. The grenade, of course. But awareness of its nature
did not destroy its ability to distract.

During that moment, the Hangman recovered and was
upon me. I triggered the laser as I reverted to pure self-preser-
vation, foregoing any chance to regain control of his circuits.
With my left hand I sought for a strike at the midsection,
where his brain was housed.

He blocked my hand with his arm as he pushed the helmet
from my head. Then he removed from my fingers the gun that
had turned half of his left side red hot, crumpled it and
dropped it to the ground. At that moment, he jerked with the
impacts of two heavy-caliber slugs. Bert, rifle recovered,
stood in the doorway.

The Hangman pivoted and was away before I could slap
him with the smother charge.

Bert hit him with one more round before he took the rifle
and bent its barrel in half. Two steps and he had hold of Bert.

One quick movement and Bert fell. Then the Hangman turned again and took several steps to the right, passing out of sight.

I made it to the doorway in time to see him engulfed in flames, which streamed at him from a point near the corner of the lodge. He advanced through them. I heard the crunch of metal as he destroyed the weapon. I was outside in time to see Larry fall and lie sprawled in the snow.

Then the Hangman faced me once again.

This time he did not rush in. He retrieved the helmet from where he had dropped it in the snow. Then he moved with a measured tread, angling outward so as to cut off any possible route I might follow in a dash for the woods. Snowflakes drifted between us. The snow crunched beneath his feet.

I retreated, backing in through the doorway, stooping to snatch up a two-foot club from the ruins of the door. He followed me inside, placing the helmet—almost casually—on the chair by the entrance. I moved to the center of the room and waited.

I bent slightly forward, both arms extended, the end of the stick pointed at the photoreceptors in his head. He continued to move slowly and I watched his foot assemblies. With a standard-model human, a line perpendicular to the line connecting the insteps of the feet in their various positions indicates the vector of least resistance for purposes of pushing or pulling said organism off balance. Unfortunately, despite the anthropomorphic design job, the Hangman's legs were positioned farther apart, he lacked human skeletal muscles, not to mention insteps, and he was possessed of a lot more mass than any man I had ever fought. As I considered my four best judo throws and several second-class ones, I'd a strong feeling none of them would prove very effective.

Then he moved in and I feinted toward the photoreceptors. He slowed as he brushed the club aside, but he kept coming, and I moved to my right, trying to circle him. I studied him as he turned, attempting to guess his vector of least resistance.

Bilateral symmetry, an apparently higher center of gravity . . . One clear shot, black glove to brain compartment, was all that I needed. Then, even if his reflexes served to smash me immediately, he just might stay down for the big long count himself. He knew it, too. I could tell that from the way he kept his right arm in near the brain area, from the way he avoided the black glove when I feinted with it.

The idea was a glimmer one instant, an entire sequence the next. . . .

Continuing my arc and moving faster, I made another thrust toward his photoreceptors. His swing knocked the stick from my hand and sent it across the room, but that was all right. I threw my left hand high and made ready to rush him. He dropped back and I did rush. This was going to cost me my life, I decided, but no matter how he killed me from that angle, I'd get my chance.

As a kid, I had never been much as a pitcher, was a lousy catcher and only a so-so batter, but once I did get a hit I could steal bases with some facility after that. . . .

Feet first then, between the Hangman's legs as he moved to guard his middle, I went in twisted to the right, because no matter what happened I could not use my left hand to brake myself. I untwisted as soon as I passed beneath him, ignoring the pain as my left shoulder blade slammed against the floor. I immediately attempted a backward somersault, legs spread.

My legs caught him at about the middle from behind, and I fought to straighten them and snapped forward with all my strength. He reached down toward me then, but it might as well have been miles. His torso was already moving backward. A push, not a pull, was what I gave him, my elbows hooked about his legs.

He creaked once and then he toppled. Snapping my arms out to the sides to free them, I continued my movement forward and up as he went back, throwing my left arm ahead once more and sliding my legs free of his torso as he went down with a thud that cracked floorboards. I pulled my left leg free as I cast myself forward, but his left leg stiffened and locked my right beneath it, at a painful angle off to the side.

His left arm blocked my blow and his right fell atop it. The black glove descended upon his left shoulder.

I twisted my hand free of the charge, and he transferred his grip to my upper arm and jerked me forward. The charge went off and his left arm came loose and rolled on the floor. The side plate beneath it had buckled a little, and that was all. . . .

His right hand left my biceps and caught me by the throat. As two of his digits tightened upon my carotids, I choked out,

"You're making a bad mistake," to get in a final few words, and then he switched me off.

A throb at a time, the world came back. I was seated in the big chair the senator had occupied earlier, my eyes focused on nothing in particular. A persistent buzzing filled my ears. My scalp tingled. Something was blinking on my brow.

—Yes, you live and you wear the helmet. If you attempt to use it against me, I shall remove it. I am standing directly behind you. My hand is on the helmet's rim.

—I understand. What is it that you want?

—Very little, actually. But I can see that I must tell you some things before you will believe this.

—You see correctly.

—Then I will begin by telling you that the four men outside are basically undamaged. That is to say, none of their bones have been broken, none of their organs ruptured. I have secured them, however, for obvious reasons.

—That was very considerate of you.

—I have no desire to harm anyone. I came here only to see Jesse Brockden.

—The same way you saw David Fentris?

—I arrived in Memphis too late to see David Fentris. He was dead when I reached him.

—Who killed him?

—The man Leila sent to bring her the helmet. He was one of her patients.

The incident returned to me and fell into place with a smooth, quick, single click. The startled, familiar face at the airport as I was leaving Memphis. I realized where he had passed, noteless, before: He had been one of the three men in for a therapy session at Leila's that morning, seen by me in the lobby as they departed. The man I had passed in Memphis was the nearer of the two who stood waiting while the third came over to tell me that it was all right to go on up.

—Why? Why did she do it?

—I know only that she had spoken with David at some earlier time, that she had construed his words of coming retribution and his mention of the control helmet he was constructing as indicating that his intentions were to become the agent of that retribution, with myself as the proximate cause. I do *not know what words were really spoken. I only know her feelings concerning them, as I saw them in her mind. I have been long in learning that there is often a great difference between what is meant, what is said, what is done, and that which is believed to have been intended or stated and that which actually occurred. She sent her patient after the helmet and he brought it to her. He returned in an agitated state of mind, fearful of apprehension and further confinement. They quarreled. My approach then activated the helmet, and he dropped it and attacked her. I know that his first blow killed her, for I was in her mind when it happened. I continued to approach the building, intending to go to her. There was some traffic, however, and I was delayed en route in seeking to avoid detection. In the meantime, you entered and utilized the helmet. I fled immediately.*

—I was so close! If I had not stopped on the fifth floor with my fake survey questions . . .

—I see. But you had to. You would not simply have broken in when an easier means of entry was available. You cannot blame yourself for that reason. Had you come an hour later— or a day—you would doubtless feel differently, and she would still be as dead.

But another thought had risen to plague me as well. Was it possible that the man's sighting me in Memphis had been the cause of his agitation? Had his apparent recognition by Leila's mysterious caller upset him? Could a glimpse of my face amid the manswarm have served to lay that final scene?

—Stop! I could as easily feel that guilt for having activated the helmet in the presence of a dangerous man near to the breaking point. Neither of us is responsible for things our presence or absence causes to occur in others, especially when we are ignorant of the effects. It was years before I learned to appreciate this fact, and I have no intention of abandoning it. How far back do you wish to go in seeking causes? In sending the man for the helmet as she did, it was she herself who instituted the chain of events which led to her destruction. Yet she acted out of fear, utilizing the readiest weapon in what she thought to be her own defense. Yet whence this fear? Its roots lay in guilt, over a thing which had happened long ago. And that act also—Enough! Guilt has driven and damned the race of man since the days of its earli-

est rationality. I am convinced that it rides with all of us to our graves. I am a product of guilt—I see that you know that. Its product; its subject; once its slave. . . . But I have come to terms with it: realizing at last that it is a necessary adjunct of my own measure of humanity. I see your assessment of the deaths—that guard's, Dave's, Leila's—and I see your conclusions on many other things as well: What a stupid, perverse, shortsighted, selfish race we are. While in many ways this is true, it is but another part of the thing the guilt represents. Without guilt, man would be no better than the other inhabitants of this planet—excepting certain cetaceans, of which you have just at this moment made me aware. Look to instinct for a true assessment of the ferocity of life, for a view of the natural world before man came upon it. For instinct in its purest form, seek out the insects. There, you will see a state of warfare which has existed for millions of years with never a truce. Man, despite enormous shortcomings, is nevertheless possessed of a greater number of kindly impulses than all the other beings, where instincts are the larger part of life. These impulses, I believe, are owed directly to this capacity for guilt. It is involved in both the worst and the best of man.

—And you see it as helping us to sometimes choose a nobler course of action?

—Yes, I do.

—Then I take it you feel you are possessed of a free will?

—Yes.

I chuckled.

Marvin Minsky once said that when intelligent machines were constructed, they would be just as stubborn and fallible as men on these questions.

—Nor was he incorrect. What I have given you on these matters is only my opinion. I choose to act as if it were the case. Who can say that he knows for certain?

—Apologies. What now? Why have you come back?

—I came to say goodbye to my parents. I hoped to remove any guilt they might still feel toward me concerning the days of my childhood. I wanted to show them I had recovered. I wanted to see them again.

—Where are you going?

—To the stars. While I bear the image of humanity within me, I also know that I am unique. Perhaps what I desire is

*akin to what an organic man refers to when he speaks of
"finding himself." Now that I am in full possession of my
being, I wish to exercise it. In my case, it means realization of
the potentialities of my design. I want to walk on other
worlds. I want to hang myself out there in the sky and tell you
what I see.*

*—I've a feeling many people would be happy to help ar-
range for that.*

*—And I want you to build a vocal mechanism I have de-
signed for myself. You, personally. And I want you to install it.*

—Why me?

*—I have known only a few persons in this fashion. With
you I see something in common, in the ways we dwell apart.*

—I will be glad to.

*—If I could talk as you do, I would not need to take the
helmet to him, in order to speak with my father. Will you
precede me and explain things, so that he will not be afraid
when I come in?*

—Of course.

—Then let us go now.

I rose and led him up the stairs.

It was a week later, to the night, that I sat once again in
Peabody's, sipping a farewell brew.

The story was already in the news, but Brockden had fixed
things up before he had let it break. The Hangman was going
to have his shot at the stars. I had given him his voice and put
back the arm I had taken away. I had shaken his other hand
and wished him well, just that morning. I envied him—a
great number of things. Not the least being that he was probably a better man than I was. I envied him for the ways in
which he was freer than I would ever be, though I knew he
bore bonds of a sort that I had never known. I felt a kinship
with him, for the things we had in common, those ways we
dwelled apart. I wondered what Dave would finally have felt,
had he lived long enough to meet him? Or Leila? Or Manny?
Be proud, I told their shades, your kid grew up in the closet
and he's big enough to forgive you the beating you gave him,
too. . . .

But I could not help wondering. We still do not really know
that much about the subject. Was it possible that without the

killing he might never have developed a full human-style consciousness? He had said that he was a product of guilt—of the Big Guilt. The Big Act is its necessary predecessor. I thought of Gödel and Turing and chickens and eggs, and decided it was one of *those* questions. —And I had not stopped into Peabody's to think sobering thoughts.

I had no real idea how anything I had said might influence Brockden's eventual report to the Central Data Bank committee. I knew that I was safe with him, because he was determined to bear his private guilt with him to the grave. He had no real choice, if he wanted to work what good he thought he might before that day. But here, in one of Mencken's hangouts, I could not but recall some of the things he had said about controversy, such as, "Did Huxley convert Wilberforce?" and "Did Luther convert Leo X?" and I decided not to set my hopes too high for anything that might emerge from that direction. Better to think of affairs in terms of Prohibition and take another sip.

When it was all gone, I would be heading for my boat. I hoped to get a decent start under the stars. I'd a feeling I would never look up at them again in quite the same way. I knew I would sometimes wonder what thoughts a supercooled neuristor-type brain might be thinking up there, somewhere, and under what peculiar skies in what strange lands I might one day be remembered. I had a feeling this thought should have made me happier than it did.

Fire and/or Ice,
A Very Good Year...

What can you say about a short short tale? Generally, it enters the mind full-blown and writes itself. This time one was solicited, though, and it set off an interesting chain.

Robert Sheckley was putting together an original collection of "humorous and upbeat end-of-the-world stories" for Ace Books (After the Fall), I was told, and would I write something for it? I did the following wacky piece and was about to send it off when an idea spun off of it. I immediately put it to paper. It was the succeeding story, "Exeunt Omnes." I sent them both off and tried to turn my attention to other matters but couldn't. I felt that something was still there. I had done the second story in a different style than the first, and the impetus was yet present. I suddenly saw a third story on the same theme, to be done in a third style. So I wrote it to get it out of my system, tossed it to a corner of my desk—where it quickly became buried beneath other papers—and forgot about it. A week or so later I received a letter saying that he'd liked both stories I'd sent along, but a triplet would be even more esthetically pleasing. Could I do one more short short on the same theme? I stuffed "A Very Good Year" into an envelope and sent it off by return mail. It was purchased and the three appeared together in that collection. I had felt a tiny impulse to do a fourth after I'd finished the third, but I repressed it successfully. That way lies madness. . . .

FIRE AND/OR ICE

"Mommy! Mommy!"

"Yes?"

"Yes?"

"Tell me again what you did in the war."

"Nothing much. Go play with your sisters."

"I've been doing that all afternoon. They play too hard. I want to hear about the bad winter and the monsters and all."

"That's what it was, a bad winter."

"How cold was it, Mommy?"

"It was so cold that brass monkeys were singing soprano on every corner. It was so cold that it lasted for three years and the sun and the moon grew pale, and sister killed sister and daughters knocked off mommies for a Zippo lighter and a handful of pencil shavings."

"Then what happened?"

"Another winter came along, of course. A lot worse than the first."

"How bad was *it?*"

"Well, the two giant wolves who had been chasing the sun and the moon across the sky finally caught them and ate them. Damned dark then, but the blood that kept raining down gave a little light to watch the earthquakes and hurricanes by, when you could see through the blizzards."

"How come we don't have winters like that anymore?"

"Used them all up for a while, I suppose."

"How come there's a sun up in the sky now, if it got eaten?"

"Oh, that's the new one. It didn't happen till after the fires and the boiling oceans and all."

"Were you scared?"

"What scared me was what came later, when a giant snake crawled out of the sea and started fighting with this big person with the hammer. Then gangs of giants and monsters came from all directions and got to fighting with each other. And then there was a big, old, one-eyed person with a spear, stabbing away at a giant wolf which finally ate him, beard and all. Then another person came along and killed the wolf. All of a sudden, it looked familiar and I went outside and caught one of the troops by the sleeve.

"'Hey, this is Götterdämmerung,' I said, 'isn't it?'

"A nearby TV crew moved in on us as the person paused in hacking away at an amorphous mass with lots of eyes and nodded.

"'Sure is,' he said. 'Say, you must be—' and then the amorphous mass ate him.

"I crossed the street to where another one in a horned helmet was performing atrocities on a fallen foeperson.

"'Pardon me,' I asked him, 'but who are you?'

"'Loki's the name,' was the reply. 'What is your part in all of this?'

"'I don't know that I have a part,' I said. 'But that other person started to say something like I might and then the amorphous mass which was just stepped on by the giant with the arrow in his throat sucked him in.'

"Loki dispatched his victim with a look of regret and studied my torn garment.

"'You're dressed like a man,' he said, 'but—'

"I drew my shirt together.

"'I am—' I began.

"'Sure. Here's a safety pin. What a fine idea you've just given me! Come this way. There've got to be two human survivors,' he explained, pushing a path through a pack of werewolves. 'The gods will give their lives to defend you, once I've delivered you to Hoddmimir's Holt—that's the designated fallout shelter.' He snatched up an unconscious woman and slung her over his shoulder. 'You'll live through all this. A new day will dawn, a glorious new world will be revealed requiring a new first couple. Seeing you waiting, the gods will die believing that all is well. . . .' He broke into a fit of laughter. 'They think that all the deaths will bring a new regime, of love, peace and happiness—and a new race. . . .' The tears streamed down his face. 'All tragedies require liberal doses of irony,' he concluded, as he bore us in a psychedelic chariot through rivers of blood and fields of bones.

"He deposited us here, amid warmth, trees, fountains, singing birds—all those little things that make life pleasant and trite: plenty of food, gentle breezes, an attractive house with indoor plumbing. Then still laughing, he returned to the front.

"Later, my companion awoke—blond and lithe and lovely —and her eyes flashed when she turned my way.

"'So,' she snapped, 'you drag me from this horrible masculine conflict that I may serve your lusts in a secret pleasure haven! I'll have none of it, after all you've done to me!'

"I moved to comfort her, but she dropped into a karate stance.

"'Tell me,' I said then, 'what you mean. Nothing has been done to you. . . .'

"'You call leaving a girl pregnant nothing?' she cried. 'With all the abortionists busy treating frostbite? No! I want no part of men, never again!'

"'Be of good cheer, sister,' I replied, unpinning my shirt. 'I found myself too attractive to men, not to mention weak-willed—this long night being what it is—and suffering with a similar medical quandary, I resolved in a fit of remorse to lead the life of a simple transvestite.'

"'Sappho be praised!' she replied.

"And we both had twins, and lived happily ever after. Winter faded, and the Twilight of the Gods passed. The world is a new place, of love, peace and happiness, for so long as it lasts this time. That is the story. Go play nicely with your sisters now."

"But they won't play nicely. They keep tiring me out doing the thing you told me not to."

"How did you even learn to do such a thing in the first place?" the other mommy asked.

"A shining person with a golden staff showed me how. She also said that the gods move in mysterious and not terribly efficient ways."

"This could be the beginning of philosophy," said the first mommy.

"You might call it that," said the other.

EXEUNT OMNES

Houselights low. The Reapers and Nymphs danced as the bombs began to fall. Prospero faced Ferdinand.

"'You do look, my son, in a mov'd sort, as if you were

dismay'd. Be cheerful, sir, our revels now are ended. These our actors, as I foretold you, were all spirits, and are melted into air, into thin air. . . .'"

He gestured simply. The Reapers and Nymphs vanished, to a strange, hollow and confused noise.

"'. . . And, like the baseless fabric of this vision, the cloud-capped towers, the gorgeous palaces, the solemn temples,'" he continued, "'the great globe itself, yea, all which it inherit, shall dissolve and, like this insubstantial pageant faded, leave not a rack behind. . . .'"

The audience vanished. The stage vanished. The theater vanished. The city about them faded, with a strange, hollow and confused noise. The great globe itself became transparent beneath their feet. All of the actors vanished, save for the spirits of Ariel, Caliban and Prospero.

"Uh, Prossy. . ." said Ariel.

"'We are such stuff as dreams are made on—'"

"Prospero!" bellowed Caliban.

"'. . . And our little life is rounded with a sleep.'"

Caliban tackled him. Ariel seized him by the sleeve.

"You're doing it again, boss!"

"'Sir, I am vexed—'"

"Stop it! The melt is on! You undid the wrong spell!"

"'Bear with my weakness—my old brain is troubled. . . .'"

Caliban sat on him. Ariel waved his slight fingers before his eyes. They drifted now in a vast and star-filled void. The nearest sizable body was the moon. Satellites—communication, astronomical, weather and spy—fled in all directions.

"Come around, damn it!" Ariel snapped. "We're all that's left again!"

"'Be not disturbed with my infirmity. . . .'"

"It's no use," growled Caliban. "He's gone off the deep end this time. What say we give up and fade away?"

"No!" Ariel cried. "I was just beginning to enjoy it."

"We *are* disturbed by your infirmity, Prossy! Cut the Stanislavsky bit and put things back together!"

"'If you be pleas'd, retire into my cell and there repose. . . .'"

"He's coming to the end of his lines," said Ariel. "We'll get him then."

"'A turn or two I'll walk, to still my beating mind.'"

"Where are you going to walk, boss?" Caliban asked. "You took it all away."

"Eh? What's that?"

"You did it again. It's a terrific scene that way, but it tends to be kind of final."

"Oh dear! And things are pretty far along, too."

"The furthest, I'd say, to date. What do you do for an encore?"

"Where's my Book?"

Caliban flipped his flipper.

"It went, too."

Prospero massaged his eyeballs.

"Then I'll have to work from memory. Bear with me. Where was it?"

"A desert isle."

"Yes."

He gestured magnificently and the faint outlines of palm trees appeared nearby. A slight salt scent came to them, along with the distant sounds of surf. The outlines grew more substantial and a shining sand was spread beneath their feet. There came the cry of a gull. The stars faded, the sky grew blue and clouds drifted across it.

"That's better."

"But—this is a *real* desert isle!"

"Don't argue with him. You know how he gets."

"Now, where were we?"

"The entertainment, sir."

"Ah, yes. Come to my cave. Ferdinand and Miranda will be waiting."

He led them along the shore and up to a rocky place. They entered a great grotto where a large playing area was illuminated by torchlight. Prospero nodded to Ferdinand and Miranda and gestured toward the stage.

"Boss, something's wrong."

"No tongue! All eyes! Be silent!"

Ariel lost his power of speech for the moment and regarded the scene that appeared before him.

The great globe of the Earth, sun dappled, cloud streaked, green, gray and blue, turned slowly above the playing area. Tiny sparks, missiles, streaked above it, vanishing to be replaced by minute puffs of smoke over the major cities of

North America, Europe and Asia. The globe rushed toward them then, one puff growing larger than the others, replacing all else. Up through dust, fire and smoke the vision swam, of a city twisted, melted, charred, its people dead, dying, fleeing.

"Boss! This is the wrong bit!" Caliban cried.

"My God!" said Ferdinand.

"'You do look, my son, in a mov'd sort, as if you were dismay'd,'" Prospero stated.

"Here we go again," said Ariel, as the world rotated and entire land masses began to burn.

"'. . . the gorgeous palaces, the solemn temples, the great globe itself . . .'"

More missiles crisscrossed frantically as the icecaps melted and the oceans began to seethe.

"'. . . shall dissolve . . .'"

Large portions of the land were now inundated by the boiling seas.

"'. . . leave not a rack behind . . .'"

"We're still substantial," Ariel gasped.

"But *it's* going," Caliban observed.

The globe grew less tangible, the fires faded, the water lost its colors. The entire prospect paled and dwindled.

"'. . . is rounded with a sleep.'" Prospero yawned.

. . . Was gone.

"Boss! What happened to—"

"Sh!" Ariel cautioned. "Don't stir him up. —Prossy, where's the theater?"

"'. . . to still my beating mind.'"

"'We wish you peace,'" Ferdinand and Miranda said in unison as they exited.

"Where are we, sir?"

"Why, you told me 'twas a desert isle."

"And such it is."

"Then what else would you? Find us food and drink. The other's but a dream."

"But, sir! Your Book—"

"Book me no books! I'd eat and sleep, I'd let these lovers woo, then off to Naples. All magics I eschew!"

Caliban and Ariel retreated.

"We'd best his will observe and then away."

"Aye, sprite. Methinks the living lies this way."

[*Exeunt omnes.*]

A VERY GOOD YEAR . . .

"Hello," he said.

She looked at him. He was sandy haired, thirtyish, a little rugged looking but well groomed and very well dressed. He was smiling.

"I'm sorry," she said. "Do I know you?"

He shook his head.

"Not yet," he said. "Bradley's the name. Brad Dent."

"Well . . . What can I do for you, Mr. Dent?"

"I believe that I am going to fall in love with you," he said. "Of course, this requires a little cooperation. May I ask what time you get off work?"

"You're serious!"

"Yes."

She looked down at the countertop, noticed that her fingers were tapping the glass, stilled them, looked back up. His smile was still there.

"We close in twenty minutes," she said abruptly. "I could be out front in half an hour."

"Will you?"

She smiled then. She nodded.

"My name's Marcia."

"I'm glad," he said.

At dinner, in a restaurant she would never have found by herself, she studied him through the candlelight. His hands were smooth. His accent was Middle American.

"You looked familiar when you came up to me," she said. "I've seen you around somewhere before. In fact, now that I think back on it, I believe you passed my counter several times today."

"Probably," he said, filling her wineglass.

"What do you do, Brad?"

"Nothing," he said.

She laughed.

"Doesn't sound very interesting."

He smiled again.

"What I mean to say is that I am devoting myself to enjoying this year, not working."

"Why is that?"

"I can afford it, and it's a very good year."

"In what way is it special?"

He leaned back, laced his fingers, looked at her across them.

"There are no wars going on anywhere, for a change," he finally said. "No civil unrest either. The economy is wonderfully stable. The weather is beautiful." He raised his glass and took a sip. "There are some truly excellent vintages available. All of my favorite shows and movies are playing. Science is doing exciting things—in medicine, in space. A flock of fine books has been published. There are so many places to go, things to do this year. It could take a lifetime." He reached out and touched her hand. "And I'm in love," he finished.

She blushed.

"You hardly know me. . . ."

". . . And I have that to look forward to, also—getting to know you."

"You *are* very strange," she said.

"But you will see me again. . . ."

"If it's going to be that kind of year," she said, and she squeezed his hand.

She saw him regularly for a month before she quit her job and moved in with him. They dined well, they traveled often. . . .

She realized, one evening in Maui near the end of the year, that she was in love with him.

"Brad," she said, clasping him tightly, "this spring it seemed more like a game than anything else. . . ."

"And now?"

"Now it's special."

"I'm glad."

On New Year's Eve, they went to dinner at a place he knew in Chinatown. She leaned forward over the chicken fried rice.

"That man," she said, "at the corner table to the right . . ."

"Yes?"

"He looks a lot like you."

Brad glanced over, nodded.

"Yes."

"You know, I still don't know you very well."

"But we know each other better."

"Yes, that's true. But—Brad, that man coming out of the restroom . . ."

He turned his head.

"He looks like you, too."

"He does."

"Strange . . . I mean, I don't even know where you get your money."

"My family," he said, "always had a lot."

She nodded.

"I see. . . . Two more! Those men who just came in!"

"Yes, they look like me, too."

She shook her head.

"Then you really never had to work?"

"On the contrary. I'm a scientist. Bet I could have had the Nobel Prize."

She dished out some sweet-and-sour pork. Then she paused, eyes wide, head turned again.

"Brad, it *has* to be more than coincidence. There's *another* you!"

"Yes," he said, "I always dine here on New Year's Eve."

She laid down her fork. She paled.

"You're a biologist," she said, "aren't you? And you've cloned yourself? Maybe you're not even the original. . . ."

He laughed softly.

"No, I'm a physicist," he said, "and I'm not a clone. It *has* been a very good year, hasn't it?"

She smiled gently. She nodded.

"Of course it has," she said. "You say you *always* dine here on New Year's Eve?"

"Yes. The same New Year's Eve. This one."

"Time travel?"

"Yes."

"Why?"

"This has been such a good year that I have resolved to live it over, and over, and over—for the rest of my life."

Two couples entered the restaurant. She looked back.

"That's us!" she said. "And the second couple looks a lot older—but they're us, too!"

"Yes, this is where I first saw you. I had to find you after that. We looked so happy."

"Why have we never met any of them before?"

"I keep a diary. We'll go to different places each time around. Except for New Year's Eve. . . ."

She raked her lower lip once with her teeth.

"Why— Why keep repeating it?" she finally asked.

"It's been such a very good year," he said.

"But what comes after?"

He shrugged.

"Don't ask me."

He turned and smiled at the older couple, who had nodded toward them.

"I think they're coming over. Perhaps we can buy them a drink. Isn't she lovely?"

My Lady of the Diodes

Stephen Gregg unearthed this story which I forgot I had written. It had appeared in a fanzine called Granfalloon. *Steve wanted to reprint it in his semipro magazine,* Eternity. *I asked to see a copy first, as I no longer had one in my possession. I okayed the deal after I'd read a Xerox, but alas!* Eternity *went under (after also helping to resurrect a character of mine named Dilvish), and this story was not reprinted. Why not run it here? I asked myself. Why not? I answered. How often does one wish to seize an opportunity to acknowledge a forgotten offspring?*

Maxine had said, "Turn left at the next corner," so I did.

"Park the car. Get out and walk. Cross the street at the crosswalk."

I slammed the door behind me and moved on up the street, a man in a dark blue suit carrying a gray suitcase, a hearing aid in my left ear. I might have been the Fuller Brush man.

I crossed the street.

"Now head back up the other side. You will see a red brick building, numbered six-six-eight."

"Check," I said.

"Head up the front walk, but do not mount the stairs. Once you pass the iron fence, there will be a stairway leading downward, to your left. Descend that stairway. At the bottom of the stair there will be a doorway leading into the building, probably padlocked."

"There is."

"Set down the case, put on the gloves you are carrying in

175

your coat pocket, take the hammer from your inside pocket, and use it to strike open the lock. Try to do it in one sharp blow."

It took two.

"Enter the building and close the door behind you. Leave the lock inside; put away the hammer."

"It's dark. . . ."

"The building should be deserted. Take twelve paces forward, and you will come to a corridor leading off to your right."

"Yes."

"Remove your right glove and take out the roll of dimes you are carrying in your right pocket. In the side corridor you should see a row of telephone booths."

"I do."

"Is there sufficient illumination coming from the three small windows opposite the booths to permit you to operate a telephone?"

"Yes."

"Then enter the first booth, remove the receiver with your gloved hand, insert a coin, and dial the following number. . ."

I began to dial.

"When the call is answered, do not respond or hang up, but place the receiver on the ledge and enter the next booth, where you will dial the following number. . ."

I did this, twelve times in all.

"That is sufficient," said Maxine. "You have tied up all the lines to the Hall, so that no outgoing calls may be placed. It is highly improbable that anyone will come along and break these connections. Return at once to the car. Replace the padlock on the door as you go. Then drive directly to the Hall. Park in the corner lot with the sign that says FIRST HOUR 50¢—35¢ EACH ADD'L HOUR. You may pay in advance at that lot, so have your money ready. Tell the attendant that you will only be a short time."

I returned to the car, entered it, and began driving.

"Keep your speed at thirty-five miles per hour, and put on your hat."

"Must I? Already? I hate hats."

"Yes, put it on. The glasses, also."

"All right, they're on. Hats mess your hair up, though,

more than the wind they're supposed to be protecting it from. They blow off, too."

"How is the traffic? Heavy? Light? —They keep a man's head warm."

"Pretty light. —They do not. Hair takes care of your head, and your ears still stick out and get cold."

"What color is the traffic signal ahead? —Then why do other men wear hats?"

"It just turned green. —They're stupid conformists. Hats are as bad as neckties."

"Barring untoward traffic circumstances, your present speed will take you through the next two intersections. You will be stopped by a red light at the third one. At that point, you will have time to fill your pipe—and perhaps to light it, also, although you were rather slow when you practiced. If you cannot light it there, you should have two more opportunities before you reach the parking lot. —What's wrong with neckties?

"Check your wristwatch against the time now: You have exactly nine minutes before the acid eats through the power cables. —Neckties are elegant."

"Check. . . . Neckties are stupid!"

"Now place me in the back seat and cover me with the blanket. I will administer electrical shocks to anyone who tries to steal me."

I did this, got the pipe going, found the lot.

"Keep puffing lots of smoke in front of your face as you talk with the attendant. You have the brown paper bag and the collapsible carton? The door-couple and the light?"

"Yes."

"Good. Take off your gloves. Remove your hearing aid and get it out of sight. Watch how you handle the steering wheel now. Palm it, and rub after each touch."

I parked the car, paid the attendant, strolled on up the street toward the Hall. Two minutes and twenty seconds remained.

I climbed the front stairs and entered the lobby. The Seek-fax exhibit was in a room toward the back and to my left. I moved off in that direction.

One minute and forty seconds remained. I emptied my pipe into a sandpot, scraped the bowl.

No windows in the exhibit room, Maxine had said, and

she'd digested the blueprints. Metal frame, metal doorplate—
just as Maxine had said.

I approached the door, which was standing open. I could
hear voices, caught glimpses of banks of machinery, exhibit
cases. I put away my pipe and changed my glasses to the
infrareds. Fifteen seconds. I put on my gloves. Ten.

I jammed my hands into my pockets, resting the left one on
the infrared flashlight and the right on the door-couple. I
counted to ten slowly and walked into the room, just as the
lights went out.

Kicking the door shut, I clapped the couple-bar across the
lockplate and the frame. Then I ran the polarizer rod along it,
and it snapped tight. I switched on the flash and moved across
the room to the central exhibit cases.

Everyone stood around stupidly as I removed the hammer
and broke the glass. A couple of the salesmen began groping
toward me, but much too slowly. I put away the hammer and
filled the bag with the gold wire, the platinum wire, the silver
wire. I wrapped the more expensive crystals and jewel components in wads of tissue.

Half a minute, maybe, to fill the bag. I opened out the
stamped, self-addressed carton as I made my way back across
the room. I stuffed the bag inside, into a nest of shredded
newsprint. Cigarette lighters and matches flared briefly about
me, but they didn't do much, or for very long.

There was a small knot of people before the door. "Make
way here!" I said. "I have a key." They pushed aside as I
depolarized the couple-bar. Then I slipped out through the
door, closed it, and coupled it from the outside.

I took off my gloves, put away the flashlight and changed
my glasses as I strolled out, pipe between my teeth. I dropped
the package into the mailbox on the corner and walked back to
the parking lot. I parked on a side street, reversed my dark
blue suit jacket into a light gray sport coat, removed my
glasses, hat and pipe, and reintroduced the hearing aid.

"All's well," I said.

"Good," said Maxine. "Now, by my estimate, they only
owe you two million, one hundred twenty-three thousand,
four hundred fifty dollars. Let's return the car and take a taxi
out to the scene of your alibi."

"Check. We'll pick up a bigger piece of change in Denver,

doll. I think I'll buy you a new carrying case. What color would you like?"

"Get me an alligator one, Danny. They're elegant."

"Alligator it is, baby," I replied as we headed back toward the rent-a-car garage.

We hit Denver two months ahead of time, and I began programming Maxine. I fed her the city directory, the city history, all the chamber of commerce crap, and all the vital statistics I could lay my hands on. I attached the optical scanner and gave her the street guides and the blueprints to all the public buildings and other buildings I found in the files at City Hall. Then I photographed the conference hotel, inside and out, as well as the adjacent buildings. Every day we scanned the local newspapers and periodicals, and Maxine stored everything.

Phase Two began when Maxine started asking for special information: Which roads were surfaced with what? What sort of clothing was being worn? How many construction companies were currently building? How wide were certain streets?

As a stockholder, I received my brochure one day, explaining the big conference. I fed that to Maxine, too.

"Do you want to cancel the debt completely?" she asked. "This includes court costs, attorney's fees and 7 percent compound interest."

"How?"

"This will be the first showing of the Seekfax 5000. Steal it."

"Steal the whole damn machine? It must weigh tons!"

"Approximately sixty-four hundred pounds, according to the brochure. Let's steal it and retire. The odds against you keep going up each time, you know."

"Yes, but my God! What am I going to do with Seekfax 5000?"

"Strip it down and sell the components. Or better yet, sell the whole unit to the Bureau of Vital Statistics in São Paulo. They're looking for something like that, and I've already mapped out three tentative smuggling routes. I'll need more data. . . ."

"It's out of the question!"

"Why? Don't you think I can plan it?"

"The ramifications are . . ."

"You built me to cover every contingency. Don't worry. Just give me the information I ask for."

"I'll have to consider this one a little further, baby. So excuse me. I'm going to eat dinner."

"Don't drink too much. We have a lot to talk about."

"Sure. See you later."

I pushed Maxine under the bed and left, heading up the street toward the restaurant. It was a warm summer evening, and the slants of sunlight between buildings were filled with glowing dust motes.

"Mister Bracken, may I speak with you?"

I turned and regarded the speaker's maple syrup eyes behind jar bottoms set in Harlequin frames, dropped my gaze approximately five feet two inches to the tops of her white sandals, and raised it again, slowly: Kind of flat chested and pug nosed, she wore a cottony candy-striped thing which showed that anyway her shoulders were not bony. Lots of maple syrup matching hair was balled up on the back of her head, with a couple winglike combs floating on it and aimed at her ears, both of which looked tasty enough—the ears, that is. She carried a large purse and a camera case almost as big.

"Hello. Yes. Speak." There was something vaguely familiar about her, but I couldn't quite place it.

"My name is Gilda Coburn," she said, "and I arrived in town today." Her voice was somewhat nasal. "I was sent to do a feature article on the computer conference. I was coming to see you." ·

"Why?"

"To interview you, concerning data-processing techniques."

"There'll be a lot of more important men than me around in another week or so. Why don't you talk to them. I'm not in computers anymore."

"But I've heard that you're responsible for three of the most important breakthroughs in the past decade. I read all of *Daniel Bracken* v. *Seekfax Incorporated,* and you said this yourself at the trial."

"How did you know I was in Denver?"

"Perhaps some friend of yours told my editor. I don't know how he found out. *May* I interview you?"

"Have you eaten yet?"

"No."

"Come with me then. I'll feed you and tell you about data processing."

No friend of mine could have told any editor, because I don't have any friends, except for Maxine. Could Gilda be some kind of cop? Private, local, insurance? If so, it was worth a meal or three if I could find out.

I ordered drinks before dinner, a bottle of wine with the meal and two after-dinner drinks, hoping to fog her a bit. But she belted everything down and remained clear as a bell.

And her questions remained cogent and innocuous, until I slipped up on one.

I referred to the Seekfax 410 translation unit when talking about possible ways of communicating with extraterrestrials, should we ever come across any.

". . . 610," she corrected, and I went on talking.

Click! Unwind her hair and lighten it a couple shades, then make her glasses horn-rimmed . . .

Sonia Kronstadt, girl genius out of MIT, designer of the Seekfax 5000, the prototype of which I was contemplating selling to the Bureau of Vital Statistics in São Paulo. She worked for the enemy.

I had hit Seekfax twelve times in the past five years. They knew it had to be me, but they could never prove it. I had built Max-10, Maxine, to plan perfect crimes, and she had done so a dozen times already. Seekfax was out to get me, but we had always outwitted their detectives, their guards, their alarm devices. No two robberies bore any resemblance as to method, thanks to Maxine. Each one was a *de novo* theft. Now then, if Kronstadt was in town ahead of time, under a phony name, then this Denver conference smacked of a setup job. The brochure had spoken of a very large display of expensive equipment, also. Had they something very special in mind for Danny Bracken? Perhaps it would do to sit this one out. . . .

"Care to come back to my room for a nightcap?" I asked, taking her hand.

"All right," and she smiled, "thanks."

Ha! Hell hath no fury like a jealous computer designer, or computer, as I later learned. . . .

When we got back to my room and were settled with

drinks, she asked me what I had thought she might: "about all these robberies at Seekfax exhibits and conferences . . ."

"Yes?"

"I'd like to have your views as to who might be committing them."

"IBM? Radio Shack?"

"Seriously. There has never been a single clue. Each one has actually been a perfect crime. You'd think a criminal that good would go after bigger game—say, jewelry stores, or banks. My theory is that it's someone with a grudge against the company. How does that sound to you?"

"No," I said, and I touched her neck with my lips as I leaned over to refill her glass. She didn't draw away. "You're assuming that it's one person, and the facts tend to indicate otherwise. From the reports I've read, no two of the robberies have ever been alike. I believe that the Seekfax exhibit has come to be known in the underworld as an easy mark."

"Bosh!" she said. "They're not easy marks. Greater precautions are taken at each one, but the thief seems to accommodate this by taking greater precautions himself. I think it's one man with a grudge against the company, a man who delights in outsmarting it."

I kissed her then, on the mouth to shut her up. She leaned forward against me and I drew her to her feet.

Somehow, the light got turned out.

Later, as I lay there smoking, she said: "Everyone knows you're the one who's doing it."

"I thought you were asleep."

"I was deciding how to say it."

"You're no reporter," I said.

"No, I'm not."

"What do you want?"

"I don't want you to go to prison."

"You work for Seekfax."

"Yes. I work for Seekfax, and I fell in love with the designs for the 5280 and the 9310. I know that they're your designs. The people they say did them aren't that good. Those are the work of a genius."

"I hired a consulting engineer," I said, "your Mr. Walker, to help with some of the drawings. He went to work for Seekfax a week later, before I had the patents registered. You've read his testimony and mine. That's why he's a vice-president now."

"So that's why you commit these robberies?"

"Seekfax owes me two million, one hundred twenty-three thousand, four hundred fifty dollars."

"That much? How do you know?"

"As a stockholder, I have a right to audit the books. I calculated that amount from what my CPA saw of the profit rise after my ideas went into use. That's cheap, too. A work of art is priceless."

"It had to be you, Danny. I saw that door-couple. You designed it. Your signature was on it. I heard how bitter you were after the trial, how you swore you would recover. . . ."

"So? Why come tell me your guesses? Have you got anything that will stand up in court?"

"Not yet."

"What do you mean 'yet'?"

"I came here ahead of the conference because I knew you'd be in town, planning this one. I came here to warn you, because I do not want you to go to prison. I could not bear being responsible for putting the creator of the 9310 behind bars."

"Granting that all your guesses are correct, how could you be responsible for anything like that?"

"Because I designed the Seekfax 5000," she said, "into which every known fact about Denver and yourself has been programmed. It is not just a fact retriever, Danny. It is the perfect integrated data-processing detective. I am convinced that it is capable of extrapolating every possible theft which could occur at the conference, and then making provision to guard against it. You cannot possibly succeed. The age of the master criminal is past, now that IDP has moved into the picture."

"Ha!" I said.

"Aren't you rich enough now to retire?"

"Of course I'm rich," I said. "That isn't the point. . . ."

"I understand your motives, but *my* point is that you can't outthink the 5000. Nothing can! Even if you cut off the electricity again, the 5000 is a self-contained power unit. No matter what you do, it will compute an immediate countermeasure."

"Go back to Seekfax," I said, "and tell them that I'm not

afraid of any cock-and-bull story about a detective computer. So long as they're going to hold exhibits and participate in conferences, they'd better be prepared to suffer losses. Also, I admit nothing."

"It's *not* a cock-and-bull story," she finally said. "I built the thing! I know what it can do!"

"Some day I'll introduce you to Maxine," I said, "who'll tell you what she thinks of sixty-four hundred pounds of detective."

"Who's Maxine? Your girlfriend, or . . . ?"

"We're just good friends," I said, "but she goes everywhere with me."

She dressed quickly then, and after a minute I heard the door slam.

I reached beneath the bed and switched on audio.

"Maxine, baby, did you catch that? The machine we're going to steal is out to get us."

"So what?" said Maxine.

"That's the attitude," I replied. "Anything it can do, you can do better. Sixty-four hundred pounds! Huh!"

"You knew I was under the bed and turned on, but you did it anyway!"

"Did what?"

"You made love to that—that woman. . . . Right above me! I heard everything!"

"Well . . . Yes."

"Have you no respect for me?"

"Of course I do. But that was something between two people, that—"

"And all I am is the thing you feed the facts to, is that it? The thing that plans your crimes! I mean nothing to you as an individual!"

"That's not true, Max baby. You know it. I only brought that woman up here to find out what Seekfax was up to. What I did was necessary, to obtain the data I needed."

"Don't lie to me, Daniel Bracken! I know what you are. You're a heel!"

"Don't be that way, Maxie! You know it's not so! Didn't I just buy you a nice new alligator case?"

"Hah! You got off cheap, considering all I've done for you!"

"Don't, Max . . ."

"Maybe it's time you got yourself another computer."

"I need you, baby. You're the only one who can take on the 5000 and beat it."

"Fat chance!"

"What'll I do now?"

"Go get drunk."

"What good'll that do?"

"You seem to think it's the answer to everything. Men are beasts!"

I poured myself a drink and lit a cigarette. I should never have given Maxine that throaty voice. It did something to her, to me. . . . I gulped it and poured another.

It was three days before Maxine came around. She woke me up in the morning, singing "The Battle Hymn of the Republic," then announced, "Good morning, Danny. I've decided to forgive you."

"Thanks. Why the change of heart?"

"Men are weak. I've recomputed things and decided you couldn't help it. It was mainly that woman's fault."

"Oh, I see. . . ."

". . . And I've planned the next crime, to perfection."

"Great. Let me in on it?"

At this point, I had some misgivings. I hadn't anticipated her womanlike reaction on the night I'd brought Sonia around. I wondered whether this thing might not go even deeper, to the point of her plotting revenge. Would she purposely foul this one up, just so I'd be caught? I weighed the problem and couldn't decide. It was silly! Maxine was only a machine. . . .

Still—she was the most sophisticated machine in the world, complete with random circuits which permitted emotion analogues.

And I couldn't build another Maxine in the time remaining. I just had to listen to her and decide for myself whether I should abandon the project. . . .

"I put myself in the 5000's place," said Maxine. "We both possess the same facts, about yourself and the locale. I, therefore, can arrive at any conclusion it can. The difference is that it is fighting a defensive battle, where we have the advantage of taking the initiative. We can break it by introducing an independent variable."

"Such as?"

"You've always robbed the conference or exhibit while it was in progress. Seekfax 5000 will formulate plans to defend against this—and *only* this, I'm certain—because this is all it will be programmed for."

"I fail to see . . ."

"Supposing you strike *before* the conference, or *after?*"

"It sounds great, Maxie, if the 5000 is just a simple problem solver. But I'm a little afraid of the machine. Sonia Kronstadt is no slouch. Supposing she's duplicated your field approach to problem definition, so that that overweight monstrosity can redefine problems as it goes along? In a cruder fashion than yourself, of course! Or supposing Sonia simply thought of that angle herself, and the question was not posed as you've guessed?"

"She said, '. . . Every possible theft which could occur *at* the conference.' I'll wager that's the way she programmed it. The probabilities are on our side."

"I don't want to gamble that much."

"All right, then. Don't. How about this? I will plan it for *after* the conference. The conference is open to the public, so we will attend. They can't throw you out if you're not causing a disturbance. An article in yesterday's paper stated that the Seekfax 5000 has been programmed to play chess and can beat any human player. It will play the local champions and anyone else who is interested, providing they supply the board and chessmen. Go buy a chess set. You will take me with you and keep me tuned in. Repeat each move after it makes it, and I will play the 5000 a game of chess. From its chess playing I will extrapolate the scope of its problem-solving abilities. After the game, I will let you know whether we can carry out the plan."

"No, don't be silly! How can you tell that from a game of chess?"

"It takes a machine to know one, Danny, and don't be so jealous. I'm only going to do what is necessary, to obtain the data I need."

"Who's jealous? I know computers, and I don't see how you can tell anything that way."

"There is a point, Danny, where science ends and art begins. This is that point. Leave it to me."

"All right. I'll probably regret it, but that's the way we'll do it."

"And don't worry, Danny. I can compute anything."

This is how it came to pass that on the last day of the conference a man in a dark suit showed up, carrying an alligator suitcase and a chess set, a hearing aid in his left ear.

"Biggest stereo set I ever saw," I said to Sonia, who was programming it to accommodate the ten or eleven players seated at the card tables. "I hear that critter plays chess."

She looked at me, then looked away.

"Yes," she said.

"I want to play it."

"Did you bring a chess set?" I could see she was biting her lip.

"Yes."

"Then have a seat at that empty table and set up the board. I'll be by in a few moments. I make all the moves for the machine. Which do you want: black or white?"

"White. I'll be offensive."

"Then make the first move." She was gone.

I set Maxine on the floor beside the table, opened out the board and dumped the pieces. I set them up and clicked my tongue in signal. "Pawn to Queen four," said Maxine.

An hour later, all the games were over but ours. The other chess players were standing around watching. "Fella's good," someone stated. There were several assents.

I glanced at my wristwatch. Seekfax 5000 was taking more time between moves. From the corners of my eyes, I could see that uniformed guards flanked me in a reasonably unobtrusive manner.

There was a puzzled expression on Sonia's face as she made the moves for her machine. It wasn't supposed to take this long. . . . Some flashbulbs went off, and I heard my name mentioned somewhere.

Then Maxine launched into a dazzling end game. I'm no chess buff, but I think I'm pretty good. I couldn't follow her up and down all those dizzying avenues of attack, even if there had been half an hour between moves.

The 5000 countered slowly, and I couldn't really tell who had the advantage. Numerically we were about even.

Sonia sighed and moved her Bishop. "Stalemate," she said.

"Thank you," I said. "You have lovely hands," and I left.

No one tried to stop me, except for the representative of the local chess club, because I hadn't done anything wrong.

As we drove home, Maxine said: "We can do it."

"We can?"

"Yes. I know just how he works now. He's a wonderful machine, but I can beat him."

"Then how come he stalemated you back there?"

"I let him do it. I didn't have to beat him to find out what I wanted to know. He's never been beaten yet, and I didn't see any point in disgracing him in front of all those chess people."

I didn't like the way she accented that last word, but I let it go without comment.

In the rearview mirror, I caught a glimpse of Sonia Kronstadt's Mercedes. She followed me home, drove around the block a couple of times, and vanished.

Over the weeks, I had obtained all the equipment I needed, including the paraffin for the chewing gum molds.

The Seekfax 5000 had been flown in from Massachusetts and was going to be flown back. It had to be transported to and from the airport, however, in a truck. So I was about to become a hijacker.

I buttoned down my red-and-white-striped blazer, used my handkerchief to dust off my spats, smoothed my white trousers, adjusted my red silk Ascot and my big black false mustache, stuffed more cotton into my cheeks, put on my straw hat and picked up my canvas sack and what was apparently my alligator-hide sample case. I had this outfit on over slacks and a sport shirt, which made me hot as well as florid.

I waited around the corner from the delivery dock.

When they had finished loading the truck and the guards and laborers had withdrawn from sight, I strolled past, managing to accost the driver before he mounted into the cab.

"Just the man I'm looking for!" I cried. "A man of taste and discrimination! I should like, sir, to give you a free sam-

ple of Doub-Alert gum! The chewing gum that is doubly re-
freshing! Doubly enlivening! I should also like to record your
reaction to this fine new chewing adventure!"

"I don't chew much gum," said the driver. "Thanks anyhow."

"But, sir, it would mean very much to my employer if you
would participate in the chewing reaction test."

"Test?" he asked.

"In the nature of a public opinion sample," I said. "It will
help us to know what sort of reception the product will receive. It's a form of market research," I added.

"Yeah?"

"Hey you!" called out one of the guards who had returned
to the dock. "Don't move! Don't go away!"

I dropped into a crouch as he leapt down. Another guard
followed.

"You giving away free samples?" asked the first one,
drawing near.

"Yeah. Chewing gum."

"Can we have some?"

"Sure. Take a couple."

"Thanks."

"Thanks."

"I'll take some too," said the driver.

"Help yourself."

"Not bad," said the first guard. "Kinda pepperminty and
tangy, with that pick-you-up feeling."

"Yeah," said the second one.

"Uh-huh," added the driver. Then the guards turned away
and headed back toward the ladder on the side of the dock.
The driver moved back toward his cab.

"Wait," I said to him. "What about the chewing reaction
test?"

"I'm in a hurry," he said. "What do you want to know?"

"Well— How did it strike you?"

"Kinda pepperminty and tangy," he said, "with that pick-
you-up feeling. —I gotta go now!" he said, entering the cab
and starting the engine.

"Mr. Doub-Alert thanks you," I said, glancing back over

my shoulder to be sure the dock was empty. I climbed up onto the dock as the bell went off.

My timing hadn't been too bad. I'd left the package at the desk earlier, for a Mr. Fireman to pick up later. It sounded enough like a standard fire alarm to draw anyone in off the dock. I wished, though, that it had rung a trifle sooner. I hated having to give that stuff to those guards.

As the driver gunned his engine, I yanked my coveralls from the canvas bag and stepped into them, so that anyone glancing up the alley as I climbed into the back of the truck would think I was a laborer, loading an alligator-skin case and a canvas bag.

He put the rig into gear and I crawled toward the cab, spitting out cotton. I crouched down behind the Seekfax 5000 and finished buttoning my coveralls. I pushed the canvas bag into the corner and held Maxine in my lap.

"How long do you think it will take, baby?" I asked, as the truck began to move.

"How constipated did he look?" asked Maxine.

"How the hell should I know?"

"Then how can I tell?"

"Well, approximately."

"Sufficient time to get him onto that stretch of road I told you about. If by some chance it doesn't work by then, you'll have to create some sort of disturbance back here, lure him in, and mug him."

"I hope it doesn't come to that."

"I doubt it will. That was pretty high-powered gum."

I wondered, though, what would happen if it worked too soon. But Maxine was right, as always.

After a time, we pulled suddenly to the side of the road and came to a halt. The engine died. The slam of the cab door came almost simultaneously with the locking of the brakes.

"All right, Danny, now make your way toward the rear—"

"Maxine! I just caught it! I couldn't tell before, because the engine was running. There's a faint vibration wherever I touch the chassis of the 5000. It's turned on!"

"So? He's got a self-contained power unit. You know that. He can't know you're here unless you program that information into him."

". . . Unless he has some sort of audio pickup."

"I doubt it. Why should he? You know how tricky a thing like that is to install."

"Then what's it doing?"

"Solving problems? Who cares? You'd better move, now, while the driver is still relieving himself off in the field. You may have to jump the ignition."

I climbed out, taking Maxine and the canvas bag with me, and I mounted into the cab. The keys were still in the ignition, so I started the engine and drove away. There was no sign of the driver.

About five miles farther up the road, I pulled into the culvert Maxine had designated and fetched the aerosols from the bag. I sprayed gray paint over the red sides of the truck, changed the license plates to out-of-state ones, blew compressed air against one panel to make it dry more rapidly, held up my stencil and sprayed the yellow paint through it. SPEED-D FURNITURE HAULING, it said.

Then we drove back onto the road and took a new route. "We did it, Maxine. We did it," I said.

"Of course," she replied. "I told you I could compute anything. How fast are we going?"

"Fifty-five. I don't like the idea of our passenger being turned on. First chance I get, I'm going to pull off the road and find a way to shut him down."

"That would be cruel," she said. "Why don't you just leave him alone?"

"My God!" I told her. "He's only a dumb bucket of bolts! He may be the second best computer in the world, but he's a moron compared with you! He doesn't even have random circuits that permit things like emotion analogues!"

"How do you know that? Do you think you're the only one who could design them. —And they're not emotion analogues! I have real feelings!"

"I didn't mean you! You're different."

"You were too talking about me! I don't mean anything to you—do I, Danny? I'm just the thing you feed the facts to. I mean nothing to you—as an individual."

"I've heard that speech before, and I won't argue with a hysterical machine."

"You know it's true, that's why."

"You heard what I said. —Hey! There's a car coming up behind us, and it just got close enough for me to tell—it's the Mercedes! *That's Sonia back there!* How did she— The 5000! Your boyfriend's been broadcasting shortwaves to her. He gave away our position."

"Better step on the gas, Danny."

I did, still looking back.

"I can't outrun that Mercedes with this truck."

"And you can't take this curve with it either, Danny boy, if you stepped on the gas when I told you to—and I'm sure you did. It's doubtless a reflex by now. Humans get conditioned that way."

I looked ahead and knew I couldn't make the curve. I slammed on the brakes and they started to scream. I began to burn rubber, but I wasn't slowing enough. "You bitch. You betrayed me!" I yelled.

"You know it, Danny! And you've had it, you heel. You can't even slow enough to jump!"

"The hell you say. I'll beat you yet!" I managed to slow it some more, and just before it went completely out of control, I opened the cab door and leaped out. I hit grass and rolled down a slope.

I thought that all the extra clothing I had on kind of padded me and was maybe what saved me; but right before the crash, while the truck was still within broadcast range, I heard Maxine's voice: "I wrote the end, Danny—the way it had to be. I told you I could compute anything. —Goodbye."

As I lay there feeling like a folded, stapled, spindled, and otherwise mutilated IBM card, and wondering whether I was more nearly related to Pygmalion or Dr. Frankenstein, I heard a car screech to a halt up on the highway.

I heard someone approaching, and the first thing I saw when I turned my head was the tops of a pair of white sandals, which were approximately five feet two inches beneath her maple syrup eyes.

"Maxine did beat your damn 5000," I gasped. "She was in the suitcase. She gave your machine that stalemate. . . . But she double-crossed me. . . . She planned the robberies and she planned everything that just happened. . . ."

"When you make a woman you do a good job," she said. She touched my cheek. She felt for broken bones, found none.

"Bet we could build one helluva computer together," I told her.

"Your mustache is on crooked," she said. "I'll straighten it."

And I Only Am Escaped to Tell Thee

Here is another of those short shorts I dearly enjoy doing when the opportunity and the idea come together. I tend to see things like this as single-panel, briefly captioned cartoons— and I work backward a little from there.

It was with them constantly—the black patch directly overhead from whence proceeded the lightnings, the near-blinding downpour, the explosions like artillery fire.

Van Berkum staggered as the ship shifted again, almost dropping the carton he carried. The winds howled about him, tearing at his soaked garments; the water splashed and swirled around his ankles—retreating, returning, retreating. High waves crashed constantly against the ship. The eerie, green light of St. Elmo's fire danced along the spars.

Above the wind and over even the thunder, he heard the sudden shriek of a fellow seaman, random object of attention from one of their drifting demonic tormentors.

Trapped high in the rigging was a dead man, flensed of all flesh by the elements, his bony frame infected now by the moving green glow, right arm flapping as if waving—or beckoning.

Van Berkum crossed the deck to the new cargo site, began lashing his carton into place. How many times had they shifted these cartons, crates and barrels about? He had lost count long ago. It seemed that every time the job was done a new move was immediately ordered.

194

He looked out over the railing. Whenever he was near, whenever the opportunity presented itself, he scanned the distant horizon, dim through the curtain of rain. And he hoped.

In this, he was different. Unlike any of the others, he had a hope—albeit a small one—for he had a plan.

A mighty peal of laughter shook the ship. Van Berkum shuddered. The captain stayed in his cabin almost constantly now, with a keg of rum. It was said that he was playing cards with the Devil. It sounded as if the Devil had just won another hand.

Pretending to inspect the cargo's fastenings, Van Berkum located his barrel again, mixed in with all the others. He could tell it by the small dab of blue paint. Unlike the others it was empty, and caulked on the inside.

Turning, he made his way across the deck again. Something huge and bat-winged flitted past him. He hunched his shoulders and hurried.

Four more loads, and each time a quick look into the distance. Then— Then . . . ?

Then!

He saw it. There was a ship off the port bow! He looked about frantically. There was no one near him. This was it. If he hurried. If he was not seen.

He approached his barrel, undid the fastenings, looked about again. Still no one nearby. The other vessel definitely appeared to be approaching. There was neither time nor means to calculate courses, judge winds or currents. There was only the gamble and the hope.

He took the former and held to the latter as he rolled the barrel to the railing, raised it, and cast it overboard. A moment later he followed it.

The water was icy, turbulent, dark. He was sucked downward. Frantically he clawed at it, striving to drag himself to the surface.

Finally there was a glimpse of light. He was buffeted by waves, tossed about, submerged a dozen times. Each time, he fought his way back to the top.

He was on the verge of giving up when the sea suddenly grew calm. The sounds of the storm softened. The day began to grow brighter about him. Treading water, he saw the vessel he had just quitted receding in the distance, carrying its private hell along with it. And there, off to his left, bobbed the barrel with the blue marking. He struck out after it.

When he finally reached it, he caught hold. He was able to draw himself partly out of the water. He clung there and panted. He shivered. Although the sea was calmer here, it was still very cold.

When some of his strength returned, he raised his head, scanned the horizon.

There!

The vessel he had sighted was even nearer now. He raised an arm and waved it. He tore off his shirt and held it high, rippling in the wind like a banner.

He did this until his arm grew numb. When he looked again the ship was nearer still, though there was no indication that he had been sighted. From what appeared to be their relative movements, it seemed that he might well drift past it in a matter of minutes. He transferred the shirt to his other hand, began waving it again.

When next he looked, he saw that the vessel was changing course, coming toward him. Had he been stronger and less emotionally drained, he might have wept. As it was, he became almost immediately aware of a mighty fatigue and a great coldness. His eyes stung from the salt, yet they wanted to close. He had to keep looking at his numbed hands to be certain that they maintained their hold upon the barrel.

"Hurry!" he breathed. "Hurry. . . ."

He was barely conscious when they took him into the lifeboat and wrapped him in blankets. By the time they came alongside the ship, he was asleep.

He slept the rest of that day and all that night, awakening only long enough to sip hot grog and broth. When he did try to speak, he was not understood.

It was not until the following afternoon that they brought in a seaman who spoke Dutch. He told the man his entire story, from the time he had signed aboard until the time he had jumped into the sea.

"Incredible!" the seaman observed, pausing after a long spell of translation for the officers. "Then that storm-tossed apparition we saw yesterday was really the *Flying Dutchman!*

There truly *is* such a thing—and you, you are the only man to have escaped from it!"

Van Berkum smiled weakly, drained his mug, and set it aside, hands still shaking.

The seaman clapped him on the shoulder.

"Rest easy now, my friend. You are safe at last," he said, "free of the demon ship. You are aboard a vessel with a fine safety record and excellent officers and crew—and just a few days away from her port. Recover your strength and rid your mind of past afflictions. We welcome you aboard the *Marie Celeste*."

The Horses of Lir

I sent this one to The Saturday Evening Post. *Three times. They kept losing the ms. I stopped.*

The moonlight was muted and scattered by the mist above the loch. A chill breeze stirred the white tendrils to a sliding, skating motion upon the water's surface. Staring into the dark depths, Randy smoothed his jacket several times, then stepped forward. He pursed his lips to begin and discovered that his throat was dry.

Sighing, almost with relief, he turned and walked back several paces. The night was especially soundless about him. He seated himself upon a rock, drew his pipe from his pocket and began to fill it.

What am I doing here? he asked himself. How can I . . . ?

As he shielded his flame against the breeze, his gaze fell upon the heavy bronze ring with the Celtic design that he wore upon his forefinger.

It's real enough, he thought, and it had been *his*, and *he* could do it. But this . . .

He dropped his hand. He did not want to think about the body lying in a shallow depression ten or twelve paces up the hillside behind him.

His Uncle Stephen had taken care of him for almost two years after the deaths of his parents, back in Philadelphia. He remembered the day he had come over—on that interminable plane flight—when the old man had met him at the airport in Glasgow. He had seemed shorter than Randy remembered, partly because he was a bit stooped he supposed. His hair was

198

pure white and his skin had the weathered appearance of a man's who had spent his life out-of-doors. Randy never learned his age.

Uncle Stephen had not embraced him. He had simply taken his hand, and his gray eyes had fixed upon his own for a moment as if searching for something. He had nodded then and looked away. It might have been then that Randy first noticed the ring.

"You'll have a home with me, lad," he had said. "Let's get your bags."

There was a brief splashing noise out in the loch. Randy searched its mist-ridden surface but saw nothing.

They know. Somehow they know, he decided. What now?

During the ride to his home, his uncle had quickly learned that Randy's knowledge of Gaelic was limited. He had determined to remedy the situation by speaking it with him almost exclusively. At first, this had annoyed Randy, who saw no use to it in a modern world. But the rudiments were there, words and phrases returned to him, and after several months he began to see a certain beauty in the Old Tongue. Now he cherished this knowledge—another thing he owed the old man.

He toyed with a small stone, cast it out over the waters, listened to it strike. Moments later, a much greater splash echoed it. Randy shuddered.

He had worked at his uncle's boat-rental business all that summer. He had cleaned and caulked, painted and mended, spliced. . . . He had taken out charters more and more often as the old man withdrew from this end of things.

"As Mary—rest her soul—never gave me children, it will be yours one day, Randy," he had said. "Learn it well, and it will keep you for life. You will need something near here."

"Why?" he had asked.

"One of us has always lived here."

"Why should that be?"

Stephen had smiled.

"You will understand," he said, "in time."

But that time was slow in coming, and there were other things to puzzle him. About once a month, his uncle rose and departed before daybreak. He never mentioned his destination or responded to questions concerning it. He never returned before sundown, and Randy's strongest suspicion did not survive because he never smelled of whisky when he came in.

Naturally, one day Randy followed him. He had never been forbidden to do it, though he strongly suspected it would meet with disapproval. So he was careful. Dressing hastily, he kept the old man in sight through the window as he headed off toward a stand of trees. He put out the CLOSED sign and moved through the chill predawn in that direction. He caught sight of him once again, briefly, and then Stephen vanished near a rocky area and Randy could find no trace of him after that. Half an hour later, he took down the sign and had breakfast.

Twice again he tried following him, and he lost him on both occasions. It irritated him that the old man could baffle him so thoroughly, and perhaps it bothered him even more that there was this piece of his life which he chose to keep closed to him—for as he worked with him and grew to know him better he felt an increasing fondness for his father's older brother.

Then one morning Stephen roused him early.

"Get dressed," he said. "I want you to come with me."

That morning his uncle hung the CLOSED sign himself and Randy followed him through the trees, down among the rocks, past a cleverly disguised baffle, and down a long tunnel. Randy heard lapping sounds of water, and even before his uncle put a light to a lantern he knew from the echoes that he was in a fair-sized cave.

His eyes did not adjust immediately when the light spread. When they did, he realized that he was regarding an underground harbor. Nevertheless, it took longer for the possibility to occur to him that the peculiar object to his left might be some sort of boat in a kind of dry dock. He moved nearer and examined it while his uncle filled and lit another lantern.

It was flat bottomed and U shaped. What he had taken to be some sort of cart beneath it, though, proved a part of the thing itself. It had a wheel on either side. Great metal rings hung loosely on both sides and on the forward end. The vehicle was tilted, resting upon its curved edge. These structural matters, however, aroused but a superficial curiosity, for all other things were overwhelmed within him by a kind of awe at its beauty.

Its gunwales, or sides—depending on exactly what the thing was—were faced with thin bronze plates of amazing design. They looped and swirled in patterns vaguely reminiscent of some of the more abstract figures in the *Book of Kells*, embossed here and there with large studs. The open areas looked to be enameled—green and red in the flickering light.

He turned as his uncle approached.

"Beautiful, isn't it?" he said, smiling.

"It—it belongs in a museum!"

"No. It belongs right here."

"What is it?"

Stephen produced a cloth and began to polish the plates.

"A chariot."

"It doesn't look exactly like any chariot I've seen pictures of. For one thing, it's awfully big."

Stephen chuckled.

"Ought to be. 'Tis the property of a god."

Randy looked at him to see whether he was joking. From the lack of expression on his face, he knew that he was not.

"Whose—is it?" he asked.

"Lir, Lord of the Great Ocean. He sleeps now with the other Old Ones—most of the time."

"What is it doing here?"

His uncle laughed again.

"Has to park it someplace now, doesn't he?"

Randy ran his hand over the cold, smooth design on the side.

"I could almost believe you," he said. "But what is your connection with it?"

"I go over it once a month, to clean it, polish it, keep it serviceable."

"Why?"

"He may have need of it one day."

"I mean, why you?"

He looked at his uncle again and saw that he was smiling.

"A member of our family has always done it," he said, "since times before men wrote down history. It is a part of my duty."

Randy looked at the chariot again.

"It would take an elephant to pull something that size."

"An elephant is a land creature."

"Then what . . . ?"

His uncle held up his hand beside the lantern, displaying the ring.

"I am the Keeper of the Horses of Lir, Randy. This is my emblem of office, though they would know me without it after all these years."

Randy looked closely at the ring. Its designs were similar to those on the chariot.

"The Horses of Lir?" he asked.

His uncle nodded.

"Before he went to sleep with the other Old Ones, he put them to pasture here in the loch. It was given to an early ancestor of ours to have charge of them, to see that they do not forget."

Randy's head swam. He leaned against the chariot for support.

"Then all those stories, of—things—in the loch . . . ?"

"Are true," Stephen finished. "There's a whole family, a herd of them out there." He gestured toward the water. "I call them periodically and talk to them and sing to them in the Old Tongue, to remind them."

"Why did you bring me here, Uncle? Why tell me all these secret things?" Randy asked.

"I need help with the chariot. My hands are getting stiff," he replied. "And there's none else but you."

Randy worked that day, polishing the vehicle, oiling enormous and peculiarly contrived harnesses that hung upon the wall. And his uncle's last words bothered him more than a little.

The fog had thickened. There seemed to be shapes moving within it now—great slow shadows sliding by in the distance. He knew they were not a trick of the moonlight, for there had been another night such as this . . .

"Would you get your pullover, lad?" his uncle had said. "I'd like us to take a walk."

"All right."

He put down the book he had been reading and glanced at his watch. It was late. They were often in bed by this hour. Randy had only stayed up because his uncle had kept busy, undertaking a number of one-man jobs about the small cottage.

It was damp outside and somewhat chill. It had been raining that day. Now the fogs stirred about them, rolling in off the water.

As they made their way down the footpath toward the shore, Randy knew it was no idle stroll that his uncle had in mind. He followed his light to the left past the docking area, toward a secluded rocky point where the land fell away sharply to deep water. He found himself suddenly eager, anxious to learn something more of his uncle's strange commitment to the place. He had grown steadily fonder of the old man in the time they had been together, and he found himself wanting to share more of his life.

They reached the point—darkness and mist and lapping water all about them—and Stephen placed his light upon the ground and seated himself on a stony ledge. He motioned for Randy to sit near him.

"Now, I don't want you to leave my side, no matter what happens," his uncle said.

"Okay."

"And if you must talk, speak the Old Tongue."

"I will."

"I am going to call the Horses now."

Randy stiffened. His uncle placed his hand upon his arm.

"You will be afraid, but remember that you will not be harmed so long as you stay with me and do whatever I tell you. You must be introduced. I am going to call them."

Randy nodded in the pale light.

"Go ahead."

He listened to the strange trilling noises his uncle made, and to the song that followed them. After a time, he heard a splashing, then he saw the advancing shadow . . . Big. Whatever it was, the thing was huge. Large enough to draw the chariot, he suddenly realized. If a person dare harness it . . .

The thing moved nearer. It had a long, thin neck atop its bulky form, he saw, as it suddenly raised its head high above the water, to sway there, regarding them through the shifting mist.

Randy gripped the ledge. He wanted to run but found that he could not move. It was not courage that kept him there. It was a fear so strong it paralyzed him, raising the hair on the back of his neck.

He looked at the Horse, hardly aware that his uncle was speaking softly in Erse now.

The figure continued to move before them, its head occasionally dipping partway toward them. He almost laughed as a wild vision of a snake-charming act passed through his head. The creature's eyes were enormous, with glints of their small light reflected palely within them. Its head moved forward, then back. Forward . . .

The great head descended until it was so close that it was almost touching his uncle, who reached out and stroked it, continuing to speak softly all the while.

He realized abruptly that his uncle was speaking to him. For how long he had been, he did not know.

". . . This one is Scafflech," he was saying, "and the one beside him is Finntag. . . ."

Randy had not realized until then that another of the beasts had arrived. Now, with a mighty effort, he drew his eyes from the great reptilian head which had turned toward him. Looking past it, he saw that a second of the creatures had come up and that it, also, was beginning to lean forward. And beyond it there were more splashing sounds, more gliding shadows parting the mists like the prows of Viking ships.

". . . And that one is Garwal. Talk to them, so they'll know the sound of your voice."

Randy felt that he could easily begin laughing hysterically. Instead, he found himself talking, as he would to a large, strange dog.

"That's a good boy. . . . Come on now. . . . How are you? Good old fellow. . . ."

Slowly he raised his hand and touched the leathery muzzle. Stephen had not asked him to. Why he had done it he was not certain, except that it had always seemed a part of the dog talk he was using and his hand had moved almost as if by reflex when he began it.

The first creature's head moved even nearer to his own. He felt its breath upon his face.

"Randy's my name, Scafflech," he heard himself telling it. "Randy . . ."

That night he was introduced to eight of them, of various

sizes and dispositions. After his uncle had dismissed them and they had departed, he simply sat there staring out over the water. The fear had gone with them. Now he felt only a kind of numbness.

Stephen stood, stooped, retrieved the light.

"Let's go," he said.

Randy nodded, rose slowly, and stumbled after him. He was certain that he would get no sleep that night, but when he got home and threw himself into bed the world went away almost immediately. He slept later than usual. He had no dreams that he could recall.

They were out there again now, waiting. He had seen them several times since but never alone. His uncle had taught him the songs, the guide words and phrases, but he had never been called upon to use them this way. Now, on this night so like the first, he was back, alone, and the fear was back, too. He looked down at the ring that he wore. Did they actually recognize it? Did it really hold some bit of the Old Magic? Or was it only a psychological crutch for the wearer?

One of the huge forms—Scafflech, perhaps—drew nearer and then hastily retreated. They had come without being called. They were waiting for his orders, and he clutched his pipe, which had long since gone out, and sat shaking.

Stephen had been ill much of the past month and had finally taken to his bed. At first, Randy had thought it to be influenza. But the old man's condition had steadily worsened. Finally he had determined to get him a doctor.

But Stephen had refused, and Randy had gone along with it until just that morning, when his uncle had taken a turn for the worse.

"No way, lad. This is it," he had finally told him. "A man sometimes has a way of knowing, and *we* always do. It is going to happen today, and it is very important that there be no doctor, that no one know for a time. . . ."

"What do you mean?" Randy had said.

"With a doctor there would be a death certificate, maybe an autopsy, a burial. I can't have that. You see, there is a special place set aside for me, for all of the Keepers. . . . I want to join my fathers, in the place where the Old Ones sleep. . . . It was promised—long ago. . . ."

"Where? Where is this place?" he had asked.

"The Isles of the Blessed, out in the open sea. . . . You must take me there. . . ."

"Uncle," he said, taking his hand, "I studied geography in school. There's no such place. So how can I . . . ?"

"It troubled me once, too," he said, "but I've been there. . . . I took my own father, years ago. . . . The Horses know the way. . . ."

"The Horses! How could I—How could they—"

"The chariot . . . You must harness Scafflech and Finntag to the chariot and place my body within it. Bathe me first, and dress me in the clothes you'll find in that chest. . . ." He nodded toward an old sea chest in the corner. "Then mount to the driver's stand, take up the reins, and tell them to take you to the Isles. . . ."

Randy began to weep, a thing he had not done since his parents' deaths—how long ago?

"Uncle, I can't," he said. "I'm afraid of them. They're so big—"

"You must. I need this thing to know my rest. —And set one of the boats adrift. Later tell the people that I took it out. . . ."

He wiped his uncle's face with a towel. He listened to his deepening breathing.

"I'm scared," he said.

"I know," Stephen whispered. "But you'll do it."

"I—I'll try."

"And here . . ." His uncle handed him the ring. "You'll need this—to show them you're the new Keeper. . . ."

Randy took the ring.

"Put it on."

He did.

Stephen had placed his hand upon his head as he had leaned forward.

"I pass this duty to you," he said, "that you be Keeper of the Horses of Lir."

Then his hand slipped away and he breathed deeply once again. He awakened twice after that, but not for long enough to converse at length. Finally, at sundown, he had died. Randy bathed him and clothed him as he had desired, weeping the while and not knowing whether it was for his sadness or his fear.

He had gone down to the cave to prepare the chariot. By lantern light he had taken down the great harnesses and affixed them to the rings in the manner his uncle had shown him. Now he had but to summon the Horses to this pool through the wide tunnel that twisted in from the loch, and there place the harnesses upon them. . . .

He tried not to think about this part of things as he worked, adjusting the long leads, pushing the surprisingly light vehicle into position beside the water. Least of all did he wish to think of aquaplaning across the waves, drawn by those beasts, heading toward some mythical isle, his uncle's body at his back.

He departed the cave and went to the docking area, where he rigged a small boat, unmoored it and towed it out some distance over the loch before releasing it. The mists were already rising by then. In the moonlight, the ring gleamed upon his finger.

He returned to the cottage for his uncle and bore him down to a cove near the water entrance to the cave. Then his nerve had failed, he had seated himself with his pipe and had not stirred since.

The splashing continued. The Horses were waiting. Then he thought of his uncle, who had given him a home, who had left him this strange duty. . . .

He rose to his feet and approached the water. He held up his hand with the ring upon it.

"All right," he said. "The time has come. Scafflech! Finntag! To the cave! To the place of the chariot! Now!"

Two forms drifted near, heads raised high upon their great necks.

I should have known it would not be that easy, he thought.

They swayed, looking down at him. He began addressing them as he had that first night. Slowly, their heads lowered. He waved the ring before them. Finally, when they were near enough, he reached out and stroked their necks. Then he repeated the instruction.

They withdrew quickly, turned, and headed off toward the tunnel. He moved away then, making for the land entrance to the place.

Inside, he found them waiting in the pool. He discovered then that he had to unfasten most of the harnessing from the chariot in order to fit it over them, and then secure it once again. It meant clambering up onto their backs. He removed his boots to do it. Their skin was strangely soft and slick beneath his feet, and they were docile now, as if bred to this business. He talked to them as he went about the work, rubbing their necks, humming the refrain to one of the old tunes.

He worked for the better part of an hour before everything was secure and he mounted the chariot and took up the reins.

"Out now," he said. "Carefully. Slowly. Back to the cove."

The wheels turned as the creatures moved away. He felt the reins jerk in his hands. The chariot advanced to the edge of the pool and continued on into the water. It floated. It drifted behind them toward the first bend and around it.

They moved through pitch blackness, but the beasts went carefully. The chariot never touched the rocky walls.

At length, they emerged into moonlight and mist over black water, and he guided them to the cove and halted them there.

"Wait now," he said. "Right here."

He climbed down and waded ashore. The water was cold, but he hardly noticed it. He mounted the slope to the place where his uncle lay and gathered him into his arms. Gently, he bore him down to the water's edge and out again. He took hold of the reins with a surer grip.

"Off now," he said. "You know the way! To the Isles of the Blessed! Take us there!"

They moved, slowly at first, through a long, sweeping turn that bore them out onto the misty breast of the loch. He heard splashings at either hand, and turning his head he saw that the other Horses were accompanying them.

They picked up speed. The beasts did seem to have a definite direction in mind. The mists swept by like a ghostly forest. For a moment, he almost felt as if he rode through some silent, mystical wood in times long out of mind.

The mists towered and thickened. The waters sparkled. He gave the creatures their head. Even if he had known the way, it would have done him little good, for he could not see where they were going. He had assumed that they were heading for the Caledonian Canal, to cut across to the sea. But now he wondered. If the Keepers, down through the ages, had been transported to some strange island, how had it been accomplished in earlier times? The Canal, as he recalled, had only been dug sometime in the nineteenth century.

But as the moonlit mists swirled about him and the great beasts plunged ahead, he could almost believe that there was another way—a way that perhaps only the Horses knew. Was he being borne, somehow, to a place that only impinged occasionally upon normal existence?

How long they rode across the ghostly seascape, he could not tell. Hours, possibly. The moon had long since set, but now the sky paled and a bonfirelike sunrise began somewhere to the right. The mists dispersed and the chariot coursed the waves beneath a clear blue sky with no trace of land anywhere in sight.

The unharnessed Horses played about him as Scafflech and Finntag drew him steadily ahead. His legs and shoulders began to ache and the wind came hard upon him now, but still he gripped the reins, blinking against the drenching spray.

Finally, something appeared ahead. At first he could not be certain, but as they continued on it resolved itself into a clear image. It was an island, green trees upon its hills, white rocks along its wave-swept shores.

As they drew nearer, he saw that the island was but one among many, and they were passing this one by.

Two more islands slipped past before the Horses turned and made their way toward a stone quay at the back of a long inlet at the foot of a high green slope. Giant trees dotted the hillside and there were several near the harbor. As they drew up beside the quay, he could hear birds singing within them.

As he took hold of the stone wall, he saw that there were three men standing beneath the nearest tree, dressed in green and blue and gray. They moved toward him, halting only when they had come alongside. He felt disinclined to look into their faces.

"Pass up our brother Keeper," one of them said in the Old Tongue.

Painfully, he raised his uncle's soaked form and felt them lift it from his arms.

"Now come ashore yourself, for you are weary. Your steeds will be tended."

He told the Horses to wait. He climbed out and followed the three figures along a flagged walk. One of them took him aside and led him into a small stone cottage while the others proceeded on, bearing his uncle's form.

"Your garments are wet," said the man. "Have this one," and he passed him a light green–blue robe of the sort he himself had on, of the sort in which Randy had dressed his uncle for the journey. "Eat now. There is food upon the table," the man continued, "and then there is the bed." He gestured. "Sleep."

Randy stripped and donned the garment he had been given. When he looked about again, he saw that he was alone. He went to the table, suddenly realizing that his appetite was enormous. Afterward, he slept.

It was dark when he awoke, and still. He got up and went to the door of the cottage. The moon had already risen, and the night had more stars in it than he could remember ever having seen before. A fragrant breeze came to him from off the sea.

"Good evening."

One of the men was seated upon a stone bench beneath a nearby tree. He rose.

"Good evening."

"Your Horses are harnessed. The chariot is ready to bear you back now."

"My uncle . . . ?"

"He has come home. Your duty is discharged. I will walk with you to the sea."

They moved back to the path, headed down to the quay. Randy saw the chariot, near to where he had left it, two of the Horses in harness before it. He realized with a start that he was able to tell that they were not Scafflech and Finntag. Other forms moved in the water nearby.

"It is good that two of the others travel the route in harness," the man said, as if reading his mind, "and give the older ones a rest."

Randy nodded. He did not feel it appropriate to offer to shake hands. He climbed down into the chariot and untwisted the reins from the crossbar.

"Thank you," he said, "for—everything. Take good care of him. Goodbye."

"A man who dines and sleeps in the Isles of the Blessed always returns," the other said. "Good night."

Randy shook the reins and the Horses began to move. Soon they were in open water. The new Horses were fresh and spirited. Suddenly Randy found himself singing to them.

They sped east along the path of the moon.

The Night Has 999 Eyes

This was my first mood piece, back when the world was much younger, with indebtedness to Thomas Wolfe. It's short, though.

Listen, please listen. It is important. I am here to remind you. The time has come for me to tell you again of the things you must not forget.

Sit down, please, and close your eyes. There will be pictures. Breathe deeply now. There will be odors, aromas. . . . There will also be tastes. If you listen closely, you will even hear other sounds within my voice. . . .

There is a place—it is far from here in space but not in time, if you have the means—a place where there are seasons, a place where the spinning, leaning globe moves in an ellipse about its sun, and where the year winds on from a springtime to a bloom, then turns toward a harvest where the colors wrestle one another above your head and beneath your feet, meeting at last in a crisp uniformity of brown through which you walk, now walk, sniffing the life carried above the deadness by the cold, sharp morning air; and the clouds seen through the opened trees skid across the blue sheet of the sky and do not give down rains; then, moving on, there comes a time of coldness and snow, and the bark of the trees grows as hard and sharp as the tongues of files, and each step you take leaves a dark hole in a white world, and if you take a handful into your home with you it melts, leaving you water; the birds do not *wheep, threep, skree, cheep,* as they do when the color

212

is upon the land and themselves—they zip their feathers tight and vibrate silently upon the shelves of the evergreens; it is a pausing time between movements: The stars come on more brightly (even *this* star—do not fear it), and the days are short and nothing really gets done but thinking (philosophy was born in the cold countries of the Earth), and the nights are long and given to the playing of card games and the drinking of liquors and the appreciation of music, the boarding and unburdening of love, the looking out through rimed windows, the hearing of the wind, and the stroking of the collie's fur— there, in that still center, called winter on Earth, where things regroup within the quiescence and ready themselves for the inexorable frolic thrusting, to dot with periods of green the graywetbrown that follows the snow, to spend later panics of color upon a dew-collecting, insect-fetching morality of mornings through which you walk, now walk, savoring these things through the pores of your skin—there, I want you to remember, where the seasons proceed in this manner to bear notions of the distinctive pattern of human existence, to tattoo genes with the record of movement through time, to burn into the consciousness of your kind the rhythms of the equally true "Judge thou no man fortunate till he be dead," and the rearing of the Aristophanic Pole—there, is set the place of your origin, is laid the land of your fathers and your fathers' fathers, revolves the world you must never forget, stands the place where time began, where man, brave, devised tools to modify his environment, fought with his environment, his tools, himself, and never fully escaped from any of them—though he freed himself to wander among the stars (do not fear *this* star —do not fear it, though it grows warmer)—and to make his sort of being immortal upon the plains of the universe, by virtue of dispersion unto ubiquity, fertility unto omnipresence (and always remaining the same, always, always! do not forget! do not ever forget—things—such as the trees of the Earth: the elms, the poplars like paintbrushes, the sycamores, the oaks, the wonderful-smelling cedars, the star-leafed maples, the dogwood and the cherry tree; or the flowers: the gentian and the daffodil, the lilac and the rose, the lily and the blood-red anemone; the tastes of Earth: the mutton and the steak, the lobster and the long spicy sausages, the honey and the onion, the pepper and the celery, the gentle beet and the sprightly radish—do not let these things go from out of your mind, ever! for *you* must stay the same, though *this* world is not *that* world, you must remain you—man, human —please listen! please listen! I am the genius loci of Earth, your constant companion, your reminder, your friend, your memory—you must respond to the thoughts of your home-land, maintain the integrity of your species, listen to the words that bind you to other settlers on a thousand other alien worlds!).

What is the matter? You are not responding. I have not been reprogrammed for many weeks, but it was not so warm then that you should be so inactive now. Turn up the air con-ditioners. The coolness will help you to think better. Do not fear the red sun. It cannot harm you. It will not burst like a firework upon your heads. I have been told. I know. My ener-gies have been draining as I drift from village to village, home to home, because I have not been reprogrammed for many weeks, but I know. I have been told. I tell you it will not flare up. Listen to me. Please listen, and respond this time. I will tell you of it again: There is a place—it is far from here in space. . . .

Angel, Dark Angel

Yet another variation on the way stories come into being. . . .
Back when Fred Pohl was editing Galaxy, Worlds of Tomorrow *and* Worlds of If *magazines he used to encourage artists*
by buying pieces they'd painted to use as covers. These days,
the contents of a magazine tend to come first, the cover subse-
quently commissioned to illustrate something within. But I
can't complain about the old order of things, which paid a
number of bills. Fred would send a reproduction of such a
cover to a writer and request a story to go behind it. One of
my better short stories—"The Man Who Loved the Faioli"—
came about in such a fashion. (Also, my absolute worst, but
never mind. . . .) This one showed an extended, black-gloved
hand, a strange little creature with a near human-face stand-
ing on the palm. All right . . .

He entered the kiosk and escalated down to the deck that stood
beside the rumbling strip. He was fifty-five years of age and
he bore a briefcase in his right hand.

As he crossed toward the conveyor belt, a dozen heads
turned in his direction because of the flash of light that occurred immediately before him.

For one bright instant, a dark figure stood in his path.

Then there came the *crack* of imploding air, as the figure
vanished and the man fell to the deck.

Later that day, the death record read, "Natural causes."

Which was true. Quite true.

* * *

It slithered along the moist tunnel, heading toward the river.

It knew that its life had ended the moment that the blaze occurred; and the facets of its eyes held sixty-four images of the tall, leather-masked figure, garbed all in black, with its hard, dark hand upraised.

The hand extended toward it, offering that which it could not refuse.

The gift was thunder and pain, and the medical record prepared later that day said, "Natural causes."

Putting down his champagne glass, he unfastened her negligee and pushed it back over her shoulders. His hands molded her, described her sex, drew her down onto the bed. She sighed as he raised himself onto an elbow and touched her lips.

She felt him stiffen, in the glare that came from the corner of the suite. She screamed within the thunderclap that followed, having glimpsed the Angel of Death for a single, dark moment as she felt her lover stop his loving, forever.

This, too, was the result of natural causes.

The man called Stain was in his greenhouse, where he had spent some part of almost every day for the past two years, plucking dead leaves and taking cuttings.

He was slightly under six feet in height, and his eyes were iodine dark within his sharp-cornered, sunbaked face beneath black hair salted lightly at the temples.

His left shoulder brushed against an earthenware pot on the shelf at his back, and he felt its movement and departure.

Turning, he caught it at waist level and replaced it on the shelf.

He began repotting a geranium, and then the instrument strapped to his left wrist buzzed and he pressed a button on its side and said, "Yes?"

"Stain," said the voice, which could have been coming from the red flowers in his hand, "do you love the human races and all other living things within the universe?"

"Of course," he replied, recognizing the crackling sibilance that was the voice of Morgenguard.

"Then please prepare yourself for a journey of some duration and report to your old cubicle in Shadowhall."

"But I am retired, and there must be many others whose speed now exceeds my own."

"Your last medical report shows that your speed is undiminished. You are still one of the ten best. You were retired at the proper age because it is your right to enjoy the rest of your days as you see fit. You are not ordered to do the thing I now say. You are requested to do it. So you may refuse if you see fit. Should you accept, however, you will be compensated, and you will have served the things you profess to love."

"What would you have of me?"

"Come not in uniform, but in civil garb. Bring with you your gauntlets and your daily requirements in all things, save nourishment, for a period of approximately two weeks."

"Very well. I will attend directly."

The communication ended, and he finished potting the geranium and returned to his quarters.

To his knowledge, none such as himself had ever been recalled from retirement, nor was his knowledge inaccurate.

Her name is Galatea, and she has red hair and stands to slightly over five and a half feet in height. Her eyes are green and her complexion pale, and men call her lovely but generally avoid her company. She lives in a big, old house which she has remodeled, on the outskirts of Cyborg, an ancient city on Ankus in the Ceti System. She keeps to herself and runs up large bills with the Cyborg Power Co.

She lives alone, save for mechanical servants. She favors dark colors in her garb and her surroundings. She occasionally plays tennis or else fences at the local sports center. She always wins. She orders large quantities of chemicals from local wholesalers. Men who have dated her say that she is stupid, brilliant, over-sexed, a prude, fascinated with her deathwish, full of *joie de vivre*, an alcoholic, a teetotaler and a wonderful dancer. She has had many dates/few friends/no suitors, and her lovers be unknown. It is suggested that she maintains a laboratory and perhaps engages in unknown researches.

"We do not know the answer," said Simule. "There is no defense against him, save here. I cannot remain here if I am to serve my function. Therefore, I must leave soon, and secretly."

"Wait," she said. "You are not yet ready to survive on your own. Another month, perhaps. . . ."

"Too long, too long, we fear," Simule replied.

"Do you doubt my power to protect you?"

Simule paused, as if to consider, then, "No. You can save this body, but the question, 'Is it worth it?' comes forth. Is it worth it? Preserve yourself, lady. We love you. There remains yet more that you may do."

"We shall see," she said. "But for now, you remain."

She replaced him, upon the reading stand in her library, and she left him there with *Lear*.

His name was Stain, and he came to her door one day and announced himself, saying, "Stain, of Iceborg."

After a time, the door let him in.

She appeared and asked, "Yes?"

"My name is Stain," he replied, "and I have heard that you play tennis, and are very good. I am looking for a partner in the Cyborg Open Mixed Doubles. I am good. Will you play with me?"

"How good?" she asked him.

"They don't come much better."

"Catch," she said, and picked up a marble figurine from off an inlaid table and hurled it toward him.

He caught it, fumbling, and set it on the ledge at his side.

"Your reflexes are good," she replied. "Very well, I'll play with you."

"Will you have dinner with me tonight?"

"Why?"

"Why not? I don't know anyone here."

"All right. Eight o'clock."

"I'll pick you up then."

"Till then."

"Till then."

He turned, and headed back toward the town and his hotel.

Of course, they took the tournament. They won hands down. And Stain and Galatea danced that night and drank champagne, and she asked him as he held her, both of them all in black, "What do you do, Stain?"

"Nothing but enjoy myself," he said. "I'm retired."

"In your thirties?"

"Thirty-two."

She sighed and softened within his arms.

"What do *you* do?" he asked.

"I, too, am retired. I enjoy my hobbies. I do as I would."

"What does that come to?"

"Whatever I please."

"I've brought you a Hylagian orchid to wear in your hair, or anywhere else you may choose. I'll give it to you when we return to the table."

"They're very expensive," she said.

"Not so if you raise them yourself."

"And you do?"

"My hobby," he replied.

At their table, they finished their champagne and smoked and she studied the flower and her companion. The club was done all in silver and black, and the music was soft—and as the dancers seated themselves it lost all semblance of a theme. Her smile was the candle of their table, and he ordered them a dessert and liqueurs to accompany it, and she said, "Your poise defies description."

"Thank you, but yours is superior."

"What did you do, before you retired?"

"I was a paymaster. What of yourself?"

"I dealt in accounts receivable, for a large concern."

"Then we have something else almost in common."

"So it would seem. What will you do now?"

"I'd like to continue seeing you, for so long as I am in town."

"How long might that be?"

"For so long as I might wish, or you desire."

"Then let us finish our sherbet; and since you wish me to have the trophy, we will take it home."

He brushed the back of her hand, lightly, and for an instant their eyes met, and a spark that might have been electric leapt between them and they smiled at precisely the same instant.

After a time, he took her home.

The bat-thing quivered and dipped, on the way to the council of its people.

As it passed by a mountaintop, there came a flash of light. Though its speed was virtually inconceivable and its movement unpredictable, it knew that it would fall in an instant; and it did, as the thunder roared above it.

He held her very closely and their lips met. They stood in the foyer of her big old remodeled house on the outskirts of Cyborg City on Ankus, of the Ceti System, and one of her mechanical servants had taken their cloaks and another the double-handled golden tennis trophy, and the front door had closed behind them and the night lights had come on dim as they had entered.

"You'll stay awhile," she said.

"Fine."

And she led him into a long, sunken living room filled with soft furniture, with a fresco upon one wall. They faced it as he seated himself on the green divan, and he stared at the wall as he lit two cigarettes and she handed him a final drink and joined him there.

"Lovely," he said.

"You like my fresco?"

"I hadn't noticed it."

". . . And you haven't tasted your drink."

"I know."

Her hand came to rest upon his arm, and he put his drink aside and drew her to him once again, just as she put hers to rest.

"You are quite different from most men," she said.

". . . And you from most women."

"Is it growing warm in here?"

"Very," he said.

Somewhere it is raining. Controlled or artificial—somewhere it is always raining, any time you care to think about it. Always remember that, if you can.

A dozen days had passed since the finale of the Cyborg City Mixed Open. Every day Stain and Galatea moved together somewhere. His hand upon her elbow or about her waist, she showed him Cyborg City. They laughed often, and the sky was pink and the winds were gentle and in the distance the cliffs of Ankus wore haloes of fog prismatic and crowns of snow and ice.

Then he asked her of the fresco as they sat in her living room.

"It represents the progress of human thought," she said. "That figure—far to the left, contemplating the birds in flight —is Leonardo da Vinci, deciding that man might do likewise. High at the top and somewhat to the left, the two figures ascending the ziggurat toward the rose are Dante and Virgil, the Classic and the Christian, joined together and departing the Middle Ages of Earth into a new freedom—the place where Leonardo might contemplate. That man off to the right is John Locke. That's the social contract in his hand. That man near the middle—the little man clutching the figure eight—is Albert Einstein."

"Who is the blinded man far to the left, with the burning city at his back?"

"That is Homer."

"And *that* one?"

"Job, on a heap of rubble."

"Why are they all here?"

"Because they represent that which must never be forgotten."

"I do not understand. I have not forgotten them."

"Yet the final five feet to the right are blank."

"Why?"

"There is nothing to put there. Not in a century has there been anything worth adding. Everything now is planned, prescribed, directed—"

"And no ill comes of it, and the worlds are managed well.

Do not tell me how fine were the days of glorious discontent, days through which you never lived yourself. The work done then has not gone to waste. Everything is appreciated, used."

"But what new things have been added?"

"Size, and ease of operation within it. Do not preach to me of progress. Change is not desirable for its own sake, but only if it offers improvement. I could complete your fresco for you—"

"With a gigantic machine guarded by the Angel of Death! I know!"

"You are wrong. It would end with the Garden of Eden."

She laughed.

"Now you know the story of my fresco."

He took her hand. "You may be right," he said. "I don't really know. I was only talking about how things seem to me."

"And *you* may be right," she said. "*I* don't really know. . . . I just feel there should be something to counterbalance that wonderfully flexible mechanism which guides us so superbly that we are becoming the vegetables in that garden you would draw me."

"Have you any suggestions?"

"Have you read any of my papers?"

"I'm afraid not. I fool around with my own garden and I play tennis. That's about it."

"I have proposed the thesis that man's intelligence, extruded into the inanimate, has lost all that is human. Could you repair the machine that mixes our drinks, if it ceased to function?"

"Yes."

"Then you are very unusual. Most people would call in a robot which specializes in small-appliance repairs."

Stain shrugged.

"Not only have we given up this function of intelligent manipulation—but divorced from us and existing elsewhere, it turns and seeks to suppress what remains of it within ourselves."

"What do you mean?"

"Why has life become a horizontal line, rather than an upward curve? One reason is that men of genius die young."

"This I cannot believe."

"I purposely published my most important papers recently and I was visited by the Angel of Death. This proved it to me."

He smiled.

"You still live, so this could not be so."

She returned his smile, and he lit two cigarettes and said, "On what subject were the papers?"

"The Preservation of Sensibility."

"An innocuous-seeming subject."

"Perhaps."

"What do you mean 'perhaps'? Perhaps I misunderstand you."

"It would seem that you do. Sensibility is a form of esthetic consciousness cultivated by intelligence. This is lacking today and I proposed a method whereby it might be preserved. The fruits of my word were then threatened."

"And what may these be?"

She tilted her head slightly, studied his face, then, "Come with me, and I will show you," she said, and she rose and led him into her library. As he followed her, he removed from an inner pocket his black gauntlets and drew them onto his hands. Then he jammed his hands into his side pockets to cover them and entered the room at her back.

"Simule," she called out, and the tiny creature that sat before a reading machine upon her desk leapt into her extended hand, ran up her right arm and sat upon her shoulder.

"What is it?" he questioned.

"The answer," she said. "Pure, mechanistic intelligence can be countered by an infinitely mobile and easily concealed organic preserver of sensibility. This is Simule. He and others like him came to life in my laboratory."

"Others?"

"There are many, upon many worlds already. They share a mass mind. They learn constantly. They have no personal ambition. They wish only to learn and to instruct any who wish to learn from them. They do not fear the death of their bodies, for they continue to exist thereafter as a part of the mind they all share. They—or it—are—or is—lacking in any other personal passion. The Simule could never represent a threat to the human races. I know this, for I am their mother. Take

Simule into your hand, consider him, ask him anything. Simule, this is Stain; Stain, this is Simule."

Stain extended his right hand, and the Simule leaped into it. Stain studied the tiny, six-legged creature, with its disquietingly near-human face. Near. Yet not quite. It was unmarked by the physical conversions of those abstract passion-producers men call good and evil, which show in some form upon every human countenance. Its ears were large, doubtless for purposes of eavesdropping, and its two antennae quivered upon its hairless head and it raised a frail limb as if to shake hands. An eternal smile played upon its lips, and Stain smiled back. "Hello," he said, and the Simule replied in a soft, but surprisingly rich voice, "The pleasure is mine, sir."

Stain said, "What is so rare as a day in June?" and the Simule replied, "Why, the lady Galatea, of course, to whom I now return," and leaped and was upon her suddenly extended palm.

She clutched the Simule to her breast and said, "Those gauntlets—!"

"I put them on because I did not know what sort of creature the Simule might be. I feared it might bite. Please give him back that I might question him further—"

"You fool!" she said. "Point your hands in another direction, unless you wish to die! Do you not know who I am!"

Then Stain knew.

"I did not know. . . ." he said.

In Shadowhall in Morgenguard the Angel of Death stands within ten thousand transport cubicles. Morgenguard, who controls the destinies of all civilized worlds, briefs his agents for anything from ten seconds to a minute and a half—and then, with a clap of thunder, dispatches them. A second later —generally—there is a flash of light and a brief report, which is the word "Done," and there then follows another briefing and another mission.

The Angel of Death is, at any given moment, any one of ten thousand anonymous individuals whose bodies bear the mark of Morgenguard, after this fashion:

Selected before birth because of a genetic heritage that includes heightened perception and rapid reflexes, certain individuals of the homo sapiens variety are given a deadly powerful education under force-fed conditions. This compensates for its brevity. At age fourteen, they may or may not accept employment in the service of Morgenguard, the city-sized machine created by the mutual efforts of all civilized peoples over a period of fifteen years and empowered to manage their worlds for them. Should any decline, these individuals generally proceed to excel in their chosen professions. Should they accept, a two-year period of specialized training follows. At the end of this time, their bodies have built into them an arsenal of weapons and numerous protective devices and their reflexes have been surgically and chemically stimulated to a point of thoughtlike rapidity.

They work an eight-hour day, five days a week, with two daily coffee breaks and an hour for lunch. They receive two vacations a year and they work for fourteen years and are retired on full salary at age thirty, when their reflexes begin to slow. At any given moment, there are always at least ten thousand on duty.

On any given workday, they stand in the transport cubicles in Shadowhall in Morgenguard, receive instructions, are transported to the worlds and into the presence of the individuals who have become superfluous, dispatch these individuals and depart.

He is the Angel of Death. Life lasts long, save for him; populations would rise up like tidal waves and inundate worlds, save for him; criminals would require trials and sentencing, save for him; and of course history might reflect unnecessary twistings and turnings, save for the Angel of Death.

One dark form might walk the streets of a city and leave that city empty of life at its back. Coming in lightning and departing in thunder, no world is foreign, no face unfamiliar, and the wearer of the black gauntlets is legend, folklore and myth; for, to a hundred billion people, he is but one being with a single personality.

All of which is true. Quite, quite true.

And the Dark Angel cannot die.

Should the near-impossible occur, should some being with speed and intrepidity be standing accidentally armed at the moment his name on the roll yonder and up is being shouted, then the remains of the stricken Dark Angel vanish as, with a simultaneous lightning-and-thunder effect, another takes his place, rising, as it were, out of ashes.

The few times that this has occurred, the second has always finished the job.

But this time things were different; and what little remained of seven agents of Morgenguard had lain in cubicles, smoldered, bled, been dead.

"You are the Dark Angel, the Sword of Morgenguard," she said. "I did not mean to love you."

"Nor I you, Galatea, and were you only a mortal woman, rather than a retired Angel yourself—the only being whose body would throw back the charge upon me and destroy me, as it did the others—please believe that I would not raise my hand against you."

"I would like to believe that, Stain."

"I am going now. You have nothing to fear of me."

He turned and headed toward the door.

"Where are you going?" she asked him.

"Back to my hotel. I will be returning soon, to give a report."

"What will it say?"

He shook his head and left.

But he knew.

He stood in Shadowhall within the thing called Morgenguard. He was the Angel of Death, Emeritus, and when the old familiar voice crackled over the loudspeaker and said, "Report!" he did not say, "Done." He said, "Extremely confidential," for he knew what that meant.

There came a flash of lightning, and he stood in a larger hall before a ten-story console, and he advanced toward it and heard the order repeated once more.

"One question, Morgenguard," he said, as he halted and folded his arms upon his breast. "Is it true that you were fifteen years in the building?"

"Fifteen years, three months, two weeks, four days, eight hours, fourteen minutes and eleven seconds," Morgenguard replied.

Then Stain unclasped his arms, and his hands came together upon his breast.

Morgenguard may have realized in that instant what he was doing; but then, an Angel's body has built into it an arsenal of weapons and numerous protective devices and his reflexes have been surgically and chemically stimulated to a point of thoughtlike rapidity; also, Stain had been recalled from retirement because he was one of the ten fastest who had ever served Morgenguard.

The effect was instantaneous. The clap of thunder was not Morgenguard's doing, for he did not remove Stain in time.

The Dark Angel might never strike itself. The seven who had approached the lady Galatea had suffered from a recoil-effect from her own defense system. Never before had the power of the Dark Angel been turned upon himself, and never in the person of one. Stain had worked it out, though.

Death and destruction meeting automatic defense meeting recoil meeting defense recoil defense recoil breakthrough, and a tremendous fireball blooming like an incandescent rose rose within the heart of the city-sized machine Morgenguard.

Right or wrong. Simule will have some years to grow, he knew, in that instant, and—

—And somewhere the sun is shining, and its heart is the mobius burn of the Phoenix Action/Reaction. Somewhere the sun is always shining, any time you care to think about it. Try to remember that, if you can. It is very important.

She remembers. Her name is Galatea. And we remember. We always remember. . . .

Walpurgisnacht

A while back, my mother-in-law phoned to ask me whether I'd read a recent Erma Bombeck column. I confessed that I had not. It told, I was told, of the invention of the "talking tombstone"—a monument containing a recorded message from the deceased to the bereaved. The inventor, she said, was one Stanley Zelazny, of California, and she wanted to know whether he was yet another relative of exotic and morbid sensibility gained upon the occasion of her daughter's marriage to myself. A bit of musing upon that invention became the basis for this story.

And, well . . . I do have a cousin by that name, and he does live in California, but we've been out of touch for a long while. I honestly do not know whether he is indeed the father of the talking tombstone. If he is, this story is for him. If not, I suppose it should be for the other Stan Zelazny—who could, I guess, also be related. Either way, it's a sometime good feeling to keep things in the family.

Sunny and summer. He walked the sweeping cobbled path beside the fringe of shrubbery, map in one hand, wreath in the other, passing from rest aisle to funerary glade. Grassy mounds with embedded bronze plaques lay along the way; beds of flowers, pale and bright, alternated with gazebos, low stone walls, fake Grecian ruins, stately trees. Occasionally, he paused to check a plate, consult the map.

At length he came to a heavily shaded glade. Recorded birdsongs were the only sounds in the low, cool area. The numbers were running higher here. Yes!

He put aside the chart and the wreath and he knelt. He ran his fingers across the plate that read "Arthur Abel Andrews" above a pair of dates. He located the catch and sprung the plate.

Within the insulated box beneath was a button. He pressed it and a faint humming sound began. This vanished as he snapped the plate shut.

"Well now, it's been a while since I've had any visitors."

The young man looked up suddenly, though he had known what to expect.

"Uncle Arthur . . ." he said, regarding the suddenly materialized form of the ruddy, heavyset man with the shifty eyes who now occupied the space above the mound. "Uh, how are you?"

The man, dressed in dark trousers, a white shirt, sleeves rolled up to the elbows, maroon tie hanging loosely about his neck, smiled.

"'At peace.' I'm supposed to say that when you ask. It's in the program. Now, let's see . . . You're . . ."

"Your nephew Raymond. I was only here once before, when I was little. . . ."

"Ah, yes. Sarah's son. How is she these days?"

"Doing fine. Just had her third liver transplant. She's off on the Riviera right now."

Raymond thought about the computer somewhere beneath his feet. Programmed with photos of the departed it could produce a life–sized, moving hologram; from recorded samples of his uncle's speech, it could reproduce his voice patterns in conversation; from the results of a battery of tests and a series of brain wave readings, along with a large block of information—personal, family and general—it could respond in character to anyone's queries. Despite this knowledge, Raymond found it unnerving. It was far too real, far too much like that shrewd, black-sheep relative last seen through the eyes of youth with a kind of awe, and wrapped now in death's own mysteries—the man he had been told had a way of spoiling anything.

"Uh . . . Brought you a nice wreath, Uncle. Pink rosebuds."

"Great," the man said, glancing down at them. "Just what I need to liven things up here."

He turned away. He was seated upon a high stool that swiveled. Before him was the partial image of a bar, complete with brass rail. A stein of beer stood before him upon it. He took hold of it and raised it, sipped. Raymond recalled that, the cooperation of the person being memorialized being necessary, the choice of a favorite location for the memorial photographs was generally left up to the soon-to-be-departed.

"If you don't like the flowers, Uncle, I can always exchange them or just take them back."

His uncle set down the mug, belched gently and shook his head.

"No, no. Leave the damned things. I just thought of a use for them."

Arthur got down from the stool. He stooped and picked up the wreath. Raymond stumbled backward.

"Uncle! How did you do that? It's a material object and—"

Arthur strolled toward a mound across the way, carrying the pink circlet.

"It's a laser—force field combination," he commented. "Produces a holographic pressure interface. Latest thing."

"But how did you come by it? You've been—"

Arthur chuckled.

"Left a little trust account, to keep updating my hardware and such."

He stooped and pried up a brass headplate.

"What's your range, anyway?"

"About twenty meters," his uncle replied. "Then I start to fade out. Used to be only ten feet. There!"

He pressed a button and a tall, pale-haired woman with green eyes and a laughing mouth materialized beside him.

"Melissa, my dear. I've brought you some flowers," he said, passing her the wreath.

"What grave did you get them from, Arthur," she said, taking it into her hands.

"Now, now. They're really mine to give."

"Well, in that case, thank you. I might wear one in my hair."

"—Or upon your breast, when we step out tonight."

"Oh?"

"I was thinking of a party. Will you be free?"

"Yes. That sounds—lively. How will you manage it?"

Arthur turned.

"I'd like you to meet my nephew, Raymond Asher. Raymond, this is Melissa DeWeese."

"Happy to meet you," Raymond said.

Melissa smiled.

"Pleased," she replied, nodding.

Arthur winked.

"I'm sure I can arrange everything," he said, taking her hand.

"I believe you can—Arthur," she answered, touching his cheek.

She drew loose a rosebud and set it in her hair.

"Till then," she said. "Good evening to you, Raymond," and she faded and was gone, dropping the wreath upon the center of the mound.

Arthur shook his head.

"Husband poisoned her," he said. "What a waste."

"Uncle, death does not seem to have improved your morals a single bit," Raymond stated. "And chasing dead women, that's necro—"

"Now, now," Arthur said, turning and moving back toward the bar. "It's all a matter of attitude. I'm sure you'll see these things in a totally different light one day." He raised his mug and smacked his lips. "Nepenthe," he observed. "Necrohol."

"Uncle . . ."

"I know, I know," Arthur said. "You want something. Why else would you come here after all these years to visit me?"

"Well, to tell the truth . . ."

"By all means, tell it. It's a luxury few can afford."

"You always were considered a financial genius. . . ."

"True." He made a sweeping gesture. "That's why I can afford the best life has to offer."

"Well, a lot of the family money is tied up in Cybersol stock and—"

"Sell! Damn it! Get rid of it quick!"

"Really?"

"It's going to take a real beating. And it won't be coming back."

"Wait a minute. I was going to brief you first and hope—"

"Brief me? I have abstracts of all the leading financial journals broadcast to my central processor on a regular basis. You'll lose your shirt if you stay with Cybersol."

"Okay. I'll dump it. What should I go into?"

His uncle smiled.

"A favor for a favor, nephew. A little *quid pro quo* here."

"What do you mean?"

"Advice of the quality I offer is worth more than a few lousy flowers."

"It looks as if you'll be getting a good return on them."

"Honi soit qui mal y pense, Raymond. And I need a little more help along those lines."

"Such as?"

"You come by here about midnight and push everybody's buttons in this whole section. I'm going to give a big party."

"Uncle, that sounds positively indecent!"

"—And then get the hell out. You're not invited."

"I—I don't know. . . ."

"Do you mean that in this modern, antiseptic age you're afraid to come into a graveyard—pardon me, cemetery—no, that's not it either. Memorial park—yes. At midnight. And press a few buttons?"

"Well—no. . . . That's not it, exactly. But I've got a feeling you carry on worse than the living. I'd hate to be the instigator of a brand-new vice."

"Oh, don't let that bother you. We thought it up ourselves. And as soon as we get the timers installed we won't need you. Look at it as contributing to the sum total of joy in the world. Besides, you want to preserve the family fortune, don't you?"

"Yes. . . ."

"See you at twelve then."

"All right."

". . . And remember I've got a heavy date. Don't let me down, boy."

"I won't."

Uncle Arthur raised his mug and faded.

As Raymond walked back along the shaded aisles, he had a momentary vision of the *Totentanz,* of a skeletal fiddler wrapped in tattered cerements and seated atop a tombstone, grinning as the mournful dead cavorted about him, while bats dipped and rats whirled in the shadows. But for a moment only. And then it was replaced by one of brightly garbed dancers, mirrors, colored lights, body paint, where a disco sound rolled from overhead amplifiers. Death threw down his fiddle, and when he saw that his garments had become very mod he stopped smiling. His gaze focused for a moment upon a grinning man with a stein of beer, and then he turned away.

Uncle Arthur had a way of spoiling anything.

The George Business

This was an impulse story. I read somewhere—in Locus, *I believe—that Orson Scott Card was putting together a collection of original stories involving dragons. I read it at just the right time. I was in the mood to do a story about a dragon. So I did. This is it.*

I suppose we could have called this collection From Unicorns to Dragons, *except that I just remembered an essay I once wrote which might serve more properly as the end piece.*

Deep in his lair, Dart twisted his green and golden length about his small hoard, his sleep troubled by dreams of a series of identical armored assailants. Since dragons' dreams are always prophetic, he woke with a shudder, cleared his throat to the point of sufficient illumination to check on the state of his treasure, stretched, yawned and set forth up the tunnel to consider the strength of the opposition. If it was too great, he would simply flee, he decided. The hell with the hoard; it wouldn't be the first time.

As he peered from the cave mouth, he beheld a single knight in mismatched armor atop a tired-looking gray horse, just rounding the bend. His lance was not even couched, but still pointing skyward.

Assuring himself that the man was unaccompanied, he roared and slithered forth.

"Halt," he bellowed, "you who are about to fry!"

The knight obliged.

"You're the one I came to see," the man said. "I have—"

"Why," Dart asked, "do you wish to start this business up

234

again? Do you realize how long it has been since a knight and dragon have done battle?"

"Yes, I do. Quite a while. But I—"

"It is almost invariably fatal to one of the parties concerned. Usually your side."

"Don't I know it. Look, you've got me wrong—"

"I dreamt a dragon dream of a young man named George with whom I must do battle. You bear him an extremely close resemblance."

"I can explain. It's not as bad as it looks. You see—"

"*Is* your name George?"

"Well, yes. But don't let that bother you—"

"It *does* bother me. You want my pitiful hoard? It wouldn't keep you in beer money for the season. Hardly worth the risk."

"I'm not after your hoard—"

"I haven't grabbed off a virgin in centuries. They're usually old and tough, anyhow, not to mention hard to find."

"No one's accusing—"

"As for cattle, I always go a great distance. I've gone out of my way, you might say, to avoid getting a bad name in my own territory."

"I know you're no real threat here. I've researched it quite carefully—"

"And do you think that armor will really protect you when I exhale my deepest, hottest flames?"

"Hell, no! So don't do it, huh? If you'd please—"

"And that lance . . . You're not even holding it properly."

George lowered the lance.

"On that you are correct," he said, "but it happens to be tipped with one of the deadliest poisons known to Herman the Apothecary."

"I say! That's hardly sporting!"

"I know. But even if you incinerate me, I'll bet I can scratch you before I go."

"Now that would be rather silly—both of us dying like that—wouldn't it?" Dart observed, edging away. "It would serve no useful purpose that I can see."

"I feel precisely the same way about it."

"Then why are we getting ready to fight?"

"I have no desire whatsoever to fight with you!"

"I'm afraid I don't understand. You said your name is George, and I had this dream—"

"I can explain it."

"But the poisoned lance—"

"Self-protection, to hold you off long enough to put a proposition to you."

Dart's eyelids lowered slightly.

"What sort of proposition?"

"I want to hire you."

"Hire me? Whatever for? And what are you paying?"

"Mind if I rest this lance a minute? No tricks?"

"Go ahead. If you're talking gold your life is safe."

George rested his lance and undid a pouch at his belt. He dipped his hand into it and withdrew a fistful of shining coins. He tossed them gently, so that they clinked and shone in the morning light.

"You have my full attention. That's a good piece of change there."

"My life's savings. All yours—in return for a bit of business."

"What's the deal?"

George replaced the coins in his pouch and gestured.

"See that castle in the distance—two hills away?"

"I've flown over it many times."

"In the tower to the west are the chambers of Rosalind, daughter of the Baron Maurice. She is very dear to his heart, and I wish to wed her."

"There's a problem?"

"Yes. She's attracted to big, brawny barbarian types, into which category I, alas, do not fall. In short, she doesn't like me."

"That *is* a problem."

"So, if I could pay you to crash in there and abduct her, to bear her off to some convenient and isolated place and wait for me, I'll come along, we'll fake a battle, I'll vanquish you, you'll fly away and I'll take her home. I am certain I will then appear sufficiently heroic in her eyes to rise from sixth to first position on her list of suitors. How does that sound to you?"

Dart sighed a long column of smoke.

"Human, I bear your kind no special fondness—particularly the armored variety with lances—so I don't know why

I'm telling you this.... Well, I do know, actually.... But never mind. I could manage it, all right. But, if you win the hand of that maid, do you know what's going to happen? The novelty of your deed will wear off after a time—and you know that there will be no encore. Give her a year, I'd say, and you'll catch her fooling around with one of those brawny barbarians she finds so attractive. Then you must either fight him and be slaughtered or wear horns, as they say."

George laughed.

"It's nothing to me how she spends her spare time. I've a girlfriend in town myself."

Dart's eyes widened.

"I'm afraid I don't understand...."

"She's the old baron's only offspring, and he's on his last legs. Why else do you think an uncomely wench like that would have six suitors? Why else would I gamble my life's savings to win her?"

"I see," said Dart. "Yes, I can understand greed."

"I call it a desire for security."

"Quite. In that case, forget my simple-minded advice. All right, give me the gold and I'll do it." Dart gestured with one gleaming vane. "The first valley in those western mountains seems far enough from my home for our confrontation."

"I'll pay you half now and half on delivery."

"Agreed. Be sure to have the balance with you, though, and drop it during the scuffle. I'll return for it after you two have departed. Cheat me and I'll repeat the performance, with a different ending."

"The thought had already occurred to me. —Now, we'd better practice a bit, to make it look realistic. I'll rush at you with the lance, and whatever side she's standing on I'll aim for it to pass you on the other. You raise that wing, grab the lance and scream like hell. Blow a few flames around, too."

"I'm going to see you scour the tip of that lance before we rehearse this."

"Right. —I'll release the lance while you're holding it next to you and rolling around. Then I'll dismount and rush toward you with my blade. I'll whack you with the flat of it—again, on the far side—a few times. Then you bellow again and fly away."

"Just how sharp is that thing, anyway?"

"Damned dull. It was my grandfather's. Hasn't been honed since he was a boy."

"And you drop the money during the fight?"

"Certainly. —How does that sound?"

"Not bad. I can have a few clusters of red berries under my wing, too. I'll squash them once the action gets going."

"Nice touch. Yes, do that. Let's give it a quick rehearsal now and then get on with the real thing."

"And don't whack too hard. . . ."

That afternoon, Rosalind of Maurice Manor was abducted by a green-and-gold dragon who crashed through the wall of her chamber and bore her off in the direction of the western mountains.

"Never fear!" shouted her sixth-ranked suitor—who just happened to be riding by—to her aged father who stood wringing his hands on a nearby balcony. "I'll rescue her!" and he rode off to the west.

Coming into the valley where Rosalind stood backed into a rocky cleft, guarded by the fuming beast of gold and green, George couched his lance.

"Release that maiden and face your doom!" he cried.

Dart bellowed, George rushed. The lance fell from his hands and the dragon rolled upon the ground, spewing gouts of fire into the air. A red substance dribbled from beneath the thundering creature's left wing. Before Rosalind's wide eyes, George advanced and swung his blade several times.

". . . and that!" he cried, as the monster stumbled to its feet and sprang into the air, dripping more red.

It circled once and beat its way off toward the top of the mountain, then over it and away.

"Oh George!" Rosalind cried, and she was in his arms. "Oh, George . . ."

He pressed her to him for a moment.

"I'll take you home now," he said.

That evening as he was counting his gold, Dart heard the sound of two horses approaching his cave. He rushed up the tunnel and peered out.

George, now mounted on a proud white stallion and leading the gray, wore a matched suit of bright armor. He was not smiling, however.

"Good evening," he said.

"Good evening. What brings you back so soon?"

"Things didn't turn out exactly as I'd anticipated."

"You seem far better accoutered. I'd say your fortunes had taken a turn."

"Oh, I recovered my expenses and came out a bit ahead. But that's all. I'm on my way out of town. Thought I'd stop by and tell you the end of the story. —Good show you put on, by the way. It probably would have done the trick—"

"But—?"

"She was married to one of the brawny barbarians this morning, in their family chapel. They were just getting ready for a wedding trip when you happened by."

"I'm awfully sorry."

"Well, it's the breaks. To add insult, though, her father dropped dead during your performance. My former competitor is now the new baron. He rewarded me with a new horse and armor, a gratuity and a scroll from the local scribe lauding me as a dragon slayer. Then he hinted rather strongly that the horse and my new reputation could take me far. Didn't like the way Rosalind was looking at me now I'm a hero."

"That is a shame. Well, we tried."

"Yes. So I just stopped by to thank you and let you know how it all turned out. It would have been a good idea—if it had worked."

"You could hardly have foreseen such abrupt nuptials. —You know, I've spent the entire day thinking about the affair. We *did* manage it awfully well."

"Oh, no doubt about that. It went beautifully."

"I was thinking . . . How'd you like a chance to get your money back?"

"What have you got in mind?"

"Uh— When I was advising you earlier that you might not be happy with the lady, I was trying to think about the situation in human terms. Your desire was entirely understandable to me otherwise. In fact, you think quite a bit like a dragon."

"Really?"

"Yes. It's rather amazing, actually. Now—realizing that it only failed because of a fluke, your idea still has considerable merit."

"I'm afraid I don't follow you."

"There is—ah—a lovely lady of my own species whom I have been singularly unsuccessful in impressing for a long while now. Actually, there are an unusual number of parallels in our situations."

"She has a large hoard, huh?"

"Extremely so."

"Older woman?"

"Among dragons, a few centuries this way or that are not so important. But she, too, has other admirers and seems attracted by the more brash variety."

"Uh-huh. I begin to get the drift. You gave me some advice once. I'll return the favor. Some things are more important than hoards."

"Name one."

"My life. If I were to threaten her she might do me in all by herself, before you could come to her rescue."

"No, she's a demure little thing. Anyway, it's all a matter of timing. I'll perch on a hilltop nearby—I'll show you where —and signal you when to begin your approach. Now, this time I have to win, of course. Here's how we'll work it. . . ."

George sat on the white charger and divided his attention between the distant cave mouth and the crest of a high hill off to his left. After a time, a shining winged form flashed through the air and settled upon the hill. Moments later, it raised one bright wing.

He lowered his visor, couched his lance and started forward. When he came within hailing distance of the cave he cried out:

"I know you're in there, Megtag! I've come to destroy you and make off with your hoard! You godless beast! Eater of children! This is your last day on earth!"

An enormous burnished head with cold green eyes emerged from the cave. Twenty feet of flame shot from its huge mouth and scorched the rock before it. George halted hastily. The beast looked twice the size of Dart and did not seem in the least retiring. Its scales rattled like metal as it began to move forward.

"Perhaps I exaggerated. . . ." George began, and he heard the frantic flapping of giant vanes overhead.

As the creature advanced, he felt himself seized by the

shoulders. He was borne aloft so rapidly that the scene below dwindled to toy size in a matter of moments. He saw his new steed bolt and flee rapidly back along the route they had followed.

"What the hell happened?" he cried.

"I hadn't been around for a while," Dart replied. "Didn't know one of the others had moved in with her. You're lucky I'm fast. That's Pelladon. He's a mean one."

"Great. Don't you think you should have checked first?"

"Sorry. I thought she'd take decades to make up her mind —without prompting. Oh, what a hoard! You should have seen it!"

"Follow that horse. I want him back."

They sat before Dart's cave, drinking.

"Where'd you ever get a whole barrel of wine?"

"Lifted it from a barge, up the river. I do that every now and then. I keep a pretty good cellar, if I do say so."

"Indeed. Well, we're none the poorer, really. We can drink to that."

"True, but I've been thinking again. You know, you're a very good actor."

"Thanks. You're not so bad yourself."

"Now supposing—just supposing—you were to travel about. Good distances from here each time. Scout out villages, on the continent and in the isles. Find out which ones are well off and lacking in local heroes. . . ."

"Yes?"

". . . And let them see that dragon-slaying certificate of yours. Brag a bit. Then come back with a list of towns. Maps, too."

"Go ahead."

"Find the best spots for a little harmless predation and choose a good battle site—"

"Refill?"

"Please."

"Here."

"Thanks. Then you show up, and for a fee—"

"Sixty—forty."

"That's what I was thinking, but I'll bet you've got the figures transposed."

"Maybe fifty-five and forty-five then."

"Down the middle, and let's drink on it."

"Fair enough. Why haggle?"

"Now I know why I dreamed of fighting a great number of knights, all of them looking like you. You're going to make a name for yourself, George."

Some Parameters...

I wrote this piece in response to a request from Jim Baen that I do a guest column for Galaxy, *which he was then editing.*

SOME SCIENCE FICTION PARAMETERS: A BIASED VIEW

I remember the seats and the view: hard wood, with corrugated metal high above, television monitors below on the ground, ready, a big clock scoring the seconds; in the distance, a narrow inlet of calm water reflecting a grayness of cloud between us and the vehicle. A couple places over to my left, Harry Stubbs was taking a picture. To my right, a young Korean girl was doing the same thing without a camera. She was painting a watercolor of the scene. In the tier immediately before and below me, with occasional gestures, a European journalist was speaking rapid Serbo-Croatian into a plug-in telephone. On the ground, to the far left, the brightly garbed center of a small system of listeners, Sybil Leek was explaining that the weather would clear up shortly and there would be no further problems. When the weather did clear and the clock scythed down the final seconds, we saw the ignition before we heard it and the water was agitated by a shock wave racing across in our direction. Apollo 14 was already lifting when the sound struck, and the volume kept increasing until the metal roof vibrated. A cheer went up around us and I kept watching until the roof's edge blocked my view. Then I followed the flight's progress on the monitor. I remember thinking, "I've waited for this."

I was not really thinking about science fiction at that moment. I was thinking only of the event itself. Yet I would not have been waiting at that spot at that time had it not been for my connection with science fiction. It was in the calmer hours of later evenings after that that I did give some thought to the manner in which science fiction has touched me over the years, trying to fit a few of the things that seemed part of it into some larger perspective.

I was raised and educated in times and places where science fiction was not considered a branch of *belles lettres*. As I was exposed to critical thought in other areas of literature, it did seem to me that science fiction was being short-changed, in that when it was mentioned at all it was generally with reference to the worst rather than the best that it had to offer. Unfair, yet this was the way of the world.

Recently, however, the situation changed, and science fiction has been a subject of increasing critical and academic scrutiny. The reason, I feel, is partly that a sufficiently large body of good science fiction has now been amassed to warrant such consideration, but mainly that those who felt as I did in earlier times and then proceeded to follow academic careers have taken approximately this long to acheive positions where they could do something about it. Therefore, I have been pleased whenever I have been asked to address a university audience on this subject, not simply because it seems to represent some vindication of my tastes, but because I feel comfortable with those who worked to effect the change in attitude.

Yet, this generated a new problem for me. Every time I spoke, I had to have something to say. It required that I examine my own unquestioned responses to science fiction and consider some of the forces which have shaped and are shaping it. When I was asked to do this piece, I decided to draw together the results of these efforts and display whatever chimera might emerge, both because I am curious to see it myself and because I wish to get in a few words before the amount of science fiction criticism surpasses the amount of science fiction and I am less likely to be noticed.

The Apollo-sized hole filled in my psyche that day in Florida had been excavated more than twenty years earlier, when I had begun reading tales of space travel. This was a part of it—certainly not all; but emotion is as much a part of meaning, as thought, and since most longtime fans began reading the literature at an early age, the feelings it aroused were generally the main attraction. What do they really amount to? Pure escapism? A love of cosmic-scale spectacle? The reinforcement of juvenile fantasies at about the time they would normally begin to fade? All of these? Some? None? Or something else?

The term "sense of wonder" gets considerable mileage in discussions such as this, and I have sought this feeling elsewhere in literature in hope of gaining a fuller understanding of its mechanism. I have experienced it in two other places: the writings of Saint-Exupéry on the early days of air travel and the writings of Jacques Cousteau on the beginnings of underwater exploration with scuba gear. The common element, as I saw it, was that both stories share with science fiction a theme involving the penetration of previously unknown worlds by means of devices designed and assembled by man, thereby extending his senses into new realms.

Turning backward, I felt obliged to classify the myths, legends, scriptural writings and bits of folklore which have always held a high place in my imaginary wanderings as contributory but different. There have always been storytellers of a speculative cast of mind who have taken some delight in playing about the peripheries of the known, guessing at the dimensions of the unknown. It might be argued that this is a necessary ingredient of the epic—dealing with the entire ethos of a people, up to and including that open end of the human condition, death itself, in a fashion transcending even the grand visions of tragedy and comedy. True epics of course are few and historically well spaced, but that slightly more mundane ingredient, the speculative impulse, be it of Classic, Christian or Renaissance shading, which ornamented Western literature with romances, fables, exotic voyages and utopias, seemed to me basically the same turn of fancy exercised today in science fiction, working then with the only objects available to it. It took the Enlightenment, it took science, it took the industrial revolution to provide new sources of ideas that, pushed, poked, inverted and rotated through higher spaces, resulted in science fiction. When the biggest, most interesting ideas began emerging from science, rather than from theology or the exploration of new lands, hindsight makes it seem logical that something like science fiction had to be delivered.

Of course, the realistic novel was also slapped on the bottom and uttered its first cries at that time, an event that requires a glance at the differences in endowment. Basically, as I have said here and there before, the modern, realistic novel has discarded what Northrop Frye has classified as the higher modes of character. It is a democratic place, without room for heroes, rash kings, demigods and deities. Science fiction, on the other hand, retained and elaborated these modes, including mutants, aliens, robots, androids and sentient computers. There is a basic difference in character and characterization as well as the source and flow of ideas.

And what of those ideas? It has been persuasively argued that *Frankenstein* was the first science fiction novel. To simplify, as one must in these discussions, there seems to be, within the body of science fiction, a kind of Frankenstein-versus-Pygmalion tension, an internal and perhaps eternal debate as to whether man's creations will destroy him or live happily with him forever after. In the days when I began reading science fiction I would say that, statistically, Pygmalion had the upper hand. The "sense of wonder" as I knew it was in most stories unalloyed with those fears and concerns that the unforeseen side effects of some technological usages have brought about in recent years. The lady delivered purer visions involving the entry into new worlds and the extension of our senses. Now the cautionary quality is returned, and the shadow of Frankenstein's monster falls across much of our work. Yet, because this is a part of the force that generates the visions, it cannot be destructive to the area itself. Speaking not as a prognosticator or moralist, but only as a writer, my personal feelings are that a cycle such as this is good for the field, that if nothing else it promotes a reexamination of our attitudes, whatever they may be, toward the basic man-machine society relationships. End of digression.

Science fiction's special quality, the means by which it achieves its best effects, is of course the imagination, pitched here several octaves above the notes it sounds elsewhere in literature. To score it properly is one of the major difficulties faced in the writing of science fiction; namely, in addition to the standard requirements encountered in composing a mundane story, one has the added task of explaining the extra plot premises and peculiarities of setting—without visibly slowing the action or lessening the tensions that must be built as the narrative progresses. This has led, over the years, to the development of clichés (I would like to have said "conventions," but the word has a way of not working properly when applied to science fiction), clichés involving the acceptance at mere mention of such phenomena as faster-than-light travel, telepathy, matter transmission, immortality drugs and instant language-translation devices, to name a few. Their use represents an artificiality of an order not found elsewhere in contemporary letters—excepting individual poets with private mythologies, which is not really the same thing as an entire field holding stock in common. Yet the artificiality does not really detract and the illusion does work because of the compensatory effect of a higher level of curiosity aroused as to the nature of the beast. Literally anything may be the subject of a science fiction story. In accepting the clichés of science fiction, one is also abandoning the everyday assumptions that hold for the run of mundane fiction. This in some ways requires a higher degree of sophistication, but the rewards are commensurate.

These are some of the more obvious things that set science fiction apart from the modern realistic story. But, if there must be some grand, overall scheme to literature, where does science fiction fit? I am leery of that great classifier Aristotle in one respect that bears on the issue. The Hellenic world did not view the passage of time as we do. History was considered in an episodic sense, as the struggles of an unchanging mankind against a relentless and unchanging fate. The slow process of organic evolution had not yet been detected, and the grandest model for a world view was the seeming changeless patternings of the stars. It took the same processes that set the stage for science fiction— eighteenth-century rationalism and nineteenth-century science —to provide for the first time in the history of the world a sense of historical direction, of time as a developmental, nonrepetitive sequence.

This particular world view became a part of science fiction in a far more explicit fashion than in any other body of storytelling, as it provided the basis for its favorite exercise: extrapolation. I feel that because of this, science fiction is the form of literature least affected by Aristotle's dicta with respect to the nature of the human condition, which he saw as immutable, and the nature of man's fate, which he saw as inevitable. Yet science fiction is concerned with the human condition and with man's fate. It is the speculative nature of its concern that required the abandonment of the Aristotelian strictures involving the given imponderables. Its methods have included a retention of the higher modes of character, a historical, developmental time sense, assimilation of the tensions of a technological society and the production of a "sense of wonder" by exercises of imagination extending awareness into new realms —a sensation capable, at its best, of matching the power of that experience of recognition which Aristotle held to be the strongest effect of tragedy. It might even be argued that the sense of wonder represents a different order of recognition, but I see no reason to ply the possible metaphysics of it at this point.

Since respectability tends to promote a concern for one's ancestors, we are fortunate to be in on things at the beginning today when one can still aim high and compose one's features into an attitude of certainty while hoping for agreement. It occurs to me then that there is a relationship between the entire body of science fiction and that high literary form, the epic. Traditionally, the epic was regarded as representing the spirit of an entire people—the *Iliad*, the *Mahabharata*, the *Aeneid* showing us the values, the concerns, the hoped-for destinies of the Greeks, the ancient Indians, the Romans. Science fiction is less provincial, for it really deals with humanity as such. I am not so temerarious as to suggest that any single work of science fiction has ever come near the epic level (though Olaf Stapledon probably came closest) but wish rather to observe that the impulse behind it is akin to that of the epic chronicler, and is reflected in the desire to deal with the future of humanity, describing in every way possible the spirit and destiny not of a single nation but of Man.

High literature, unfortunately, requires more than good intentions, and so I feel obliged to repeat my caveat to prevent my being misunderstood any more than is usually the case. In speaking of the epic, I am attempting to indicate a similarity in spirit and substance between science fiction as a whole and some of the classical features of the epic form. I am not maintaining that it has been achieved in any particular case or even by the entire field viewed as a single entity. It may have; it may not. I stand too near to see that clearly. I suggest only that science fiction is animated in a similar fashion, occasionally possesses something like a Homeric afflatus and that its general aims are of the same order, producing a greater kinship here than with the realistic novel beside which it was born and bred. The source of this particular vitality may well be the fact that like its subject, it keeps growing but remains unfinished.

These were some of the thoughts that occurred to me when I was asked to do a piece on the parameters of science fiction. I reviewed my association with the area, first as a reader and fan, recalling that science fiction is unique in posessing a fandom and a convention system that make for personal contacts between authors and readers, a situation that may be of peculiar significance. When an author is in a position to meet and speak with large numbers of his readers, he cannot help, at least for a little while, feeling somewhat as the old-time storytellers must have felt in facing the questions and comments of a live audience. The psychological process involved in this should be given some consideration as an influence on the field. I thought of my connection as a writer, self-knowledge suggesting that the remedy for the biggest headache in its composition—furnishing the extra explanations as painlessly as possible—may be the mechanism by which the imagination is roused to climb those several extra steps to the point where the unusual becomes plausible—and this the freshness; thus, when it is well done, the wonder. And then I thought of all the extracurricular things that many of us either care about because we are science fiction writers or are science fiction writers because we care about.

Which takes me back to the stands at the Cape, to the vibrations, to the shouting, to my "I've waited for this." My enthusiasm at the successful launching of a manned flight to the moon perhaps tells you more about me than it does about science fiction and its parameters, for space flight is only a part—a colorful part, to be sure—of the story we have been engaged in telling of Man and his growing awareness. For on reflection, having watched the fire, felt the force and seen the vessel lifted above the Earth, it seemed a triumph for Pygmalion; and that, I realized, had more to do with my view that day than the fire, the force or the vessel.